The Chicago Story

The Chicago Story

A SPENCER MARLOWE ADVENTURE
ONE MAN, TWO CENTURIES

Kelvin White

This book, as always, is dedicated to my wife Jenny for her indispensable literary advice and ongoing support of my writing.

I would also like to acknowledge the bikers I have ridden with over the years. My love of motor bike riding started when I bought my first Harley Davidson Softail over thirty years ago. A beer at the Queens Hotel in Highgate, Western Australia, followed by ridiculous high-powered rides through the Perth Hills, became our group's adrenaline rush for many years. Dangerous? Oh yeah. Stupid? Without a doubt, but what a blast.

Not only have we traversed the vast continent of Australia several times, but our motor bike adventures have also taken us to Vietnam, Sumatra, Thailand, Bali, India and across the United States. The Harley Davidson Sturgis Rally in South Dakoata USA, 2013, was an unforgettable experience and is an integral part of the Chicago Story.

The names of the core group of these desperadoes have already appeared in earlier Spencer Marlowe stories. I'm sorry if I leave anyone out, but in no particular order I would like to acknowledge Phil 'The Doc' Beinart, Ian 'The Toad' Lenane, Wayne and Keith Ginbey, Peter 'Popeye' Collings, Marty Farrand, Alan Lambert, Dave Bidstrup, Dave Weadley, John Tomes, George 'The Framer' Demmer and Dave Glendinning. Thanks for the good times, guys.

CONTENTS

CHAPTER ONE
WELCOME TO YOUR NIGHTMARE

First it was the meld of odours; the sanitary tang of antiseptic, the slaughterhouse stench of blood and vomit, the incongruous scent of get-well carnations. Then slowly a dark veil began to lift. Through lidded eyes he saw a starched angel in white, a crisp cap perched primly on her head. The angel chatted, not to him. He noticed her elongated vowels. 'Would you like a carfee, arrfercer?' *Where in hell am I?* The veil dropped, the voices grew fainter, like he was being sucked into a tunnel. Then again, darkness.

The man jerked. An alarm beeped. An intercom crackled. Running feet thudded on linoleum floors. Somewhere in the background came the muffled sound of a TV. He turned his head. Dozing in a chair by his bed sprawled a police officer, his navy pea jacket slung casually over the back of the steel-framed hospital chair. On the cop's shirt sleeve, he saw an octagonal Chicago police logo.

I'm in Chicago? He tried to speak; his mouth was dry.

'Water, please, may I have some water?' He noticed a jug resting on a cabinet by his bed. He reached for it. His hand pulled up short, shackled to the steel rung of the bed. The cop folded his arms across his chest.

'So, sleeping beauty awakes. About fucking time. You want water, eh? When I fucking say so.'

'Where am I? What's happened?'

'I wasn't born yesterday, Marlowe. Save it for the judge. Shut the fuck up. When I'm good and ready you can have a drink.'

Who am I? What have I done?

The door swung open; a woman burst into the room. From her dark grey worsted suit to her thick black stockings, sensible court shoes and large unfashionable black leather bag, she looked corporate; an accountant? Maybe she's a lawyer? She held a hand to her mouth.

Someone I know? A friend?

'My God, Spencer, what have they done to you?'

The lady's voice opened the floodgates. The man's body screamed as a jarring flash of lightning split his brain. His whole body felt like it'd been hit by a train.

'Who the fuck are you? Get out!' The cop sprung to his feet; his teeth bared as he gripped his holstered 0.38 revolver.

The lady was authoritative: brusque, imposing. She held up a badge, thrusting it like a clenched fist within an inch of the cop's nose. The cop flinched. He looked like a veteran, maybe early forties; the beginning of a paunch, red hair, Irish heritage the man thought. *This's a cop used to dealing with low life and crims.* He looked solid, dependable, nobody's fool, but he visibly quailed at the sight of this commanding female. He caught a glimpse of a shoulder holster. Her revolver was large, its worn, scarred walnut grip sending a clear message.

In a voice barely a whisper, the lady daggered a finger, 'You listen to me, flatfoot. Undo those God damn handcuffs. You better believe I mean now. Right now!'

The cop whined, 'Lady I got orders. I can't just undo the cuffs. Be reasonable.'

'It's not "Lady". It's Special Agent Steele of the FBI. Listen up you son of a bitch, and listen carefully. Undo those cuffs now or I'll have you walking the beat on the Southside for the rest of your miserable career. Now do it.'

'Yes, Ma'am.' The cop fumbled; he dropped the keys. 'Sorry Ma'am.' He hastily scooped them up, and in a practiced motion, unlocked the cuffs.

Special Agent of the FBI furious lady stared at the officer long enough that even Spencer started to feel the heat of her displeasure.

'Do you mind?'

'Huh?'

The cop goggled at her.

'Do you mind?' she repeated.

The cop blushed.

'Sorry Ma'am.' He sprung to his feet, indicating the empty chair.

Savannah Steele sat down as if she were the Queen of England and the throne had just been vacated.

'Oh my God, what a day.' She smiled at the cop. 'My feet are killing me. Now, officer…?'

'Officer Doolan, Ma'am.'

'Officer Doolan, would you be so kind as to go to the canteen and fetch cups of coffee? Black. Mine has two sugars and Mister Marlowe's does not.'

The cop hesitated. *In his world women don't tell him what to do.*

Savannah Steele's gaze was unblinking.

'Yes, Ma'am. One with two and one without.'

She didn't waste a moment once Doolan was out of the room before leaning forward and talking to him like they knew each other. Like they were old pals from uni.

'Spencer…Spencer, just what have you been up to?'

Spencer Marlowe gazed at the apparition before him. *Who is she? who am I? Apparently, I'm someone called Spencer Marlowe.*

The woman leant back in her chair.

'The question is…is this more Spencer Marlowe bullshit, or…have you really no memory? Well, one thing's certainly not bullshit; you've been worked over, good and proper. Seeing as you were unconscious when they picked you up, I guess it's reasonable to assume you don't remember everything. By the way, Inez sends her love.'

'Inez?'

'Spencer, you'd better not be bullshitting me. Inez is very fond of you; she was distraught when you fell off the Santa Monica Pier all those years ago. Everybody believed you'd drowned. Aha!' Savannah Steele waved a finger. 'I was suspicious from the get go. You'd been acting peculiar before you fell. But I remembered the last time you'd disappeared when we were travelling back from Tokyo in 55. I'm glad you didn't pick the depths of winter to suddenly turn up like a bad penny. Spring is bad enough. The winters here in Illinois are brutal. Inez and I are still living in LA and loving it. Capone, remember Capone?'

Spencer Marlowe gazed, blank-faced.

'No, I guess you wouldn't remember. Capone's our cat, he's fat and old, but still with us.'

'Excuse me, Ma'am.'

'Ah…Officer Doolan with coffee.'

Spencer Marlowe watched as the police officer handed Savannah the coffees and stood awkwardly.

'Doolan, grab a chair. Sit in the corridor. Shut the door and keep watch. Mister Marlowe and I have a lot to catch up on.'

'Ma'am, exactly who am I looking out for?'

'In particular, Officer Doolan, anyone who looks like he may be associated with outlaw bikers.'

'And what should I do if such a person or persons wants to enter the room?'

Savannah Steele smiled sweetly. 'Shoot them, Officer Doolan. Shoot them.'

CHAPTER TWO

THE STORY UNFOLDS

'I'm sorry, I really have no memory. It's obvious you and I go back a long way. You mention Tokyo in 1955, and then Santa Monica at a later date. I'm completely confused.'

'Call me stupid, but I believe you. We worked together in New York and then Tokyo on an operation called the Manhattan Sting and then we both went…ah…sort of undercover in LA to deal with some…some traffickers, some sex trade traffickers in Mexico and LA. Even now the FBI don't know all the details. We ahh…sort of…Oh my God, I really shouldn't be talking about this. I'll…look, I think I'll leave this until you get your memory back.'

'You mention someone called Inez.'

'You don't remember Inez?' Savannah fidgeted with a handkerchief.

Spencer shook his head.

'I feel like it's a waste of time telling you stuff but I guess we have to start somewhere. Inez is flying into O'Hare this morning. We've managed to get an FBI safe house in Long Grove. I'm sure whoever is after you won't find us there.'

'This really is embarrassing and I feel ridiculous, but where exactly are we? You said Inez is flying into O'Hare. What's O'Hare? And who in hell is after me?'

Savannah's sharp gaze cut into him,' Jesus, this really is a doozy this time Spencer. We're in Chicago. It's March 1965 and it's as cold as a brass toilet seat in the Yukon. Oh boy, do I miss California? O'Hare is the airport. Long Grove is a small town in Illinois not far away. And who is after you? For Christ's sake Spencer you're the one who killed the bastard, you mean to say you don't remember who you killed or why? Kiss my go to hell, this's is just fine and dandy. So, we're going to be holed up with unknown gangsters searching high and low for you. Great, this's just great.'

Savannah called out to the uniformed officer nervously waiting in the hallway.

'Officer Doolan, yoo hoo.'

Officer Doolan bolted into the room. 'Yes, Ma'am?'

'Officer Doolan, by the way, what's your first name?'

'Seamus Ma'am.'

Savannah grinned at Spencer, muttering, 'It would be, wouldn't it?'

Doolan managed to blush, yet again.

'Seamus, be a darling, grab Mister Marlowe's personal effects, and a wheelchair, follow me down to the car park.'

'Umm with umm Mister Marlowe?'

'No Seamus, you and I are going to run away together and the wheelchair may be needed in case I shoot you because of your Irish stupidity. Of course, with Mister Marlowe,' she barked.

'Yes, Ma'am. Of course, Ma'am. Sorry, Ma'am.'

Officer Doolan followed them down the halls, into the elevator, and then all the way outside to where this FBI lady's car sat parked. He clearly wanted to say something, and

Spencer (that was probably his name) felt like chuckling at the poor cop's uneasiness. Didn't want to be put in his place by a woman, didn't want to explain to the hospital or his superiors what had happened, probably wouldn't live this down with his fellow cops. He looked like nothing more than a petulant child.

'Well, there she is Spencer, another Plymouth. Do you remember the last one was a God-awful battleship grey? The red looks great, what do you think?'

'Yep, real nice.' Spencer smiled weakly.

'You really haven't changed, have you? Can't shoot and know damn all about automobiles. Hell, I wonder if you can still fight? Obviously, they got the better of you this time. Anyway, I know you don't care but I managed to get the tight asses at DC to option this little jalopy with the big V8. This one's got the 440 cubic inch and a modified four-barrel carby. I can see your eyes glazing over. What sort of man isn't interested in this stuff? Officer Doolan, you like automobiles, don't you?'

'Yes Ma'am. Of course, Ma'am.'

'Oh, dear Spencer, I do remember you did enjoy that T Bird I supplied you with when you went to Shoshone Springs. I'll help you into the car. Ok, there you go.'

'Thanks. Umm Agent Steele…or are we well and truly on first name basis?' Spencer managed a cockeyed grin. He winced at the pain of all the bruising. His face had a lot of healing to do.

'I think you've been hanging around with the Irish too long. Of course, it's God damn first names. Jesus, you're practically family.'

Spencer winced as a sharp searing pain almost made him pass out. 'Christ, fair dinkum that hurts.'

'That, Seamus, is pure Australian. Now, be a darling and put the wheelchair in the trunk.'

'Ma'am, that's hospital property.'

'Doolan…picture this. The south side of Chicago, its winter, you're not sure, but you think your balls may be frozen solid. You do have balls, Seamus?'

'Yes Ma'am.'

'Put the God damn chair in the trunk.'

'Yes Ma'am. But what do I tell the hospital?'

Savannah Steele placed a hand on the officer's shoulder. 'Now Doolan. You understand the meaning of the word "initiative" don't you?'

'Yes, Ma'am.'

'Seriously Doolan if you say "yes, Ma'am", one more time I'll shoot you myself.'

'Yes, Ma…I mean Agent Steele.'

'You may tell the hospital anything that springs to mind. The chair was stolen by a vicious Southside gang. There was a shootout, you killed three of them, but there were too many and they got away with the chair.'

Officer Doolan placed the chair in the trunk, his beetroot face, complimenting his red hair and freckles.

'Oh, Doolan you're going to make a wonderful mother. Tell them that Agent Steele of the FBI has requisitioned the chair.'

'Yes, Ma'am.'

CHAPTER THREE
YOU ARE NOT ALONE

'My God, Spencer that God damn Doolan, what a putz. I reckon he could end up being commissioner, he's as bright as Alaska in December.'

Spencer laughed. 'You sure are one tough lady. If you have a husband or boyfriend, he has my sympathy.'

'Oh, Spencer you really don't remember do you?'

'Sorry, have I hit a raw spot? Is there something in your deep dark past I'm supposed to know about?'

'Actually there's a few things in both of our deep dark past as it happens. Dead Mexican bandits. Christ almighty, even a cop.'

'We killed a cop?' Spencer's face paled.

'Dear, dear, Spencer, you killed a cop.'

'I'm beginning to be happy about having no memory. How did I kill him? Why did I kill him?'

'The why's can wait. As it happened, you shot him.'

'Hang on, I thought you said I was a lousy shot.'

'That you are. It was point blank range. You missed. It was the ricochet that killed him.'

'Oh.'

'I'll fill you in on the details another time. Don't lose any sleep; he was one of the baddies.'

Savannah glanced at the rear-view mirror and put her foot down. The car roared as they tore through the lights as they turned red.

'Hey, what's the hurry?' Spencer waved as an angry driver shook a fist.

'I'm not sure.' Savannah glanced again at her rear-view.

Spencer gazed with interest at the traffic. The people. The men had longer hair than he remembered.

'Exactly where are we? I know it's Chicago.' Spencer's gaze turned upwards as he stared at the metal and glass skyscrapers. They were impressive, but he had an inkling that they should be even larger, taller, more grand. Something seemed off, but he chalked it up to his lack of memory.

'Oh, let's see. This is East Huron. This is the city. Doesn't ring any bells?'

'This's bloody awful. It's a complete blank.'

'Is there anything, anything at all that, I don't know…looks odd or that…I'm not sure what I'm trying to say?'

''Yeah, the fashion. I notice a lot of the men have quite long hair.'

'So do you.'

'What? Really? Spencer grabbed the rear-view mirror.

'Hell, you're right. Jesus, how did that happen? I look like a Beatle.'

'There you go,' Savannah said triumphantly.

'There you go, what?'

'You know about those stupid English, so-called musicians. That's a memory.'

'You're right. John, Paul, George, and Ringo. Hey, how about that?'

'So, what else do you remember. Who's the president? Surely you know that.'

'I know! Ronald Reagan.'

'This is hopeless. Ronald Reagan is a Hollywood actor, and not a very good one.'

'I don't know. I just get these, sort of flashbacks. Obviously, they're not necessarily accurate.'

'Let's just hope things become a bit clearer as days go by. Meanwhile there's been a tan Ford that seems to be following us.'

Spencer turned his head and peered through the rear window. 'Looks innocuous enough. Two business suited gentlemen, from what I can see.'

'Spencer, don't draw attention. Keep your eyes straight ahead.'

'Yes, Ma'am.' He chortled.

'Everyone's a clown. You haven't changed a bit. Your memory might be gone but you still know how to annoy me. I'm going to make a right and head out through farmland. There's no other autos on the road, if they stay with us, I'll know if it's what or who I think it is.'

Spencer wasn't in the least alarmed. He had no idea why anyone would wish him harm. His mind was revolving, a hodgepodge of strange images. He had brief glimpse of an Asian lady, long straight black hair. Then an even briefer flash of a laughing little girl. 'Daddy daddy, look what I can do.' Then the images were cruelly wrenched away.

There was something in Agent Steele's demeanour that filled him with confidence. If the occupants in the car behind meant them some harm, he had the feeling that this tough woman would take it in her stride.

'Bastards are still following, I'm going to pull over and open the bonnet, and see if I can do an impersonation of a helpless female.'

'That could be a bit of a stretch.' Spencer laughed.

Savannah ignored him, muttering 'Come on tough guys. I'm just a helpless little woman, not a God damn thing for you to fear.'

The Plymouth rolled onto the verge. Savannah glanced at the rear vision the Ford had pulled over about 200 yards behind. Savannah sprung out and opened the bonnet, bending over and peering through the gap. The Ford quietly started up and slowly crawled up behind the Plymouth. Two men warily clambered out, one heavy set, the other slim. The heavy man turning, perhaps to see if there were any other vehicles. The sky was blue, the birds chirped, the field of corn waved gently in the breeze. All around was a palette of greens, lush and cheery; nothing bad could happen here.

'Hi there, lady. You gotta problem?'

Savannah stepped to one side 'Well, well well, if it isn't T-Bone Petrelli and Ned Twinkle Toes. Two of the mob's finest. How very odd. What exactly is your interest in me or my passenger?'

'You're a bit out of your jurisdiction ain't you?' Twinkle Toes asked with sneer. 'What's a dyke like you doing in the second city?'

'Oh dear, really Ned, did you seriously think I'm restricted to California? The "F" in FBI does stand for federal, dummy. Now if you really want to start on the subject of sexuality, does the lovable T-Bone here know about you and those, how would you put it? Let me see. Ah…yes, those rather, compromising I think the word is, those photos you were caught with. Really Ned, so young, no clothes, boys and girls. I thought the mob had rules against that sort of stuff?'

'You fucking lying bitch.'

Spencer watched with interest, still not alarmed. He thought the look on the men's faces was comical.

'Shoot her, T-Bone,' Ned Twinkle Toes yelled. Anger had contorted his face. Spencer thought he looked like the boss: small, wiry, dapper. Clad in a very snazzy three-piece grey sharkskin suit and an off-white fedora.

The other man, big and heavy-set, scowled as he reached to his hip, pushing his coat aside. Spencer could see a flat black holster and a fat black automatic. Still, Spencer wasn't alarmed.

'FBI! Freeze, you son of a bitch.'

The son of a bitch didn't freeze, his hand was on his revolver when a massive handgun appeared in Savannah's hand.

The bucolic countryside reverberated to the sound of the slug from a .357 Magnum. T-Bone dropped like a stone. His chest erupted into a riot of red, as his life blood pumped onto the fertile Illinois earth.

'Now Twinkle Toes, you're not going to be silly, are you?'

'Fuck you, you fucking dyke.' Twinkle Toes, was lithe, slim and agile. Spencer was very impressed as Twinkle Toes threw himself onto the ground, rolling and at the same time grabbing his weapon. Spencer still wasn't alarmed.

'Hey Twinkle Toes. Nice.' Savannah waited for a split second as she watched the mobster's athletic antics, and then her ferocious handgun exploded twice more.

Spencer wasn't alarmed, but he was certainly nauseous as the first slug tore through the man's head, leaving a trail of grey matter splattered over his expensive tailoring. The second slug had ripped through his stomach. This was rather irrelevant as Twinkle Toes was already on his way to mobster heaven.

CHAPTER FOUR

JUST LIKE OLD TIMES

Savannah holstered her revolver, as she gazed dispassionately at the bodies.

'A word of advice, T-Bone, next time you have a chance to kill someone, don't hesitate. Ok?'

Savannah slid into the driver's seat of the Plymouth.

'I'd just love to know what you've been up to. Any ideas?'

Spencer shook his head, 'I seem to have pissed someone off, but I just can't remember a bloody thing. Meanwhile what do you do with…the late, what were the names? T-Bone and Twinkle Toes. Where do these guys get their names from?'

Spencer was mildly curious to Ned's reference to "Savannah the dyke" but figured questions about that comment were definitely out of order. She had just dispatched two people in the space of ten seconds, with the same look as someone selecting a cut of meat from the butchers. He would figure it out, and in the meantime stay on this woman's good side. He also wondered if this had anything to do with the mysterious Inez she had mentioned.

'I'm going to get onto the radio telephone to Dale. As it happens, he's been stationed in Chicago for the last couple of years. I tell you, Spencer, he's gonna get such a kick out of hearing that you've turned up. Now let's fire this gizmo up.'

Spencer's gaze turned briefly to the bulky Motorola telephone.

'You don't have a cell?'

'What was that…a cell…Why would we put these guys in a cell? Jesus Spencer what's wrong with you? They're dead meat. When I shoot people it's for keeps. I mean, you didn't see a God damn twitch, or hear a moan, I'm pretty sure. Cell, Cell…really,' Savannah muttered.

Spencer closed his eyes and grimaced. It wasn't just the pain of his wounds; he'd had a momentary flash, he's seen an Asian lady, long black hair, she'd been holding a small silver object to her ear, she was talking, a pretty little girl was dancing by her side. Then nothing. The vision disappeared. He had a momentary feeling of loss, of heartache. It hurt. Then it was gone.

'Dale, Savannah. Yep. You too. Oh, Dale you're going to love this. Yep, I have boy wonder in the automobile. Yes, it's really him no fooling. Umm but…well it seems the boy has enemies.' Savannah chortled. 'Well actually two less enemies. A ha…yep…yeah…I understand. Hang on a minute, Special Agent Fletcher, it was a God damn righteous kill. Well two kills I suppose. I have a witness. Yeah, Spencer saw it all. They went for their guns. Yes…' Savannah said wearily. 'I told them I was FBI. For Christ's sake Dale they knew who I was. Just you listen to me, we're out in hillbilly country and those two schmucks were following us. Yeah, like I said. Who? Get this, T-bone and Twinkle Toes. Only his toes or any other part him aren't twinkling anymore.'

Savannah roared with laughter.

'All right I'll give you the address. You'll send out the garbage truck? Whoa, and you're coming as well? Terrific.'

Savannah hung up the phone. 'Well Spencer it's reunion time again, Dale and the cleanup crew are on the way.'

'I have a feeling I'm meant to know Dale…?'

'Dale Fletcher, you and he are old, what? I guess colleagues of sorts. He's looking forward to seeing you. Oh, and he's finally given up smoking. Thank God for that. I know the smoke annoyed you, didn't it?'

'I'm sure it did.' Spencer shrugged, feeling more and more confused.

'Do I assume that your memory starts at the hospital bed?'

'That's it. I've had some flashes of memory but they're gone in an instant.'

Savannah was silent for a second. 'Tell me what you can remember.'

'I've had a vision of an Asian lady, Japanese, I think. Oh…and a little girl, part Asian, I know they're important.'

'Spencer, Spencer, as always, I'm completely confused where you're concerned. But that sounds like your wife Michiyo and your daughter Trilby.'

Spencer put his head in his hands. 'I have a wife and daughter; I've killed people and I have no memory. Jesus, it couldn't get much worse, could it?'

'Dale and his crew will be here shortly, in the meantime I picked up your personal effects from the hospital, as I expected there's nothing of particular interest. We have, a wallet, with ten dollars, three nickels and a quarter. You don't seem to have much in the way of worldly assets. Oh, and of course we have that God damned lucky charm of yours.

What's it called? I seem to remember you called it a cornicello. Here, catch.'

Savannah threw the trinket towards him; Spencer caught it in his right hand. 'Bloody hell.' It felt like he had been zapped with a stun gun. His mind was hit with a multitude of fleeting images like a movie on fast forward. Japanese military in their distinctive World War two uniforms, khaki with cotton forage caps, the Raffles Hotel, Waikiki Beach, the same laughing little girl, the same Asian lady. He saw a sleek midnight blue automobile nothing like the cars of today, it had a small blue and white emblem on the bonnet. Then a rock and roll band performing on a pier, happy people, ice cream, hamburgers, hot dogs, Budweiser Beer in small bottles. Everything loomed loud, louder, a scream, falling, water…and then it was gone.

Spencer's head fell forward; he moaned softly.

'Spencer, Spencer, are you ok?' He opened his eyes. Savannah was shaking him. 'What on Earth was that all about?'

'I have no idea. I saw the Asian lady again and the little girl. There was a whole lot of images that made no sense.'

'Give us a clue?'

'Honestly there were so many, one image that was distinctive was a rock and roll band. They were playing on what looked like a pier.'

'Great.' Savannah clapped her hands together 'Your memory is coming back. That would have been the Beach Buddies as they were known then, performing on the Santa Monica Pier. You were there with me Inez and Priscilla, surely you remember Priss?'

Spencer looked miserable 'It's gone, there's nothing. It's a bloody blank.'

'It's a start, that's what it is. Your memory is going to come back, I know it. Hey listen, here comes Dale and the garbagemen.'

A bland powder blue Chevy Impala station wagon pulled in front of the Plymouth. This is exactly the sort of vehicle Spencer thought you could see a suburban mum driving when she drops her 2.3 children off at the all-white day care center. Following close behind was a cream flat nose Dodge Fargo van. Spencer observed a lean older man climb out of the Impala, he gazed quickly around before speaking to the two white coverall clad men from the van. He pointed at the two bodies. It seemed a quick joke was shared as the men from the van loudly guffawed. Obviously, the sight of two corpses wasn't too disturbing. This, Spencer guessed, was Dale Fletcher.

Spencer studied Fletcher as he made his way to the Plymouth. He saw a lined honest face, a grey crewcut and a pinstripe suit, white shirt and a natty red and white polka dot tie. Everything about the man shrieked wholesome middle class.

Dale gave Savannah a wave as he opened the rear door of the Plymouth. 'Savannah.' He grinned 'Everywhere you go death seems to follow. Well, those two monkeys aren't going to be missed.'

He then clapped Spencer on the shoulder. 'My God, Spencer it's just great to see you again, Mr. "it's a long story."' Spencer turned and faced Dale wondering exactly what the long story jibe was all about. 'Do you know Spencer, ever since you disappeared in Santa Monica, Savannah here has made sure your photo was posted in every God damn field office of the FBI? I mean coast to coast.'

'Dale, Dale,' Savannah interrupted. 'Spencer has no memory, he doesn't remember a thing. He's having some flashes and I reckon it'll all come back to him. But for now, zilch.'

Dale gazed at Spencer again, mumbling, 'Who'd believe it eh?' He rubbed his hands together. 'Ok we have much to talk about. Savannah, I gather you're on the way to the safe house. Is your um…your friend there already?'

Savannah's eyes twinkled. 'Yes, Dale my um…friend Inez should already be there.'

'Good to see you Spencer, we'll have a debrief at the house.' He clapped him on the shoulder again.

Dale climbed out of the Plymouth and gave a wave to the two men who'd loaded the bodies away from prying eyes. Savannah watched, a smile on her face as Dale sedately drove away in the Chevrolet. She then burst into laughter.

'What's the joke?'

Savannah wiped her eyes 'Poor Dale, it's an open secret that Inez and I are in a long-term relationship. Officially the bureau doesn't condone same-sex unions, but they seemed to have turned a blind eye. But good old flag waving, go to church on Sunday Dale just doesn't know how to handle it. He has trouble making eye contact with Inez, he stutters and doesn't know what in hell to say.' She laughed again.

'What about Inez? It must make her uncomfortable.'

'My God, you know Inez. Well, you used to. Anyway, Inez actually likes Dale and she isn't even slightly embarrassed.

There is simply no way she's going to hide anything. Just wait, if Dale's there when we arrive, Inez will give me a particularly passionate kiss, just to make Dale uncomfortable. God, I love that woman. Do you remember that creep Seth that I was involved with?'

Spencer shook his head.

'No, I guess you don't. When I think back, and just how close I came to marrying that bastard. Maybe it's a case of God works in mysterious ways, but I've never really believed that stuff. Anyway, time to go, I'll try and jog your memory on the way. I'll tell you all about what you and I have been involved in. I hope that God damn memory of yours returns.'

Spencer sat back open mouthed as Savannah Steele re-acquainted him with a large chunk of his past life.

Savannah frowned. 'Where to start? I've just realized it started under very similar circumstances. It was New York in 55, you were in hospital, same type of circumstances. I was a green rookie FBI gal, given the God-awful assignment of baby-sitting Spencer Marlowe. You'd been worked over by crime boss's crew Tony Romano. What a story, truly. The FBI set up a restaurant in Greenwich with a view to taking down the mafia. It got pretty damn bloody, let me tell you.'

Spencer grinned. 'But I guess I didn't shoot anyone?'

Savannah grunted. 'You're just about the worst shot I've ever seen. Anyhow, don't interrupt, I have a lot to tell you. I had the job of recording all the gibberish you spouted when you were semi-conscious. Let me tell you none of it made any sense. Any way you and I were running the restaurant, they tried to burn us out, send hitmen and God knows what.

Without going into all the details, we ended up going to Japan, dealing with the Yakuza,'

'What happened to the New York gangster?'

'Stop interrupting. It was the same operation. Anyway, we were dealing with the Japs. We were supposedly there to import heroin into the US for Romano.'

'Who?'

'Tony Romano. He was the gangster.'

'Gotcha.'

'Anyway, I had my gun trained on a captured Japanese Yakuza. He'd recognized you from Hawaii in 41, just before Pearl Harbor. It was just about at that moment the schmuck swallowed a cyanide pill, so I never had a chance to ask him all about you, and what happened in Hawaii.'

Spencer stared at her in disbelief. 'What on earth are you talking about. I don't know how old I am. In fact, I don't even know what year it is.'

'It's 1965.'

'I'm only, what thirty-five, maybe thirty-six, I would imagine. You have to be loopy. Where did you dream this stuff up from? Hell, I'm in a car with a bloody madwoman. If I was involved in something in 41, I would have to have been born in, what, 1920 or something. That would make me mid to late forties at the least. I sure as hell don't look or feel that old.'

'Oh yeah, well hang on to your hat, it gets worse. You went into a coma on the airplane back from Tokyo, you were hospitalized in San Francisco. When I came back to check on you the next day, they said you'd gone disappeared.'

'Is there anything else? You mentioned Santa Monica, Mexico?'

'Is there something else? You betcha. We searched high and low for you, and it was if you had vanished off the face of the earth. We checked with the now CIA and spoke to agents Spinetti and Crabtree. Do those names ring a bell?' Spencer shook his head. 'Anyway, they confirmed absolutely you were involved in an operation in Hawaii involving a Japanese spy named Lee Tai.'

'Sounds Chinese to me.'

'Shut up, Spencer. Believe me he was Jap. In fact, you speak Jap.'

'Nutty as a fruit cake. Does this guy Dale Fletcher know that you've been spouting this bloody nonsense?'

'Spencer! Damn you. Dale knows all about it. Trust me.'

'I speak Japanese, really?'

'Konnichiwa, Spencer San.'

Spencer responded in Japanese.

'What do you reckon that was, dickhead? Latvian?'

Spencer's face paled. 'What's going on? I'm now thinking in Japanese. This is a bloody nightmare, fair dinkum.'

'Yep, that's right, you speak Australian as well.'

Spencer put his head in his hands. 'Go on tell me more.'

'Apparently you have a Japanese wife, named Michiyo and a little girl, Trilby.'

'You haven't met them?'

'We searched high and low here in the US and with the Australian government. You are Australian, you realize?'

'I suppose. I sort of feel Australian, if that makes sense.'

'Anyway, I'm positive Michiyo and Trilby exist, but where they live? I've no idea.'

She continued driving, tapping out an impatient rhythm on the steering wheel as the Chicago downtown melted into the main roads, and then the suburbs. Skyscrapers gave way to the large department stores and rows of restaurants, and those gave way finally to the rows and rows of near identical houses.

'We 're nearly home, so let me finish. Completely by accident I ran into you in LA in 61, same thing, but I think your memory wasn't quite as bad. But get this, when I confronted you with how the hell you were so young, you came up with this stupid bullshit time travel story. Give me a break.'

'I said that?'

'You sure did honey chile, as Priss would say.'

'Who?'

'Later. Anyway, you and I were involved in a big mission in Mexico, we were God damn lucky to get out alive.'

'Is that where I killed a cop?'

'Yep, and a couple of others.'

'Great, so I'm a serial killer.'

Savannah laughed, a look and sound he wouldn't have believed could come from a woman who'd just shot and killed two people just today. 'All in the name of truth, justice and the American whatever, Spencer.'

'Is there more?'

'Lots and lots, but it can keep, because we're at the house. But I'll just finish up. Dale and I figured that you had to have been on some sort of experimental anti-aging drug, or treatment or whatever, that had the side effect of causing problems with your memory. But what that's all about, we have no idea. If you ever knew what that was all about you never told us.'

'Is that why Fletcher made the comment "it's a long story?"'

Savannah laughed again. 'Every time we pressed you for details that was the standard Spencer Marlowe response.'

CHAPTER FIVE

HOME SWEET HOME

Spencer had been so engrossed in Savannah's story he hadn't paid much attention to his surroundings. The Plymouth pulled into the driveway of a pleasant two-story stucco home. He could see a manicured lawn, some rose bushes in full bloom, petunias lining the drive, and an American flag crackled in the breeze. Dale Fletcher's Impala station wagon was parked in the street.

As Savannah opened the trunk to grab out the wheelchair, Spencer observed a statuesque, elegant lady with lustrous black hair and refined Hispanic features come running out of the home, followed by a smiling Dale Fletcher. This, he guessed, had to be Inez.

'Spencer dear, what have they done to you?'

Spencer was already in the wheelchair when Inez wrapped her arms around him, planting a big kiss on his cheek.

'Hey what about me, woman?' Savannah grinned.

'Of course, my darling.'

Savannah whispered to Spencer. 'Cast your peepers on Dale. Poor bastard.'

Sure, enough Inez embraced Savannah, planting a big kiss on her lips. Spencer grinned as he observed Dale scratching his head and shuffling his feet.

'I hope you're all ungry, si. We have completos for lunch.'

Spencer wasn't sure how he remembered, but he knew this was the delicious South American hot dogs.

Overwhelmingly Spencer had a feeling of gratitude. He felt as if he was home. This felt like family.

Inez ushered them into the spacious dining room. It was obvious she had been toiling in the kitchen; dish after tantalizing dish appeared. Mushroom soup, bitter greens with tomatoes the size of peas, rare roast beef slices as thin as paper noodles in a green sauce and of course the South American staple, *completos*. The hot dog on a bun topped with sauerkraut, diced tomatoes and mashed avocado, washed down with ice cold Asahi beer.

'Inez, this really is swell. Savannah is one lucky lady.' Dale grinned from ear to ear as he wiped avocado from his chin.

Inez looked pleased. Savannah winked at Spencer.

Lunch finished Inez announced, 'I know you all have business. I'll clear away, please move to the living room and I'll leave you to it.'

Inez had made coffee as they made their way into the spacious living area. The owners clearly had good taste. The room was a mix of endearingly vibrant colours, ghost white walls and dark polished wood floors acting as a blank canvas to introduce colour in its furnishings and accessories. The floor to ceiling picture window overlooked the quiet suburban street.

'Ahem.' Dale cleared his throat. 'Well Spencer, Savannah, I'll tell you what we know. What we suspect and what "Mister It's a long story,"' here he grinned, 'has to do with everything. Oh boy, what a story.'

The three of them enjoyed Inez's cooking for another few moments, with Dale peering back and forth between them. He had the look of the cat who'd just eaten the canary: entirely too pleased with himself. As the story unfolded, Spencer realized the man loved having information other people didn't.

Eventually he leaned forward and started in. 'The cops were called out to an affray at a blues club in Wabash Avenue. You were unconscious on the ground and outlaw biker type guys were giving you a good kicking.'

Spencer interrupted, 'And I'm arrested? That sounds fair.'

Dale chuckled. 'Well considering you had already killed one of the bikers, I guess the boys in blue had a reason to be upset with you.'

'Oh.'

'Surprisingly, however, they managed to get witness statements that more or less clear you. Apparently, some biker was harassing a black couple who were simply minding their own business, when you stepped in.' Dale paused for effect as he rummaged through his pockets. He grinned, 'I was just searching for cigarettes, when I remembered I quit. Anyway, as you were telling said biker to back off, a group of them came out of the club and got involved. Witnesses said there were at least six of them and they foolishly decided to teach you a lesson. Silly move, as we know. Anyway, you let fly in your own inimitable manner. Obviously, you must have realized you were in the fight of your life. The witnesses said they had never seen anything like it. You karate chopped one guy who came at you with a knife. You killed him. The next guy you swung round kicking him in the head, he fell backwards, his head hitting the concrete. He's on life support.

Eventually you were simply outnumbered and these guys were going to kick you to death. Here's where it gets interesting.'

'Actually,' Spencer said, trying to picture the scene, 'It sounds fairly interesting so far.'

'Yeah, I guess. Anyway, about the same time as the cops arrive, perhaps a bit before, a black Continental screeched up…'

'Continental?'

'God damn, Spencer,' Savannah interrupted, 'that's a Lincoln Continental. It's an automobile.'

Spencer chuckled amiably, not at all embarrassed. 'I knew that.'

'Anyway, a big guy, smartly dressed, you know, cashmere coat, all that, jumps out of the auto, screams at the bikers something like "back off, he's mine. Help me get him in the car." Now, get this, a biker calls out, "Sorry, Mister Ramirez." Just as they are about to load you into the Lincoln, two police cruisers arrive and everyone scatters. How do you like that eh?'

Spencer moved awkwardly in his wheelchair, groaning as another bolt of pain scattered through his body, a thousand particles of red-hot needles.

'I'm really none the wiser, so what's happening? This doesn't explain Twinkle Toes and T bone.'

Dale leaned back in his chair. 'Ah, but we know more.' He waited with a mischievous grin on his face. Spencer couldn't help but mirror the infectious smile, and paid for it with more pain.

'Dale for Christ's sake, get on with it.' Savannah rolled her eyes.

'Ok, now pay attention. We, that is the FBI, had been tailing an Australian thug, gangster, outlaw biker. This piece of low life is one Peter "Popeye" Gordon.'

Spencer shook his head. 'What is it with these guys? They have to have some outrageous moniker. I mean, Popeye, really. Why Popeye? Maybe he likes spinach?'

'Well as it happens, I think it's more a case of "Popeye the Sailor Man." I'll tell you about one incident the Australian authorities have told me about. To give you an idea of this guy, he has flash houses and boats in Australia. He has a fifty-foot Bertram moored at a fancy yacht club near Perth, Western Australia. Apparently, he'd been disturbing the other boaties and the Commodore of the club, a let me see here, a Mister Dinbey, was sent to tell him to be quiet. The next thing we know, Dinbey is found dead in the water. No witnesses. Death by misadventure, the coroner rules. Death seems to surround this guy. People disappear, witnesses change their mind, all the usual stuff.'

'What has this to do with me?'

'Welllll, so glad you asked. Popeye Gordon is a charming affable, good-looking guy. You'd never guess his background.'

'So?'

'Spencer, ole buddy, you had been seen having drinkies with this guy. You appeared to be the best of friends. Any clues?'

'Great,' Spencer muttered, 'I want to tell you this isn't the sort of guy I'd hang out with, but… what can I say? I just don't remember.'

Dale seemed to be enjoying himself. 'We think we have it worked out. Popeye, we believe, simply overhead the voice of a fellow Australian in a bar. As I said he's an affable sort of guy, there's a good chance he simply struck up a conversation. You don't remember, of course?'

Spencer shook his head. 'It's a complete blank.'

'As it happens, we know you were at the Green Mill Cocktail lounge on Broadway having drinks with Gordon. We were watching him, and we noticed some other hard cases who also seemed to be watching. These we think were Ramirez's men. Our men had no idea who you were, but they got close enough to hear your Aussie accent, and one of Ramirez's crew was also close enough. Our guys assumed you were an accomplice of Gordon's; Ramirez's guys would have jumped to the same conclusion.

'We overhead him telling you about the Blues club on Wabash, and you agreeing to go. The incident with the bikers was just a coincidence, not planned. But Ramirez, by this time, obviously had you in their sights, particularly as Popeye then disappeared.'

'Well, where in hell did he go?'

Dale chuckled, 'You headed off from the Green Mill walking, Gordon came out a few minutes later and we grabbed him.'

'Don't you need something like a warrant for that?'

Savannah smiled. 'Spencer, I know as much about all this as you do, but we're FBI we're not police. Probable cause we have and warrants we can get.'

Dale cleared his throat. 'In fairness we'd just received a message from the Australian authorities to arrest Gordon on suspicion of robbery and murder. So, he's now being held, awaiting extradition. We've made sure he's isolated.'

'I still have no idea what's what.'

Dale consulted his notes. 'Have you heard of a place called Lightning Ridge?'

Spencer's brows were knitted. 'Yeah, ah, small outback town New South Wales. Opals, I think.'

'Got it in one. Popeye and an accomplice allegedly robbed and murdered an opal dealer in Lightning Ridge, getting away with a mill worth of black opals.'

'So where does Ramirez fit in?'

'Ok, our informants have told us Popeye did a deal with Ramirez for a load of guns, mainly Ceska Skorpion sub machine guns. This little beauty fires about 900 rounds of 9mm a minute. And as a side deal about twenty kilos of heroin. All destined for a motorcycle gang in Milperra New South Wales.'

'So, Ramirez has the opals, Popeye has what he wants. Why are they at odds with each other?'

'You wouldn't believe it, one of Ramirez's flunkies made a fatal mistake and sent off the guns and smack without checking. Ramirez hadn't yet got his paws on the opals.'

'You said a fatal mistake?'

Dale grimaced. 'You wouldn't believe these guys, seriously.'

'Let's hear it.' Spencer shuddered; he had an idea he really didn't want to know.

'Chainsaw.'

'Christ all mighty, Spencer's face paled. 'Are you going to tell me he was cut up, what's the terminology? Umm postmortem?'

'Correct terminology Spencer, very good. But no, he was dismembered while he was still alive.'

'Surely Gordon wouldn't want to double-cross a guy like that?'

'He obviously couldn't help himself. We had his phone tapped when he got a message from the freight company querying where the drop off was in New South Wales, he realized the merchandise was on its way and he made a snap decision to keep the opals. No honour amongst thieves.'

Spencer shook his head and smiled at Savannah. 'It sounds like what you told me of the good old days. I'm happy that we're not a part of this. These guys are bad news.'

Dale held a hand up, clearing his throat again. 'Well, here's the thing. Spencer, Savannah, ahh…well, we do have something in mind.'

CHAPTER SIX

RECUPERATION

Spencer felt his stomach lurch at Dale's seemingly throwaway line, "We do have something in mind." He glanced around at the comfortable living room. Bright and full of cushions, a bold and extravagantly thick circular scarlet rug added colour and warmth. A huge fireplace, stacked with pine logs, just waiting for the freezing winter nights. A Norman Rockwell print above the fireplace was so cheerfully American. It portrayed a typically lifelike picture of a GI spooning some food into a little girl's mouth. The picture was titled "The American Way." In one corner was a TV perched on skinny legs. A small gramophone rested on a low oak table, next to it a plastic rack with a collection of Beatle and Rolling Stones records. A bookcase occupied one wall. Spencer cast an eye over Mark Twain and Sinclair Lewis classics. He was puzzled that he remembered the authors, that he was vaguely familiar with the artist Norman Rockwell, even the Readers Digest novels scattered haphazardly across the coffee table looked familiar. What was missing was memory. He knew his name; he knew Inez and Savannah were important. Instinctively he knew as an absolute he could trust these two women.

Inez grabbed an easy chair, pulling it forward. 'Spencer, I can't tell you how delighted I was when Savannah told me you were alive. We have this house for as long as it takes for you to recuperate. I'm going to play my part and fatten you up.'

She gave him a pat on the knee. 'Do you remember my tempura and yakitori?'

'Sorry.' Spencer shrugged and frowned. He felt like a fool.

Inez started speaking in Japanese, 'I'd been working for the government as an interpreter, in both Japanese and Spanish. I guess it's probably because of you that I learnt Japanese.'

Without thinking, Spencer answered in the same language, just as Savannah stepped into the room.

'Enough already. Love the food, love the beer, but listen up you two. In this house we speak American or Spanish. Comprende?'

Inez grinned as she grabbed Savannah's hand. 'Watch yourself darling or there's no sushi or Asahi for you tonight.'

Savannah rolled her eyes, but then her face broke into a huge smile. 'Honestly, Spencer, this woman is a God damn bully. I live in fear. I kid you not.'

Spencer broke into laughter; he felt like the prodigal who had just returned home.

Dale had organized a physio to come to the home as soon as Spencer was well enough. Fortunately, Spencer's level of fitness was extraordinarily high. Alf was a gruff and grizzled veteran of the pro baseball circuit and had previously been working as a physio for the New York Yankees. He was a gentle taskmaster who managed to get that little bit extra from his patients. Spencer was reminded of someone from his past, he had vague memories of standing under a freezing waterfall. Then a flash, as an elderly Japanese looking gentlemen exhorted him to crush a brick, using only his hand. Then the vision would disappear.

'Concentrate, Spencer, you're God damn daydreaming again. You wanna spend the rest of the season on the bench?'

'Sorry Alf, I just had a bit of déjà vu.'

As weeks passed Spencer felt the shackles of injury and pain fall away. He'd started taking walks around the very pleasant Long Grove township. He'd become a regular at the Café de Flore, a French inspired coffee shop and eatery.

Nights were spent watching TV or listening to Inez's collection of British rock and roll records.

'I just love Bonanza. Ben Cartwright is such a wise father figure,' Inez commented as the Bonanza theme erupted on the TV.

'Honestly Inez, it's a bit unrealistic. He never shoots anybody. Those pistols are just for show.' Savannah snorted.

'Speaking of pistols?' Inez's face looked bleak.

'Uh oh.' Savannah closed her eyes and clenched her jaw.

'It's no good closing your eyes. I found that small pistola you have hidden in the kitchen. Honestly Savannah, you're paranoid. No one knows we live here. What were you thinking?'

'I'm sorry, Nenita, but it's the job. And yes, I'm paranoid.'

'So, this sounds interesting. A pistol in the kitchen, really?' Spencer couldn't resist the opportunity for a gentle ribbing.

'Don't you start, too. I've mounted a gun on the underside of the wall cabinet that holds all the glassware. It's just a precaution. Let's just move along.'

'Hey, let's talk about music or food. Inez, what music do you like right now?'

'Not a surprise. The Tijuana Brass, El Solo Toro.'

Spencer thought for a second. 'The Lonely Bull. Right?'

'Si, you know it?'

'Umm, ah…'

'Of course, he doesn't know it. Not everyone likes that mariachi rubbish. What's wrong with Crosby or Sinatra, Ella Fitzgerald?' Savannah threw a cushion at Inez. Peace was restored.

Spencer enjoyed being the observer of the ladies' yin and yang. Their banter helped anchor him, and alleviate the deep and unsettling sense of being adrift here.

'Hey Spencer, do you like the Beatles?' Inez queried, holding the album "With the Beatles" in one hand.

Without thinking Spencer replied, 'Great, terrific band.' He realized this was a piece of his past that had lodged in his memory, 'I loved Sergeant Peppers. What a fantastic album.'

Inez, paused. 'What are you talking about. Spencer, I have every record they have released. What is this "Sergeant Pepper?"'

'You know, "Get by with a little help from my friends." Oh and "Lucy in the Sky."

He started singing the chorus of "Lucy."

Spencer, are you feeling, ok? That's not the Beatles.'

He had a moment of panic. The music, the iconic record cover loomed large in his mind.

'Inez,' he stammered. 'I don't know what to say.'

Her gaze was thoughtful. 'I'm sure it seems real to you, but I guess the kicks to your head have brought about some delusional thoughts. It's not important. Just move on, ok?'

It wasn't ok. Spencer could see and hear all the songs from the album. *What's happening to me? Who am I? Where am I really from?*

'Of course, you're right. I guess a few blows to the head can cause all sorts of problems.'

Weeks of physio came, stretched on painfully, and left. Spencer thoroughly enjoyed the company of Inez, and not just for her cooking. He enjoyed Alf's visits less, but that feeling would fade as the therapy worked its magic and his body healed. And though he would continue to be frustrated by his lack of a past, Savannah's jovial presence in the evenings proved a welcome distraction. He couldn't say what he was doing here. He only knew he was glad to have Savannah and Inez as his personal safety net.

But the next day would be a day of surprise. Spencer had no idea he'd be involved in a new love affair. A love affair with a machine. A motorcycle. That great modern horse, galloping along the freeway. The roar of a wide-open throttle, and the robust throaty growl of a big V-twin would be his new passion.

CHAPTER SEVEN

A BIKING WE WILL GO

'So, it's a surprise, is it Dale? I hate surprises. Ok, you too. I'll tell the Aussie warrior.'

Spencer's ears pricked up when he heard Savannah's guarded response. 'What's all this about?'

Savannah gazed at the phone as if she expected it to explain all. 'These geniuses at head office come up with some strange ideas. I have a feeling this one is a real doozy. Whatever it is, it arrives by truck tomorrow.'

Nine am, the doorbell rang. Savannah with one hand on her Magnum, pulled back the shades and saw a burly man clad in white coveralls standing at the door, clipboard in hand. 'Agent Steele, sign here please. If you'd be so kind as to open the garage door, I'll wheel it in.'

The man opened the back of his flat-fronted Dodge van and pulled a ramp into place.

'What on Earth? You sure you have the right address?'

Spencer shook his head at the sight of the two-wheeled monster being wheeled out of the van. The driver, a solid blonde headed guy in blue coveralls pushed the machine into place. Looking like he'd done this before, he sat astride the bike and kicked down the stand.

'Listen up, Bud. Sure, it's one heavy mother. It's all about balance. Whatever you do don't drop it; you'll never pick it up.

You're a lucky guy. I can only afford an old knuckle. But this…'
He left the sentence unfinished. Spencer could only wonder at
what a knuckle was.

Spencer gazed in awe at the spectacular piece of Milwaukee
steel, now crouched like a mythical beast in the garage. 'Just
look at that.'

Savannah read from the paperwork that had accompanied
it. 'It's a 1962 Harley Davidson Panhead chopper. It's
magnificent. Apparently, it's a 74 cubic inch, with modified
cams. Dale has pencilled on the delivery papers "Goes like a
bat out of hell". Have a look in the accompanying crate and
you'll find the clothes. You're going to love them. Cheers
Dale.'

Spencer was gobsmacked. He couldn't take his eyes off the
extended raked forks and the vivid tank design of a scantily
clad damsel with enormous mammary glands.

'Who's the smart ass, I wonder, who came up with that
God damn artwork. Disgusting.' Savannah scowled.

'Hey, let's see if we can start it up.' Spencer's eyes gleamed
as he knelt down, examining the lavish chrome fittings.

Savannah read the instructions, 'Choke, turn on the fuel.
Make sure it's in neutral. Kick start. Watch out. Watch out,
why in hell, watch out? It's just a frigging motorcycle.'

'Can't be that hard.' Spencer gingerly sat astride the beast.
He turned the fuel on, switched on the ignition and pulled out
the choke. His muscles were still sore, but so far so good.
Standing up, he winked at Savannah and jumped on the kick
starter. There was a loud bang, smoke belched out from the
twin exhausts, the kick starter flew back, throwing Spencer off
the bike.

Savannah rushed over and knelt beside him. 'Spencer, are you ok?'

Spencer grinned. 'Yep, I might just read through the rest of the instructions. Hmm ok, have to prime it. Gentle kick, then kick again. Here goes.' There was an almighty roar, the rolling thunder of the V twin motor reverberated around the garage. Spencer gleefully gave the willing engine a few revs. 'How about that, have you ever heard anything so magnificent in your life? Love it!'

They both stood spellbound as the low guttural chunky pan-head motor settled into a rhythmic thud. It sounded like, *potato potato potato.*

Inez rushed into the garage. 'Por dios, what is this?'

'Calm down Inez, it's one of Dale's little jokes. Don't worry. God damn son of a bitch,' she muttered.

'Let's see what's in the other crate.' Spencer grabbed a screwdriver from a rack on the wall.

He pulled off the timber lid and examined the contents. 'What on earth is all this about?'

Inside the crate was a selection of hard-core biker clothing.

Savannah grabbed a leather mini skirt and a packet of fish net stockings. She grinned at Spencer. 'These better be for you Superman, if Dale thinks I'm wearing this crap, he can damn well think again. What's wrong with the man? Honestly, sometimes I think Dale has more loose screws than a hardware store in an earthquake.'

Spencer laughed as he hauled out a selection of Harley Davidson leather jackets, and leather biker trousers. 'Hey, these are pretty cool.'

As they rummaged through the crate, they could see there were complete outfits for biker guys and gals.

'Hey savannah, check this one out.' Spencer held up a T-shirt with words emblazoned on the back "If you can read this the bitch has fallen off".

Savannah just rolled her eyes and grimaced. She held up a vest. 'Yeah, well just have a look at this, Marlon Brando, this is a bit of a worry. I'm beginning to get an idea of exactly what this might be about. Oh boy, here we go again.'

Spencer's jaw dropped when he stared at the leather vest, Savannah held up. In big bold letters it spelled out "Satan's Warriors Australia". The logo in the middle, depicted a horned devil, sitting astride a Harley Davidson motorcycle.

CHAPTER EIGHT

DALE TELLS ALL

Savannah paced nervously up and down the living room floor, coffee in hand.

'You're going to wear a track in that nice rug,' Spencer warned.

'He's due about now.' Savannah glanced yet again at her watch.

It was the following day, Spencer and Savannah had tossed around ideas and thoughts about the Harley Davidson and the motor clothes.

'Hell, I'll bet you don't even know how to ride the damn thing. And if Dale thinks I'm getting on the back with you in control…'

Spencer had little interest in cars, but the moment he laid eyes on the Milwaukee Monster, as he'd mentally labelled it, he was in love. He had sat, coffee in hand, simply drinking in the vision of this glorious hunk of sculpted metal. He was going to ride it, and he knew he was going to just love it.

'Here he is!' Savannah shouted out to the garage where Spencer now sat on the beast, his long legs stretched out onto the chrome highway pegs.

She practically dragged Dale out to the garage. He barely got in a greeting to Inez before he was faced with a suspicious Savannah and a curious Spencer.

'Well, I guess you two would like to know what's going down?' Dale was all smiles.

'You bet,' Spencer answered. Savannah just nodded.

'Firstly Spencer, you're back on the payroll.'

'Nice. But I remember Shylock from the Merchant of Venice.'

Dale frowned, 'I don't follow.'

'Shylock wanted his pound of flesh. I don't think the agency is doing that because it's "be nice to Spencer Marlowe week".' He couldn't keep his hands off the chopper, honestly. He ran his fingertips over the Milwaukee Monster as the conversation went on. Savannah didn't seem to want to go near it, instead leaning against the tool bench and occasionally sipping at her coffee.

'Ok, yeah, I gotcha. Here it is. We've been wanting to get the goods on this guy Ramirez for some time, and we figure you're the guy to help us do it.'

Spencer paused with his hand on the monster's grip. 'This obviously is connected to the chopper?'

'Yep. Now listen up. Ramirez believes you and Popeye are in cahoots. We'd managed to tap a number of calls between Gordon and Ramirez. As you know Popeye was exchanging opals for heroin and guns. Popeye's crowd, Satan's Warriors, have a second-hand motor bike shop in Milperra, New South Wales. Australia. What they'd planned was ongoing trade between Ramirez and the "Warriors". Ramirez was going to send over second hand Harleys and parts, in crates. Concealed in those crates were going to be weapons and smack. Apparently, it's not easy to get things like handguns in

Australia, and of course the "Warriors" already had a distribution network for the H.'

'This guy Ramirez is no fool. Spencer would be on dangerous ground. Dammit, he sure as hell doesn't look like an outlaw biker.' Savannah stared hard at Dale.

Dale always looked so pleased with himself as the information came out. Now he looked practically diabolical. 'He will by the time we've finished with the both of you.'

'Jesus H, Dale. Oh, I get it. The leather mini skirt, the ugh, fishnet stockings. Give me a break.' Savannah rolled her eyes.

'Hey, hang on. I told you we have a plan. Dammit, woman, just listen, ok? What we thought was, Spencer you go and see Ramirez at his office in State Street, just up the road from Marshall Fields.'

'Hang on, this is the same guy that wants me dead because he thinks I had a part in pinching his black opals.'

'Yeah, well at the moment he does, sure. But.' Dale waved a finger in the air. 'You tell Ramirez you had nothing to do with the con, in fact when you found out about it, you and Gordon had a big falling out. You then tried very persuasively to get Popeye to tell you where the opals were. In any event, you'll be seeing Ramirez in his fancy corporate offices, he sure as hell won't try anything there. He's far from stupid, let me tell you.'

Spencer rolled his eyes. 'I admire your confidence with my life, Dale, but getting back to the opals, I thought they'd been shipped to Australia.' Spencer glanced sideways at Savannah.

'They had, but we intercepted the shipment, in fact.' Dale reached into his trouser pocket and like a magician pulling a rabbit out of a hat, held up a magnificent, shimmering ebony stone. 'Here, catch.' He threw it to Spencer, who deftly caught it.

'Wow.' Spencer rolled it around between his fingers. He admired its cold, hard, lustrous beauty. He tossed it to Savannah.

'So, this is one of those mythical black opals. I can see what all the fuss is about. Stunning.'

'Ok, we, or I, go and see Ramirez in his office, and hope he doesn't just shoot me. And then what?' Spencer wasn't enjoying where the conversation was going.

Dale snapped open his attaché case, pulling out an A4 sized brown envelope. 'Here, have a look.'

Spencer opened the envelope and found some coloured photos. He immediately recoiled. 'Bloody hell, Dale.'

Savannah grabbed the photos and winced. 'Nice one, Dale. You should realize the boy is sensitive.'

'Yuk, Dale, a corpse, and a messy one at that. What's the point?'

'I keep forgetting you've lost your memory. As you can see this guy's face has been pretty much blown away. That aside, he looks very similar to Peter Gordon.'

Spencer peered again at the photo, he shrugged. 'If you say so, but…?'

Dale leaned forward, arms crossed and grinning maniacally. 'You tell Ramirez you had a fight with Gordon. Things got out of hand and you had to kill him, sadly before he could tell you where the opals are. Pretty neat, huh?'

'I have to ask, what's the story on the photo? I mean, who is he?'

'He is in fact a biker. He was murdered over a year ago. I simply trolled through our murder victims on file, believe me there was no shortage of willing applicants.' Dale chuckled, 'He was a criminal in real life. So, in death you might say he's helping repay his debt to society.'

'I won't take up the whole day, but I'll tell you the broad outline. Savannah, how about some coffee, and I don't suppose you have any of those wonderful *empanadas* that Inez makes?'

Spencer and Savannah listened while Dale unfolded his bold plan.

'So, here's the thing. As always, the plan is simple, but let's not confuse simple with easy. The mafia has been successful largely due to the corporate structure Lucky Luciano put in place decades ago. They were once a disparate group of rival gangs fighting each other for territory. Luciano was one smart hombre. He got all the gangs together and established rules. They all had their own designated territory. They had a structure. First there were the chiefs, or Dons as they are called. Then came the "made men", who really were like, I suppose you would say…executives.'

Savannah interrupted, 'Yeah, sure, executives that kill people.'

'Correct, let me continue please, Special Agent Steele,' Dale said with a grin. 'Then came the foot soldiers, who did all the dirty work. The foot soldiers of course want to climb the executive ladder and become made men. To get there they would have to kill a few people, perhaps put their hand up for a crime one of the made men has committed. Oh and of course serve the obligatory jail term.'

'Dale this is fascinating, but as it happens, I know and understand exactly how the mafia works." The Magnum had somehow appeared in her hand, and she was in the process of idly cleaning it with a soft chamois cloth. 'Hell, we covered all that stuff when I did my training.'

'I know, I know, but Spencer probably doesn't. And he'll need to, ok? May I continue?'

'Coffee and empanadas.' Inez swept into the garage, bearing a tray with steaming coffees and the delightful Columbian pastries. She cast a sidelong glance at Savannah's hand cannon but said nothing.

They ended up taking the conversation into the house, where neither Spencer nor Savannah could be distracted. Dale grabbed a coffee and swooped on an empanada, sinking his teeth in with relish.

'I can see your attention span is coming to an end Savannah, so I'll cut to the chase. We know Ramirez wants to become more involved with the bikers. He knows their ability to distribute drugs is just about unlimited, and covers every God damn state in the union. What he wants is to essentially unionize, or to put it another way, organize the bike gangs on the same arrangement as the mafia. Let me tell you, this is the last thing in the world we want. But!' Dale held up a finger. 'But,' he repeated, 'with big time Australian outlaw biker Spencer "the Killer" Marlowe from down under to be the capo dei capo of the whole filthy bunch. Well, need I say more?'

'Kiss my go to hell. Yeah, in fact you need to say a whole lot more. It sounds God damned hare-brained Dale, if you don't mind me saying so?' Savannah leaned back in her chair, arms folded.

'I thought you might say that, Savannah. What about you Spencer, how's it hanging so far?'

Spencer chuckled. 'Is there perhaps more to this story?'

'Smart boy. There is more. We know that Popeye Gordon was planning all of the above when the idiot decided to double cross Ramirez and scoot with the crown jewels and all the other stuff. Now here's the thing: we know, absolutely Ramirez is dead keen to be in control of the biker gangs. The biggest problem is no one gang is going to accept another US leader taking control. There's simply no way that, for instance the Texan Comancheros are going to kowtow to the Hells Angels from California. Here is where you come in, Spencer. As a gang leader from down under you're not involved in any of the politics.'

Spencer jabbed a finger at Dale. 'Aren't you forgetting the biker I killed? Isn't that likely to make me persona non grata with our motor bike riding friends?'

Dale smiled. 'Actually, that's two. The other guy you hit in Chicago has been taken off life support.'

'Great, they're going to just love me.' Spencer rolled his eyes.

'Those two were from a small outfit from Nebraska. They're called the Pagan Brotherhood.' Dale leaned back in his chair. 'They're too small, too insignificant to carry any weight with the big four.'

'Exactly, who, what are the big four, Dale?'

'Ok, that's the Hells Angels, the Comancheros, the Outlaws and the Desperadoes. Anyway, the word on the street is you are one mean son of a bitch. The two you took down were regarded as indestructible, the fact you took them both on, well apparently, they regard you as Superman. And that, that my son is what makes you such a great candidate. You have the right machine, you both have the obligatory tattoos, and of course you have the… the sort of… tough guy resume.'

'Street cred, yeah?' Spencer said, using a term nobody knew would be invented for another fifteen years or so.

'Eh… meaning credibility? Not credit.' When Spencer nodded, Dale grinned in response. 'Perfect, that's exactly what I meant.'

Savannah bounded up from her chair. 'You are seriously out of your mind if you think I'm having God damn tattoos. You can think again. I don't care if J Edgar himself tells me to get tatts, it's not happening. You can have my resignation now.'

Spencer couldn't help himself; he was convulsed. The sight of feisty Savannah dripping with venom, her hands clenching and unclenching, and the villainous scowl on her face was worth photographing. 'I just know there's a punchline. Out with it, Dale.'

Dale burst into laughter. 'Sorry I couldn't help myself. I really just wanted to see some of that famous Agent Steele outrage. That was great. Love it.' He wiped his eyes. 'What we're going to do is have one of our makeup guys plaster your bodies with the latest fake ink. Looks just like the real thing. And you can pick the ones you want, you know, swastikas, death's heads, "death before dishonour" all that sort of rubbish.'

'All you have to do is accept the risk,' Inez said from the doorway. All heads turned to see the worries plain on her face.

'I shouldn't have to remind you that Spencer has a serious bout of amnesia, dear. He might not know what he's getting involved in.'

Spencer blinked several times. 'I could've sworn I've done this sort of thing before, and I'm some kind of superhero.' When Inez's face didn't soften, he tried again. 'These are bad blokes, Inez. Getting drugs and guns off the streets can't be bad, hey?'

'Inez, darling. You know he's right, don't you?' Savannah grabbed her hand.

'Si, but at what price, my love? What price?'

15. THE LEARNING CURVE

Spencer gingerly climbed onto the chopper, clad in his biker gear. *Oh wow, this is as cool as a bucket of Penguin shit.*

Dale had a gang expert come to the house and instruct Spencer and Savannah on every aspect of biker culture. The hierarchy, the significance of the outlaw's patch. Spencer learned he had to become racist, anti-semitic and have a mediaeval attitude to women's rights and place in the gang structure. As expected, Savannah had difficulty containing her disapproval. She'd waved a warning finger in Spencer's face. 'Don't get too carried away with this crap, Sunshine. Don't forget it's only a game.'

More because of her displeasure than anything else, Spencer got into his role with ease.

'Just get up, woman, and clean my God damn bike.' Spencer had grinned.

Now came the fun part, riding the chopper. Spencer realized he must have ridden motorbikes some time in his past.

He quickly learned how to start the beast without it kicking back.

Wearing his biker clothes and his Australian gang patch and with his new slew of offensive tattoos he roared around Long Grove attracting disapproving stares from local residents. April in Illinois, but still a chill in the air. Spencer was grateful for his heavy leather gloves and warm biker clothes.

The Harley, roared, as he practiced swerving and braking. Spencer sought out tunnels and narrow streets so the blast of the exhaust would reverberate. The louder the sound, the wider his smile.

Deciding to expand his horizons, Spencer headed off to Wheeling Illinois, he knew his biker gear would arouse the interest of law enforcement. *What the hell, I'm not breaking any laws.* Just as he turned into Old McHenry Road, revelling in the roar from the shotgun exhausts with the wind in his hair and without a care in the world, the willing Panhead had just accelerated away from the corner. The noise was deafening, but he could still hear the *wee-oww* of the police siren as the police cruiser loomed in his rear vision mirror, the stern faces of the two cops inside, glaring at him.

'This should be interesting.' Spencer pulled over and nonchalantly kicked the jiffy stand out, lazily climbing off the chopper. 'What seems to be the problem, officer?'

Two officers had clambered out of the blue and white police Fairlane, hands resting menacingly on their 0.38 revolvers. 'I'll tell you what the problem is you son of a bitch: too fast too loud and, hey Caleb, what else can we think up here?' The one named Caleb strolled up to Spencer, invading his personal space, a big wad of chewing tobacco in his mouth.

He spat it out, a foul orange blob speckling Spencer's ornate biker boots. Spencer's nose wrinkled in disgust as he stared in dismay at his stained footwear. Caleb was clearly a southerner. Caleb was advancing rapidly into a war zone. 'Gosh darn Irv, I really don't know. Reckon there may be a warrant out for Mister Tough here. We might have to take him back to the station, have a bit of a powwow. What do you reckon?'

Spencer stared hard at the two officers, clearly Irv, also had it in for him, he stood there grinning. A big guy, running to fat, with his stomach overhanging his belt. Pushing his peaked hat back on his head he winked at his partner. Spencer had the distinct impression he was meant to be the morning entertainment for the two officers.

'Sorry officers if I was speeding. Write me a citation and I'll be on my way.'

'Speak when you're spoken to, you son of a bitch,' Caleb snarled, his face now about an inch away. Spencer recoiled as the tobacco spittle sprayed onto his face.

The cop then upped the ante, removing his night stick from its holder he stepped back and prodded Spencer hard in the stomach. 'Turn around, dipshit, hands behind your back.'

Spencer sighed. *I know I shouldn't but.* Spencer grabbed the offending night stick with one hand and chopped the officer's forearm. This wasn't a serious blow, but enough for Caleb to drop the stick and bellow in pain. Spencer had hit him hard enough that the officer's arm wouldn't function for a good few minutes. Caleb grabbed hold of his arm, hugging it to his chest. The other officer, Irv, sprung forward 0.38 in hand, pushing it into Spencer's face. Spencer grabbed the gun hand, forcing it downwards. He squeezed the hand. Spencer had a vision of a Japanese man saying, "Only use the power of Kokoro for good".

Irv was screaming, 'Caleb, for Christ's sake do something.' The officer was now 0n his knees, whimpering, his hand was being compressed mercilessly into the hard metal of the gun. Caleb was trying to grab his revolver with a hand that didn't appear as if it wanted to cooperate. Spencer was more intrigued with the visions of his past flashing through his mind. There was a brief memory of another cop, aviator glasses, another time, another place, an old Ford Customline emblazoned with the word "Federales", a cop lying dead. The vision cleared, just as another police cruiser screamed to a halt. This wasn't an illusion this was the real deal. Two police officers sprung out of the car; two doors slammed. Pistols pointed at Spencer. 'Step back. Get on the ground. Do it now.'

I think this might be the time for a tactical retreat. Spencer was on the grassy verge, hands behind his back. He felt the cold steel of the handcuffs as they clicked into place.

CHAPTER NINE

DALE HAS A LAUGH

'Hey, guys, I thought I was entitled to a phone call.'

Spencer had been charged with two counts of assaulting police officers and one count of speeding. Spencer had been taken to the Long Grove Administration building, housing the police facility and courthouse. The building was a bland cream brick two story featureless late fifties complex, neat clean and conservative. Old Glory and the colourful Illinois state flag hung limply from their poles.

The bored desk sergeant took Spencer's wallet and keys and filled out the custody forms.

'Here you go. Sign this.' The sergeant appeared to be amused by the whole process he glanced at the two officers Caleb and Irving. 'Defendant was unarmed, is that right?'

'Yeah Sarge,' Trooper Caleb was quick to respond, 'son of a bitch got lucky, you know how it is.'

'Really? Two of Illinois's finest, armed with nightsticks and side arms and the defendant got lucky. Yep, I think I know how it is.'

Irving snarled. 'We might just have a little chat with Mister Marlowe once he's behind bars.' He winked at the desk sergeant.

The sergeant glared at the two patrolmen. 'Not in my lockup you don't. This ain't Mississippi. Marlowe's been charged, you never know someone might bail him out. These bikers never seem to be short of money or fancy lawyers. But meantime, leave him alone.'

Spencer heaved a sigh of relief. It was obvious it was a quiet day. Spencer stood in the foyer flanked by Caleb and Irving. He thought it looked very modern and civilized with its near new grey linoleum, plain black steel chairs and a photo of President Lyndon Johnson on the wall. Spencer turned and winked at Caleb, who stepped forward his jaw tensed and his nose flaring. 'I got a long memory, you son of a bitch.'

Spencer grinned and jerked his head forward as if he was going to headbutt the cop. Caleb yelped as he sprung back his hand on his revolver.

'Hey, patrolmen, back off. That's an order,' the desk sergeant barked.

'My phone call?' Spencer grinned.

The desk sergeant pulled his glasses forward on his nose. 'Ok. Keep it brief. Are you calling your lawyer?'

Spencer thought for a moment. 'Well…I guess. Sort of.' *There's only one person I can call. Shit, he's not gonna be happy.*

Grabbing the phone the sergeant handed him, Spencer dialled the number he'd remembered, 'Dale, I have a bit of a problem…'

The call wasn't long. Spencer hung up the phone after listening to Dale chortle just a bit too much.

'Ok Patrolman Irving, escort Marlowe to his cell. Hang on, you probably can't manage on your own take P-a-trol-man Caleb with you.' Spencer smiled at the sarcastic way the desk sergeant spoke their names.

Irving grabbed Spencer roughly by the shoulder and shoved him forward.

'Oh, and if something mysteriously happens to Marlowe, if there is one hair out of place. Do I need to say anymore?' The desk sergeant winked at Spencer.

Caleb pushed Spencer into the cell, muttering something about God damn bikers to his buddy.

The clang of the prison cell door echoed along the corridor as Spencer reclined on the hard bed, a plank of wood on legs. He recognized the institutional smells of stewed coffee, cabbage, stale urine, and something indefinable. *Do tears, anguish and hopelessness have an odour?* Why were these malodorous smells so familiar? He had a vision. Another cell. It was warm. The prisoner was Australian. It wasn't in Australia. Again, the image disappeared. *What the hell does it mean?* A thin, worn, dirty mattress and a frayed blanket scowled at him. Spencer shuddered. He knew fall in Illinois was Baltic and he had little protection against the cold night.

Gazing at the barred hole in the wall, the only link with the outside world, he had another quick memory flash, other cells, other places. *What's my life all about? Am I a career criminal? Have I blotted out my past because of the shame of my crimes? I want my memory back.* He glanced at his wrist, no watch. He had another flashback, a gold and stainless-steel band, the word "Rolex" etched on the bezel. The image disappeared, along with the old man saying, "Happy birthday, son."

Reaching into his pocket, he felt for the comforting outline of the cornicello. The desk sergeant had grinned when he'd searched Spencer. The kindly glance was almost conspiratorial, Spencer had thought.

'Here you go son, keep your trinket. It sure don't look like a weapon.'

In spite of his rather dire position, Spencer surprised himself when he realized he wasn't all that concerned. He pondered his situation. *I've killed two men; Savannah tells me there are others. I'm in big trouble with the law. Savannah tells me it's not only the two at the blues club but I've killed others as well. My God, how many? Apparently, I'm over fifty years old. I have absolutely no memory of my past. I speak fluent Japanese and I'm a lethal killing machine. Yep, why worry?* He ran his hand over his stubbled face, feeling the taut skin. 'Fifty plus. Yeah, right.' He threw his head back and laughed out loud at the absurdity of his situation.

Strange fleeting images would pop up randomly, just as they started to fall into some sort of order, the images would disappear. He saw a big man with an odd wig. He had a loud braying laugh. There was a boat, the sun was shining. He and an attractive lady were laughing as they ate pineapple. The vision was snatched away.

Spencer had been waking in the middle of the night, bathed in a cold sweat, in the throes of a nightmare. There was a corpulent Japanese man, giggling, a pool with a shark, circling lazily. Then mercifully the vision faded.

But what about the here and now? *I'm in Chicago, how long have I been here?* His flashes of memory seemed to be everywhere. *I'm Australian. I know that.* Another vision, he was young, riding a surfboard. Intuitively he knew that was an Australian beach. Every time he tried to focus and get places and times into perspective his mind would go into a whirl. Somewhere in Asia. A nice hotel. Danger. Japanese soldiers. Wartime. Fear. Canoes. Limpet mines. *For God's sake this is like a disjointed adventure movie.* Try as he might, nothing about Chicago flitted through his subconscious. Now his thoughts flashed to a pier. A beach scene. Hard muscled men, pumping iron. A tall, bright bubbly redhaired lady. They were eating ice-cream. Was she a lover? A wife? Then came the vision of New York's Times Square. Now he was in a park. A sunny day. A man was playing a violin. *Hey, I remember. I gave him a dollar.*

Chicago remained elusive. He knew he must have been here for some time, and there was obviously something criminal or he wouldn't have been arrested.

He remembered reading a story about a man who went missing, only to be found thirty years later. The man had left for work, after kissing his wife and baby son goodbye. He then disappeared. It transpired he'd had some sort of medical episode and had instant amnesia. He'd somehow found his way to another city and eventually established another life. There was a new wife, a new baby son and a successful career selling real estate. His first wife had discovered his whereabouts completely by accident when she had glanced through a newspaper from the city he'd located to and saw a photo of him, in a real estate ad. *Is that me? I certainly have amnesia.* Just as this idea was starting to take hold, he remembered Savannah telling him about Los Angeles. *And what about that nonsense in Hawaii over twenty years ago? That can't be right.* He closed his eyes and tried to focus on his current life, and the only people that mattered.

Spencer realized Dale, Savannah and Inez were in his corner. They were his life, his family. *As long as they are there, I don't have a problem.*

With time on his hands his thoughts turned towards this new life that had embraced him. Every time he tried to get a handle on his predicament his mind just threw up images, images that disappeared in a flash. He thought about the details Savannah had told him about their time together in New York, Los Angeles and Japan, it was simply too difficult. None of those images remained long enough for him to connect them solidly to what Savannah had taken him through.

Spencer gazed again at the wrist where a watch should have been. *Hurry up Dale, get me out of here.* Bored voices from the other cells, kept up a barrage of mindless chatter. Everything about the lockup was depressing, the odours of unwashed men, the smell of disinfectant, the most frightening aspect was the feeling of familiarity.

I've been locked up before. Does that make me a criminal? *Do I not remember because my crimes are so evil, I have blotted them out?* He shook his head, his natural optimism gained control, 'You can only deal with the cards you have,' he murmured to himself.

Spencer heard the sound of car doors slamming, then came voices from the reception desk. Sounds like a lot of people. *Thank God, that's Dale's voice.*

'Ok guys in here, get your shots.'

The door to the cell block was flung open, three FBI types including Dale strode into the room, along with, photographers? Eager trench-coated men with their bulky Graflex Speed cameras. A blast of flashbulbs like a fourth of July celebration flashed until Spencer's eyes hurt.

'Dale…thank…'

'Shut up, Marlowe, I'm not your fucking saviour, you've just jumped from the frying pan into the fire. Ok boys, get your pictures.'

'Smile for the camera,' one of the men sniggered as he clicked away on his Nikon SLR, the glare illuminating the harsh ingrained grime of Spencer's dank cell.

Spencer was stunned. First of all, Dale swore. *Dale doesn't swear.* The anger and aggression in his voice was palpable. *What in hell is going on?*

'Dale…?'

'I won't tell you again, Marlowe, shut it. Ok boys bundle him up, get him into the automobile.' He turned to the photographers. 'How about some more pics of Marlowe out the front of the station, another when we put him in the car?'

'Sure, thing Special Agent Fletcher.'

Spencer was thrown bodily against the wall as once again steel handcuffs bit into his wrist. 'Not so tough now you son of a bitch,' the FBI man barked. The lights of the cameras flashed again. Spencer's humiliation was being recorded for posterity and the evening edition.

'Move it.' One of the FBI men, a man who looked like a pro football quarterback, pushed him roughly in the back.

Spencer stumbled out to a black unmarked Pontiac. One of the men held open a door, the other pushed his head down and thrust him into the rear seat. The photographers, clicked, cameras continued flashing like strobe lights.

You have to be kidding, you'd think I'd shot the president.

Disinterested passers-by glanced quickly at the drama as they strolled by. Spencer was glad of his warm biker gear as he felt the coolness of the spring day.

Spencer's absolute belief Dale Fletcher was firmly on his side now appeared to be wrong.

What in hell is this all about? It's obviously serious. What about Dale? Swearing and that undercurrent of violence. Am I suddenly on the USA most wanted list?

The Pontiac, made a right into Old McHenry Road and then abruptly, a left into Country Lane, then into a quiet side street, gliding noiselessly to a stop.

'Ok boys, take off the cuffs.'

'Dale, what the…'

Dale roared with laughter, 'If you could've seen your face in the lockup. Priceless. I can't wait to tell Savannah.'

Spencer rubbed his wrist where the cuffs had chafed. The quarterback FBI guy grinned. 'How did I do Spencer? I'll just bet you wanted to hit me. My name's Gus.' He held his hand out. 'No hard feelings I hope?'

Spencer grinned; the affable Gus had a smile as wide as the Brooklyn Bridge.

'Dale, what in hell, was that all about?'

'When you called me, I realized this was the perfect opportunity. Hard man, Spencer Marlowe, Australian outlaw biker arrested for assaulting police. Marlowe is a suspect in two homicides. It doesn't get much better. This story will be in the Tribune, Ramirez will see it and it sure gives you more of that street cred.'

'Aren't you forgetting something?'

'Not that I can think of.' Dale shrugged.

'You're forgetting I've assaulted two police officers; I've been done for speeding. It'd be jail time for the assaults, surely?'

Dale waved a hand in the air. 'We're FBI, we can pretty much do as we want. But as it happens the desk sergeant had a word with me. Apparently the two clowns that tried to arrest you have had complaints about roughing people up unnecessarily. The trooper named Caleb is from Mississippi and has had a lot of complaints from negroes about racial harassment, so he's sorta on notice anyway. Let's get you back to where you parked the chopper and you can get back home. Don't forget to tell Inez and Savannah the full story.'

'Oh yeah, I'll do that. Particularly the bit where Dale Fletcher swore like a longshoreman.'

CHAPTER TEN

RAMIREZ MEETS THE TALL AUSTRALIAN

The FBI artist had enjoyed the task of applying the lifelike images. Howie wore a perpetual smile while he worked. The dapper man of slight build chuckled to himself as he applied another snarling demon to Spencer's arm. Clean shaven and impeccably styled, Howie looked like the last person who would apply these kinds of ink masterpieces.

The only catch was, they were all fake.

Aside from Howie and Spencer, the large open plan office sat empty. A briefcase perched on one of the chairs placed at two other desks. A half-eaten sandwich and a bottle of Coke sat at another. The walls were grey and the floor a mottled black and white linoleum. A 16mm projector was placed in the middle of the room with a small roll up screen on one wall.

'What on earth goes on in here, Howie? Surely you don't fill all your days just doing this stuff?'

'My God, Spencer, if only you knew.' He swivelled his head, then held a finger to his lips, whispering, 'I could tell you but…'

'I know.' Spencer laughed. 'You'd have to kill me, right?'

Howie chuckled, a deep throaty sound.

'Back to business. How do you feel about the Klan, Spencer?'

'Who?'

'The Ku Klux Klan dummy, who else?'

'Oh yeah, them. Yep, a big fan.'

'Oh and of course, a swastika.'

'Seriously, Howie. Come on.'

'It's alright for you, Kangaroo man. Remember my name's Rosenburg, it's not exactly my favourite symbol. I would warn you however, don't go visiting the synagogue, I'm not sure you'd exactly be welcome.' Howie sniggered.

Spencer had laughed out loud when he'd first stood in front of the mirror and admired the extensive fake ink adorning his body.

Dale had given Spencer a last prep talk before he headed off to meet the feared Ramirez.

'Just remember, Spencer, you're a bad guy. Don't be nice, be aggressive. You have to impress Ramirez that you're one tough mother. You want to partner with him. You're keen to do business with him, but as an equal, not a lackey. Got it?'

The chopper roared along Deerfield Parkway en route to the office of Enrique Ramirez on State Street Chicago.

Spencer weaved in and out of the traffic, startling motorists as the Harley roared its outlaw message.

The chopper's front wheel became airborne as Spencer accelerated onto the interstate, he glanced at the speedometer and realized he was doing over ninety miles an hour, he was loving it. *Better slow down, we really don't need any more police giving me the business.*

Spencer eased off and leaned back, his feet stretched out onto the highway pegs, and started to pay attention to his surroundings. The vehicles looked familiar, but different. He remembered big fins, but they seemed to have gone. The cars were squarer. He admired a low-slung red convertible, the badge said "Mustang".

'Nice, very nice.' The driver a blonde lady with her hair covered by a vibrant crimson scarf, tooted and waved, blowing him a kiss as she put her foot down. The V8 motor roared its approval.

He watched the billboards come and go. 'Aha, McDonald's five miles ahead.' He smiled when he passed the golden arches, realizing he remembered seeing them before, somewhere. Where? He couldn't remember. 'Oh yeah, I know that one.' This time it was a picture of a pretty brunette in a bathing suit, carrying two packs of Coca Cola.

Spencer had well and truly become a two-wheeled convert. For him it was a funfair ride made into a vehicle he could take anywhere.

Spencer had decided to do a bit of a tour to get a feel for the second city. His expedition had started with Lake Shore Drive with the vista of Lake Michigan. The sight of the Navy Pier at East Grand Avenue grabbed his attention, he decided to park the Harley and have a quick stroll around the iconic tourist drawcard. *Bugger Ramirez, he can damn well wait.* Spencer was enthralled with what he'd seen of Chicago. He'd noticed the stunning Chicago River lined with impressive glass and concrete skyscrapers. He wondered briefly if he'd ever travelled to Chicago sometime before, but nothing appeared remotely familiar. He bought an ice cream cone from "The Original Rainbow Cone" ice cream shop. For a brief moment in time, he was just another tourist. He wiped his face with a serviette and licked his lips. Reaching into the pocket of his jeans he felt for the outline of the cornicello. *Time to beard the lion in his den.*

Spencer easily followed the direction Dale had given him. He gazed in awe at the majesty of the wide boulevard. The words of a song briefly danced through his subconscious, "On State Street that great street." The Holy Name cathedral with its massive bronze doors momentarily caught his eye. Elegant Chicago ladies strolled between Lake Street and Jackson. Equally elegant stores appeared to be the flame to their moth. The Harley chattered its rhythmic beat as it tinkered into the parking garage on State Street.

Spencer smiled inwardly at the worried glances of the other passengers in the high-speed lift as it travelled to the thirty third floor, and the office of Enrique Ramirez.

Although Dale had painted the picture, Spencer was surprised at the plush corporate offices of Ramirez. He thought the moniker "Ramirez Entertainment" was rather cute. He remembered Dale's instructions. "Remember, be aggressive. You're a killer. Got it?"

Spencer strode confidently up to the wide oak reception desk, where a very pretty lady was fielding telephone calls. 'No, I'm sorry, Mister Ramirez is busy right now. Please call back.' The name plate on her desk said "Kimberley".

'Yes…sir.' Kimberley looked disdainfully down her pretty turned up nose.

Spencer gazed briefly at the big square grey metal box on the desk. Plugs and leads sprouted out like thick spaghetti. He wasn't entirely sure what function it served. Some sort of communication system was his guess, but he had much more important matters to occupy him presently.

Spencer put his hands on the desk and leaned forward. He did his best to muster what he hoped was a lecherous smile. 'Hi there darling, how's about you get up off your pretty little ass and tell Ramirez, Spencer Marlowe is here.'

Kimberley sat back in her chair, mouth open. 'Um…do you have an appointment?'

'Don't need one. Now, hop to it, gorgeous. C'mon, chop chop.'

Kimberley gazed wildly behind her, ripping a set of earphones from her head and sprinting to the big double polished oak doors that looked like they came from the same tree as the desk.

Spencer could just hear a flurry of voices behind the doors. In less than a minute they were flung open, Kimberley pointed to the interior.

'Um, Mister Ramirez will see you now, Mister Marlowe.'

Spencer strode into the room, slamming the door shut behind him. 'Ramirez, old sport. I believe you'd like to talk to me?'

CHAPTER ELEVEN
FRIENDS LIKE THESE

Ramirez's office had a picture window, gaping at Chicago and its famous river. Spencer had glimpses of an open topped tourist boat as it sailed towards Lake Michigan. It looked like a travelogue without the commentary. The eight-foot-tall gothic lettering advertising the Chicago Tribune glared across the river.

The man himself reclined behind the aircraft carrier sized oak desk. Tasteful modern art adorned the walls. Soft grey carpeting with stark white walls looked fresh and modern. The whole scene suggested tasteful corporate wealth. Prominently on the desk was the Chicago newspaper with Spencer's photo splashed across the front. *Aha, and there's the Tribune. Good one, Dale.* The heading in bold black type "FBI tells Aussie Crime boss Spencer Marlowe told he's not welcome here. Go back home".

Spencer had already read the article stating Spencer Marlowe was the Australian equivalent, of Al Capone, Butch Cassidy and Pretty Boy Floyd, all rolled into one. *This doesn't hurt the street cred.*

Ramirez had an amused smile plastered across his handsome Latin features. Spencer guessed he was about fifty, tall, fit, greying hair. He was clad in a conservative pin stripe suit, a blindingly white shirt with a boldly patterned blue and gold tie. He wore a carnation in his coat pocket. He was in the process of lighting a large cigar.

Two other men were in the room, definitely gangster material, Spencer thought. One man was sprawled on a Chesterfield. Second in charge, Spencer reckoned. He was well built, clad in modish clothes. Flared trousers and a paisley tie. A tight puce shirt clung to his body as if it was painted on. The other man stood, giving the impression of a coiled spring. He was as tall as Spencer with the broken nose and cauliflower ear that advertised "Street brawler, watch it pal".

'Search the prick, Hugo,' the man on the Chesterfield barked.

Hugo grinned as he came up to Spencer and threw him bodily against the wall. Spencer bounced back, grabbing the unfortunate Hugo by the lapels, he then administered a vicious headbutt. Not a killer strike, but enough to see a satisfying spread of colour over Hugo's pale pink shirt. Still holding the lapels of Hugo's very smart black Italian blazer, Spencer placed his left foot parallel to Hugo's right. He gently pushed him backwards while Spencer swung his right leg. At the same time, he threw the stunned Hugo to the floor and placed his steel tipped biker boot on Hugo's neck.

Ramirez puffed on his cigar, watching the proceedings with an amused expression on his face. The other man jumped up from his chair, reaching into his coat.

'Leave it, Jerry,' Ramirez snapped.

'Yep, leave it Jerry, unless you want some too.' Spencer chuckled. He then picked up Hugo by his lapels, and proceeded to dust him down. 'Shame about the shirt Hugo, you must admit the blood contrasts nicely with the pink.

Actually, old son, I'm not sure about pink for a man's shirt. Where I come from people would think you're a faggot. Are you a faggot, Hugo?'

Spencer cringed. He loathed the insulting epithet, "faggot" but he knew he had to play the game.

'Don't push your luck, Marlowe. What do you want?' Ramirez leaned forward on his desk.

'Ok, Ramirez, I understand you need to search me. I'd do the same.' Spencer stepped back from the sullen, still bleeding Hugo, and unbuttoned his shirt, displaying his biker tatts.

'As you can see Ramirez, no wire, no gun. Although I don't need a gun with these two pussies.'

'Alright, tough guy, you've made your point. Sit down and try and convince me why I'm not going to kill you.'

Spencer plonked himself on the swivel brocade chair in front of Ramirez's desk, leaning back with his hands clasped behind his head. He spun around lazily. 'Hugo, sweetheart, go and fetch me a coffee, black. No hard feelings I hope, petal.'

'Boss,' Hugo snarled, 'are you gonna…'

'Shut up Hugo, you haven't exactly covered yourself in glory. Tell Kim to bring two coffees.'

Hugo stormed out of the room; a handkerchief held to his still bleeding nose.

'Nice office, Ramirez. Tell me, who's that cool-looking dude?' Spencer pointed to a painting of a grinning Mediterranean man, with a scar running down the side of his face.

'I thought everyone knew who that was. That's Al Capone. He used to run this town. He had it by the balls.'

'Really, and…?'

'And nothing. The Feds got him on a bum rap, a stinking misdemeanour tax dodge. They jailed the poor bastard.'

'Very sad.' Spencer grinned. He vaguely remembered he'd heard of Scarface Capone.

'His old mansion in Palm Island Florida is coming up for auction. And me, Enrique Ramirez is going to be the new owner. Anyway, enough of the bullshit. Talk to me Marlowe. Make it good. I've had men, good men, out there trying to kill you. Give me a good reason to change my mind.' Spencer glanced at Jerry; a Colt 0.45 semi- automatic pistol dangled from his forefinger.

'Oh really, Ramirez. I'm not sure exactly how you vet your staff or your hit men. If you want to be my partner you,' Spencer pointed an accusing finger, 'you are going to have to convince me you're up to it.' For the first time Ramirez appeared flustered, even confused, Spencer thought.

'Listen to me, you son of a bitch. I run this town. Me, Enrique Ramirez.'

Spencer feigned a yawn. 'Keep your shirt on. I believe you, or I wouldn't be wasting my time talking to you. But seriously, these clowns you have working for you? Really? And the bloody hit men? Let me guess, the late Twinkle Toes and T-bone?'

'What…what happened?'

'Ah yes, honestly Enrique, talk about bloody amateurs.' Spencer grinned.

Ramirez allowed ash from his Cohiba to drop onto his shirtfront. 'You iced them? Both of them? I don't believe it. How the fuck did you do that?'

'Believe it, old darling. As for the how… actually, none of your fucking business. Let's just call it a trade secret. They are both deady-pops. Also!' Spencer reached into his jeans pocket and pulled out a polaroid photo. Leaning across the desk, he handed it to Ramirez.

'What's this. A stiff. So, who is it?'

'That Enrique, is Popeye, or should I say the late Popeye Gordon. Call it a peace offering.'

Ramirez squinted at the picture 'Jerry, take a look at this.'

'Sure looks like him boss.' Jerry grabbed the Colt firmly in his hand, pointing it at Spencer as he stepped up to the desk and examined the polaroid.

'I don't get it. You killed him. Why?'

'Here's the thing Enrique, I was gobsmacked when Popeye told me he'd managed to get the smack and the guns, and still have the opals, all because of an error by one of your idiots.'

'That idiot is now dead,' Ramirez snarled.

Spencer slowly clapped his hands. 'The horse is gone, you left the stable door open. All along I could see great business opportunities with you and your organization. Getting involved with the biker gangs and their distribution network is a licence to print money. When that fool Popeye wanted to blow it all away for a lousy million dollars' worth of opals, I couldn't believe how stupid and short-sighted he was. I don't blame you for one minute trying to get me whacked; I would have done the same. It's true Popeye and I were partners but as you can see, I decided to end the partnership. I think the moron had been sniffing too much coke. Anyway, I've done us both a favour.'

Ramirez leaned back in his chair. 'Ok, give. What happened? And where are my God damn opals?'

'Your opals are, as far as I know, on their way back to Australia. I'm confident I can recover them.'

'Why did you kill Popeye before you had the stones?'

Spencer sighed. 'I had the silly prick covered with a shotty, and he made a grab for it. As you can see from the photo, he copped a load of buckshot in his face. Couldn't be helped.'

Ramirez drew back on his cigar, his eyes narrowed 'Ok, Marlowe. Suppose we do form some sort of partnership. Now, what exactly did you have in mind?'

CHAPTER TWELVE

THE BLACK HILLS

Spearfish Canyon meanders through the beautiful Black Hills of Dakota. If you didn't believe in a God, you may well do so after visiting the Black hills; its beauty is truly unsurpassed. Razor sharp mountains soared above beatific forests and rivers in the Black Hills, but Spearfish Canyon was truly something to behold. The waterfalls practically begged to be painted. Sheer cliffs of towering stone rose up by the riverside, with tenacious trees clinging to them.

The two men tied firmly onto chairs were in all probability not thinking about the bucolic countryside immediately outside of the rustic log cabin they were confined in. It was an impressive rambling residence overlooking the Spearfish Creek, one could imagine it being a holiday retreat for movie stars or millionaires. The owner was probably a millionaire, but his wealth hadn't been accumulated by traditional means. The two unfortunates had been placed in the spacious living room. A cheery log fire burned in the expansive stone fireplace. The vaulted ceilings were made of mountain pine, the floors were ash, burnished to a welcoming warm glow. The picture window looked out upon Spearfish Creek and the canyon walls.

The men had been worked over with baseball bats. They sported an impressive array of cuts and contusions. "Big Belly"

Turner groaned in pain with his right leg shattered, and Frank "the Gunsmith" grimaced, trying hard to forget the pain shooting up his broken arm like fire.

'Jesus, Tolstoy,' Frank moaned, his face contorted. 'We sold a bit of smack. C'mon, it's not the end of the world.'

Tolstoy's answer chilled both men to the bone 'Well,' he said conversationally, 'I guess it's the end of your world.' He chuckled, an easy sound that came echoing back at the two prisoners. 'As you well know, my outfit is the "Black Hills Demons." You guys are Comancheros. It's a hell of a long way from Arizona and Oregon. I don't know what made you think you can sashay into my territory and just do a little business. Sampling your own product maybe. Now, Big Belly, how would you feel if I turned up in Phoenix or Scottsdale and set up shop? Or you Frank, if I wandered into Portland or Salem, you'd get upset. I mean, really, it's bad manners. I hate bad manners.'

"Tolstoy" Barrington was an anomaly amongst the outlaw biker fraternity. Tolstoy liked books. He liked the classics, Shakespeare, Pushkin, James Joyce, and of course Leo Tolstoy.

There was another man in the room, idly playing with an antique Colt 0.45 Peacemaker revolver. His name, or nom de plume was "Con-Rod" Jackson, a high-ranking member of the Black Hill Demons.

'Hey Tolstoy,' he muttered, rolling the toothpick back and forth in his mouth, 'Can we move things along? We're still having a cookout tonight; the boys will be here soon. I gotta go into Deadwood and pick up some more beer and some steaks.'

Con-Rod was the one who'd wielded the baseball bat. He enjoyed inflicting pain.

Tolstoy sighed. 'Always the pragmatist, eh Con-Rod.' It's unlikely the lovable Con-Rod with his third-grade education understood "Pragmatist". He was a little in awe of his boss's command of English.

'Wait!' the Gunsmith begged. "You can't just—"

Two shots from the reliable old Peacemaker reverberated around the cabin, and also bounced off the sides of the canyon itself. Con-Rod lowered the smoking pistol and used the toothpick as it had been intended, between each tooth. Slow and easy. Then he flicked it off the porch and retrieved a new one.

Tolstoy felt the two bodies for a pulse. Nothing. 'Dammit Con-Rod, now we have to carry the stiffs to the truck. You really could have organized this a little better.'

'Where do we drop 'em Tolstoy?'

'Less of the we, son. I've got a bad back, remember. We'll load them into the truck, take them to the usual spot in the,' Tolstoy laughed, 'in the cemetery, I guess. Nobody will find them. Before you pick up the grub and the beer, check on the factory. Make sure those God damn wetbacks are not slacking. Any complaints, you know how to handle it.'

'Yeah sure, there's this one guy Pedro…'

'For Christs sake Con-Rod, if he gives you any lip, shoot the prick. Make sure the others see it. It'll probably help the work ethic. Now c'mon, let's move it. Big Belly is going to be one heavy motherfucker.'

STURGIS

Spencer sprawled, legs stretched out, nursing his coffee. 'Sturgis.'

'I give up, what in hell is Sturgis?' Ramirez leaned forward at his desk, his hands steepled.

'Sturgis, Enrique my friend, is a small town in South Dakota. Ten miles from Deadwood and right next to the Badlands and the Black Hills. Early August they hold the Sturgis Harley Davidson Rally. Let me tell you, this is huge. This year it's a five-day event. All the boys will be there: the Banditos, the Angels, the Comancheros, and a whole lot of others I've probably never heard of. I'm taking my old lady and I thought if you could supply some muscle…' Spencer turned to Hugo, who was sulking on a small divan, a handkerchief still held to his nose. 'Hey Hugo, are we going to kiss and make up? You want to give me a hand in Sturgis? It'll be lots of fun: beer, booze, and dames. Mind you, you're going to need a new wardrobe. I don't think pink shirts are going to cut it.'

'Ok, Sturgis, bikers. Big event, so…?'

'I don't expect a decision right this moment.' Spencer stared, unblinking at Ramirez. 'But here's the thing. We don't have a lot of time and this is one hell of an opportunity. I tell you; this could be a partnership that makes more money than anything you're currently involved in. We could set up the biggest heroin distribution network that's ever existed in the States. If you think it's too big for you to handle, I'll call it a day and…'

'Hey, hang on. Damn you. I can't make a decision just like that. There's a lot to talk about. A lot of organizing. Yes, I'm interested.'

'Boss, look, I don't know. I mean who is this guy? Ten minutes ago you were gonna kill him, and now we're going to be partners?' Jerry glared at Spencer.

'Hang on, Jerry. In the first place, we are not going to be partners. Marlowe and I might be partners.'

'Sorry boss,' Jerry added hastily. 'I didn't mean…'

'Shut the fuck up, Jerry. If I go with this, you're going to make a few dollars, don't you worry about that. What do you reckon, Hugo?'

Hugo, glanced at Ramirez, and shrugged. 'I don't trust this guy, boss.'

Ramirez laughed, 'Yeah, get over it, Hugo. If we run with this, you will be able to take Jerry and a couple of the others. We'll work out the details.'

'So, Marlowe, obviously you have something worked out. Let's have it.'

Spencer had gone over this plan with Dale and Savannah, but not so far as a bloody script. Just the broad strokes. He was winging it.

'Ok, here's the idea. At the Sturgis rally all the gangs are there, but it's truce time. They sell their drugs, they do what they do, but they agree to behave. Sturgis is all about the bikes, and having a good time. All the gangs know about you, and the H you can supply. What I'm going to do is call a meet. I reckon that, with a bit of luck that would involve, a couple of bigshots or reps from each of the gangs, big and small. Every state of the union represented. I'll explain they'll all benefit from cooperating with each other. I'm going to suggest we mark out territories, state by state maybe… we'll work something up. Also, I'm going to make it clear they buy their product from us alone. You're going to have to guarantee consistency and quality. You can do that, Enrique?'

'Yeah, yeah. Go on. How do you plan to enforce it?'

'To a large extent it will be self-enforcing. Once these have their own territories and they see the dough roll in they'll enforce things themselves. But where I come in, along with Hugo and Jerry and few more of your guys is to establish, from the get-go, who's boss.'

Ramirez waved his hands in the air. 'And how exactly do you plan to do that?'

'As I said, me and my old lady are going to rock up to the rally. I'm going to spread the word that I'm in Sturgis to organize some business. I'm the head of a mob from Australia. I'm your partner and we are going to make them very rich.'

'And just like that they're going to say, "Yep sure, we're going to take orders from you and of course me?"'

Spencer laughed. 'You're going to supply me with a decent amount of heroin. I'm going to sell it to them at a discounted rate.'

Ramirez sneered at the audacity of it. 'And they're all going to fall into line?'

'Well getting good quality H at a bargain price is going to help, but this is where Jerry and Hugo and whoever else you can supply will help. We're going to have a show of force. The first smart ass who objects is going to be made an example of. But at the end of the day, these guys aren't stupid, I believe that simple honest to goodness greed, and,' Spencer waved a finger at Ramirez. 'The fact is it's a bloody good plan. Everyone wins.'

Ramirez nodded. 'There is one big stumbling block.'

'That is?'

'That's one Tolstoy Barrington, he's the leader of the Black Hills Demons. He controls all of South and North Dakota. There is simply no way he'll accept anyone else muscling in. And let me tell you, his Sergeant at Arms, Con-Rod Jackson, is one mean mother. You'll have to sort him out, and pronto.'

'Well, Enrique,' Spencer said slowly, 'I'm going to have to make him an offer he can't refuse.'

Spencer placed his cup on the table, 'Nice furniture, Enrique, I can see you're a man of taste and breeding. I just hope your boys are up to the job. So far, they haven't inspired me with confidence. We have a month until Sturgis cranks up. Hugo, Jerry, get rid of those faggot clothes. Get some biker gear. Jeans, leathers, you get the picture.'

Jerry jumped up from the Chesterfield, a snarl seared onto his face. 'Boss, you gonna let this…'

This time it was Ramirez who bristled with anger. 'Listen to me, you morons, Marlowe has made you look like the idiots you are. When you're in South Dakota, you take orders from him. Now get over it, unless…'

Hugo glanced at Jerry. Spencer noticed both men had gone white. Jerry was the first to speak. 'No, Boss, no problem. Marlowe's the man. There won't be a problem.'

Spencer lazily uncoiled his six-foot four frame from the chair. 'Ok Enrique, I gotta go. I'll be in touch.'

OH, WHAT A WICKED WEB WE WEAVE

Dale roared with laughter when Spencer regaled him with the tale of his meet with Ramirez.

'So…he fell for it?'

'Hook line and sinker,' Spencer said with a big grin.

Dale started searching through his pockets. 'I'm still not over the tobacco cravings. It's my wife, you know. She's swallowed this balderdash about smoking being unhealthy. Hell, even my doctor says it's good for you. He smokes Chesterfields, apparently most doctors recommend them. Anyway, I'll tell you what I reckon. You and Agent Steele ride the chopper to South Dakota, establish yourself. Make yourself known…'

'Just one cotton pickin minute, Dale.' Savannah jumped up from her chair. 'I'm not riding on the back of that God damn machine, all the way to Sturgis. Forget it.' She plonked back down on the chair, her arms folded and mouth a thin hard line.

Dale chuckled. 'I sort of figured that, Savannah. Take the Plymouth. Spencer rides the bike. I've got you both checked in to Hickok House. That's a motel in Deadwood. This is right smack in the territory of some guy, name is, let me see…'

'That'd be Tolstoy Barrington, head of the local biker gang,' Spencer added.

Dale started pacing the room. Spencer had another flashback: Dale pacing a room, the same bundle of nervous energy. This time Spencer remembered the tobacco fumes, that had accompanied him. *When was it? Where was I?*

'Just like old times, eh?' Savannah nudged Spencer.

'I guess. If you say so.' *So close!* Spencer groped for the cornicello hoping for his memory to return, but it was not to be.

'Here we go, troops. Spencer, when you and Savannah get to Deadwood. Meet up at some point and ride in together on the chopper. Make a beeline to Saloon 10, on Main Street.'

'Hey!' Savannah yelled triumphantly. 'I've heard of that bar. That's where Wild Bill himself was killed. How about that, eh?'

'Thanks for the history lesson, Savannah. It also happens to be where this Tolstoy Barrington and his cohort Con-Rod Jackson hang out.' Dale handed Savannah a manila envelope. 'Have a peep at these two sweethearts.'

Savannah pulled out two photos. 'Let me guess?' She smiled.

Spencer glanced at the police mug shots. 'Tolstoy what's-his-name and Con-Rod thing-a-me-bob.'

'In fact, their names are Lester Barrington aka Tolstoy, and Leopold Jackson, or, yes, Con-Rod.'

'Vicious looking brutes,' Savannah remarked.

Spencer studied the two photos. Barrington's face was set in a sneer as he held up the police sign. Spencer noticed the long well-cut hair and the cold hard eyes. He appeared to be glaring at the photographer. Spencer concluded he exuded a well-crafted air of malice.

The bearded Con-Rod appeared bored; his face adorned with a cynical grimace.

'The first thing the two of you need to do is sort them out. Not only them, I might add. There's another thug, who goes by the moniker Trunk. He's not a decision maker, but he's a nasty piece of work. He's been indicted for rape a few times and then the victims have been coerced not to testify, know what I mean?'

Spencer nodded, 'I'm sure I'll find him.'

'I'm sure you will, but he really is a tough guy,' Dale warned. 'But anyway, tread carefully. You can't just turn up advertising a new distribution network. You're going to have to get their approval, or not. But one way or another those two thugs have to be on side or neutralized. I know it's a big ask. But you Savannah, and that God damn Magnum of yours, and you, Spencer, with your special talents, I reckon you can do it. Remember we'll have men there as well.'

'Anybody we know?' Spencer enquired.

Dale chuckled. 'Well, Gus and Ty will be there. Let me tell you they're both tough guys.'

'I remember.' Spencer smiled. 'Tell them to not wear their bloody FBI suits. Jeans and leathers, ok?'

'They're going to have more than that. We're the FBI, Spencer. We will have a safe house set up nearby, and law enforcement on call in the event of an emergency.' Dale was now rubbing his hands together, his enthusiasm radiating like a fire and brimstone preacher. 'We've taken over an old outbuilding on the edge of the Black Hills. The idea is you're going to call a meeting with all the gang leaders. We're going to have a cookout, plenty of beer, strippers, you name it.'

Predictably Savannah jumped to her feet 'God dammit Dale, are you deliberately trying to antagonize me or what? You have to be kidding, strippers. What in hell do you think I'm going to do? I'm not having that. It's disgusting.'

Dale rarely showed anger, Spencer had noticed. This time he let fly. 'You listen to me, Special Agent Steele, this show isn't there for your approval or otherwise. We have an opportunity to get a lot of bad people off the streets all at once and I'm not jeopardising that chance because it turns your stomach. These guys are God damn bikers. It's what they expect. This is a direct order. I've had enough of your grandstanding. You will do as you're told. Understand?'

The two operatives glared at each other, Spencer turned his gaze to Savannah and then to Dale, there was an unhealthy silence, finally broken by Savannah. 'Sorry Dale. You're right. I'll grin and bear it. God damn strippers I don't believe it.' She muttered.

CHAPTER THIRTEEN
WARBONNET

The big lumbering V8 Jeep Wagoneer, distinctive with its cherry red duco and its fake wood panelling set off for the old ghost town of Warbonnet, located in a remote hollow in the picturesque Black Hills. Warbonnet had a brief reign of activity in the halcyon days of the gold rush, beginning in 1874. Now looking like a movie set, it boasted a dry goods store, a bank, a saloon, a courthouse and a livery stable. Warbonnet even had its own "Boot Hill" full of ancient and weatherbeaten grave markers. Warbonnet was also the private domain of the Black Hill Demons. It was owned by Lester Barrington. Curious history loving tourists were discouraged. The sight of tooled up members of the outlaw biking fraternity swaggering along the historic main street was generally enough to deter camera wielding strangers.

Con-Rod had carried the heavy ends of the two bodies as they were unceremoniously manhandled into the back of the Jeep. Where an old tarpaulin was draped over their remains, a crude funeral shroud. He'd mentally cursed his impetuousness, shooting the two men in Tolstoy's home. He realized he'd been just too eager to watch the men die.

This job required a new toothpick. He flicked his current one aside and shook another one out of a tiny metal flask, bit it, and savored the taste on his tongue.

Far easier to have ordered them to climb into the God damn Jeep and shot them there. On the other hand, he reflected it was exciting to watch that brief moment of terror flit across Big Belly's face, followed by the sheer horror exhibited by Frank. *Oh my God, his eyes bulged. I swear, you could see it. The way his mouth moved. And he pissed himself. Jesus that was some show. I hate to say it but, hell, that really is better than sex.*

CHAPTER FOURTEEN
THE PARTNERSHIP

Everything was falling into place. Dale was sending Agents Gus Horsley and Ty Brookman to be Spencer's backup. Both men were ex Special Forces. Ty was a Harley Davidson enthusiast and owned an Electra-glide, with its innovative electric start. This Harley monster with its wide saddle and leather panniers, resplendent in its red and cream livery, was bold and loud.

Ramirez had decided to travel to Sturgis in his Lincoln, accompanied with Hugo and Jerry.

Savannah had reluctantly embarked on some exploratory runs on the back of Spencer's chopper. Dale had given her free rein in choosing her fake tattoos.

'I would have thought being a woman you might have chosen things like flowers, birds, butterflies, that sort of thing?' Dale had shaken his head when Savannah proudly showed off her ink. Mostly they were lifelike images of handguns. The only concession to femininity was a drawing of her cat "Capone" on one shoulder.

Savannah was driving her Plymouth to Deadwood. She had reluctantly agreed to then discard the Detroit metal and become a legitimate biker "Old lady" and only been seen on the back of the Harley.

Fearless crime fighter Savannah had turned to jelly when she'd first climbed on the back of the chopper. When Spencer accelerated with a roar down their quiet residential street, she clung on and prayed.

'Slow down, you bastard, I'll damn well arrest you for endangering the life of an agent. Oh God, this isn't happening. God damn Dale I'll shoot the fool, so help me.'

Spencer eased the chopper back and then wound the willing Panhead motor up a notch until they were doing sixty miles an hour on the interstate. It was a delightful day, Savannah was wearing her biker jeans and leather jacket, with a scarf, tying down her locks.

Spencer kept the bike steady, as the V twin emitted its low burbling chatter.

Savannah had been clinging on to Spencer's waist so tightly he could hardly breathe. He could then feel her beginning to relax as she leaned back, now holding the sissy bar.

'Hey, you know what? This isn't too bad. How about you take Inez for a quick spin when we get back?'

They pulled off the interstate, deciding to wend their way back through the suburbs to Long Grove. Spencer yelled out to Savannah, 'There's a white Chevy convertible, with its top down, that seems to be following. It was behind us on the interstate. I've made a few turns, but it's still there. They look like kids, I don't know. Students perhaps. But you never know.'

The chopper had just pulled up to traffic lights in Arlington Heights when the Chevrolet sidled up alongside of them. Savannah and Spencer glanced at the occupants. A quartet of football jocks, big loud and drunk were laughing and singing. The two in the back were brandishing bottles of Coors Beer.

'Hey, darling, why don't you split from the pussy on the bike? Come and join us.' One of the other jocks piped up. 'We got a party to go to. We got grass, some really good shit. We got beer.'

'Yeah, babe and you got us. Tell that candy ass punk to pull over before we run him off the road.'

'What do you reckon, Superman?' Savannah tapped Spencer on the shoulder.

'Well, I guess they do need to learn a lesson. I'll pull over.' Spencer grinned.

Potato, potato, potato. The V twin fell silent. Spencer nonchalantly kicked down the jiffy stand.

Savannah jumped off the bike, leaning on the car, she pointed at the last guy who spoke. 'If you reckon you can show a girl a good time, ok guys, let's do it.'

Spencer thought he saw a look of uncertainty on the college students faces as he unfolded his six foot four heavily tattooed frame from the chopper and strolled over to the convertible.

'So, boys, you're going to sort me out, right?'

One turned to his buddy, 'Go on Buzz, give this clown a whack, show him what for.'

Spencer stared long and hard at the unfortunate buzz cut freshman.

'Y'know Buzz, you guys spend your time playing games with a ball. Savannah and I, well we spend our time killing people. Now Buzz, I believe it's about time for the playoffs. I'll just bet you're going to be a star player, am I right? '

Before he could answer, Savannah turned her gaze to the unfortunate Buzz. 'Buzz, tell me, with your college education, did you learn about the praying mantis?' Buzz just stared, his eyes like saucers. 'Well, you see Buzz, after sex, the female kills and eats the male. The thing is, that's me to a T. I have these performance expectations. Now before you and I get to know each other a little better, I want you to think, praying mantis.' Savannah opened her jacket exposing the shoulder holster and the .357 Magnum.

Buzz was clearly the leader, he glanced at his now worried colleagues. 'You don't scare me, bitch,' he snarled.

Spencer leaned over the Chevy, and grabbed Buzz by the throat, 'Sunshine, if you're not scared of this lady, you're a bigger fool than I took you for. Step out of this car, and I guarantee you'll be watching the playoffs from the bench. Your choice, dear.'

One of the other jocks whined, 'Guys, let's just go.'

Savannah grinned 'Wise advice, but I'm afraid you're not driving.' She pointed to the empty beer bottles strewn through the Chevy.

'You're walking home.' Savannah leaned over and grabbed the keys from the ignition.

The front passenger spoke. 'You can't do that. Who do you think you are, bitch?'

'Who do I think I am? I know who I am. I'm your worst nightmare.' She flashed her badge. 'I'm FBI Special Agent Savannah Steele. 'Now, boys, out of the car and start walking.'

CHAPTER FIFTEEN
WE HAVE A PLAN

Jerry paced up and down his boss's lavish office. 'Boss, I'm really not sure about this guy.'

Enrique Ramirez sipped at his Templeton Rye, Al Capone's favorite whiskey, and rolled his eyes at his subordinates. 'Just listen to me, you two. This guy's a stone-cold killer. Just look at what he did to Popeye. He's got one hell of a plan, and we're gonna make a shit load.' He strode to his desk and grabbed the Tribune. 'You did read this, if you can read. Look at what it says. For Christ's sake, this guy has been targeted by the fucking FBI.'

'Yeah, yeah, we both read it, boss. It could still be a set-up.'

'Are you guys for real? He's a fucking Australian. Since when did the FBI recruit anyone who wasn't a God damn American? Just listen to his accent. He's Australian. Check out the God damn tatts. FBI guys all look like Mormon door knockers. The same suits, the same haircuts. He's not FBI, he's not the law, I'm telling you. I have a nose for this. This guy made you look like the idiots you are.'

'Yeah well, still. Maybe you're right. Maybe he's not FBI. That doesn't mean we can trust him. I'm with Jerry, I don't like him.' Hugo spoke quietly, sitting on the couch his head between his hands.

'Let's not get ahead of ourselves here,' Ramirez repeated himself. 'Listen up you morons, Marlowe's going to help us make a shit load of greenbacks, so for the time being, do as he says. Trust? Who says anything about trust. Of course, I don't trust the son of a bitch. He wants something from us, and vice versa. We watch him. We make sure there's no double cross. We catch him…then…at the right time, the right place, the fucker is dead meat. Comprende?'

'Sure thing, boss. I just hope I'm the one to pull the trigger. God damn Aussie son of a bitch.' Hugo seemed to brighten up.

'This guy has what it takes to pull this thing off. Just look at what we have. He's going to rock up to Deadwood with you, Jerry, and you, Hugo. He's going to have his woman. What's her name again?'

'Savannah,' Jerry piped up.

'He's going to use Deadwood as the base. From there it's ten miles to Sturgis. He's going to network with the bikers. Hell, if he can do that, I tell you we're cooking.'

Ramirez secretly had been very impressed with the way Spencer had so quickly taken control of his two lieutenants. Already he was beginning to think he and Marlowe could go on to bigger things. He liked the confident way he addressed Hugo and jerry as he was leaving,

Listen up Hugo, Jerry, to do this thing right, we have to kick a bit of ass. Got it?

Spencer had explained to Ramirez about the disused outbuilding Dale had hired. It was a remnant from the gold mining days. What Ramirez didn't know was that although the old hall was well away from prying eyes. It wasn't away from prying ears.

Dale Fletcher and a crew of technicians flew from Chicago to Rapid City, and then covertly driven to the Black Hills, fitting the building with sophisticated listening devices. They would turn it into a mountain of evidence against Enrique and the bikers, at the kingpin's expense.

'Enrique, here's what's going down. You're going to fork out for strippers, a band, food and booze. Got it?'

This was something new for Ramirez, someone else was calling the shots. He'd stared long and hard at Spencer, 'And what about you? What are you paying for? Why am I the dummy who foots the bill eh?' He kept running through his mind at the conversation that had transpired. He didn't like it, but he consoled himself with the thought, that at some point he'd turn the tables on the Australian loudmouth.

'Cos, Enrique, I'm the show, I'm the guy who's going to put it all together. You want to hand it over to him?' Spencer pointed to Hugo. 'Or perhaps Jerry? By the way Jerry, I hope you've bought some new gear, those flared trousers and your paisley shirt I'm sure knocks them dead in the disco, but where we are going, they're going to think you're taking the piss.'

Jerry held his hands out, mouthing silently to Ramirez. 'What the fuck is he talking about?'

Spencer had roared with laughter. 'Sorry sport, it's an Aussie saying "taking the piss. Having a lend". In short it simply means they're going to think you're a big city wanker.' So, for fuck's sake I'm not telling you again, go to the Harley shop. Jacket, jeans, boots, comprende?'

The more Enrique thought about it, the more he thought Spencer wasn't going to live long after the Sturgis biker convention bullshit. Once Marlowe set up the distribution network, there was no reason to keep the cocky Aussie asshole around. He'd have to try running things with a couple of holes in the head.

CHAPTER SIXTEEN

ON THE ROAD AGAIN

Ty and Gus were making their own way to Sturgis. Spencer and Savannah left the leafy suburb of Long Grove early in the morning. A tearful Inez embraced them.

'Spencer, you make sure you look after Savannah. And Savannah, look out for Spencer. Por dios Savannah, I know what you put in the trunk.' She wagged a finger. Her face was drawn, she had wrapped her arms tight around Savannah, whispering in her ear.

Inez had risen early, bustling around the spacious, well-appointed kitchen, cooking up a mountain of *arepas*, the Columbian corn cakes along with crispy bacon, fried eggs and of course fresh Indiana orange juice and steaming coffee.

Savannah had attempted to load the trunk while Inez was busy in the kitchen. Spencer had smiled when he caught a glimpse of grenades, sawn off shotguns, pistols and an assault rifle.

'I'm not sure Dale wants us to murder every biker who's going to be in Sturgis. What on Earth is that?' Spencer pointed at the assault rifle.

'Keep your God damn voice down.' Savannah gazed nervously at the house.

'I think Inez actually has a bit of an idea what you're doing. Now, that piece of hardware what is it?'

Savannah's eyes gleamed. 'Oh boy, isn't she a beaut. That's an MI6. 5.56 mm, seven hundred rounds a minute, semi-automatic. Of course, you noticed the sawn-offs, just the thing for Spencer Marlowe, who couldn't hit the Sears Roebuck building if he was standing out the front.'

'Exactly who in hell am I expected to shoot, anyway?'

'Keep your God damn voice down. Hopefully you're not going to shoot anybody…but…well you never know.'

Spencer climbed aboard the Harley Davidson chopper. In a now practiced motion, he stood and gently primed the kick starter, then pushed down hard. The twin pipes emitted their usual thunderous roar. He turned around and grinned at Savannah who was ready to go in the pillar box red Plymouth.

First stop was South Beloit, Illinois. As much as possible they avoided the anonymity of the interstate, choosing the byways, the scenic route. They made a stop at Dee Dee's in Pearl Lake for coffee. The friendly waiter didn't bat an eye at the vision of two outlaw biker types plastered with outrageous tattoos. They relaxed on the patio; Spencer stretched his legs full length. The tables had old fashioned black and white check tabletop with the usual assortment of ketchup, mustard and the famous Illinois corn relish.

Spencer had revelled on the journey so far. He'd found the vista of corn and apple orchards soothing. This was middle America the land of homespun values, church on Sunday, with old glory waving in the breeze from every other home. Well maintained clapboard homes surrounded by lawns and gardens completed the picture of communities confident and at peace. Spencer quickly realized his outlaw biker image was not what the locals felt comfortable with. He was aware of hostile stares, children pointing, suspicious parents guarding their broods like mother hens with their chicks.

Mickey's Diner at Madison, Wisconsin reluctantly served them some mediocre coffee.

Bemused onlookers stared as the chopper rumbled up to the diner. Spencer kicked the jiffy stand down, stood and stretched. Mickey's looked like an old Pullman car, transformed into a chrome and steel classic American diner. Standard design, with a long lunch counter and a clapboard kitchen bolted onto the back. It was compact but bright and clean. Booths lined the far side. Spencer grinned and gave Savannah the thumbs up as they noticed the black and white police cruiser parked in the lot.

It seemed as if the tattooed Spencer and Savannah were as welcome as a reggae band at a Ku Klux Klan rally. Everything stopped. The pair slid into their red leather booth with at least thirty eyes following their every move. A big man clad in white shirt, trousers, apron and a white side cap emblazoned with the words "Welcome to Mickey's" slouched up to their table, fixing them with a baleful stare, a roll up cigarette dangled limply from fleshy lips.

'Yeah, help you?' His demeanour and manner suggesting otherwise.

Spencer smiled a big toothy grin. 'Yep, buddy, two coffees, black, if you please.'

Spencer was a little concerned Savannah would display some anger, but in fact she appeared to have difficulty controlling her mirth. She leaned forward, whispering, 'Don't you just love it? I think they're just waiting for one of us to jump up and yell, "This is a stick up."'

The surly waiter slammed the coffees down in front of them, spilling the watery liquid onto their saucers. He threw the check down at the same time. 'I guess you folks won't be dining…will you?'

Spencer grinned at Savannah. 'I think that translates to "You definitely won't be dining, and bugger off."'

They drunk their watery coffee and sauntered back to their waiting vehicles, the eyes of the diner's patrons watching, relief etched on their faces. Savannah turned her gaze to them, giving a saucy wave.

The two patrolmen gulped the last of their sandwiches, nodded to each other and followed them into the car park.

'Wait up,' one of the officers, a granite like chunk of a man with a big gun and a no-nonsense attitude growled. His partner who looked like a rookie, stood nervously next to him.

'Licence and ID?'

'Certainly, officer.' Spencer smiled his most engaging smile. He pulled out his newly minted driver's licence and social security card. Savannah leaned against the Plymouth, trying hard not to laugh.

The rookie now seemed to have gained a little courage. He stepped up to Savannah, invading her personal space. 'Hey, didn't you hear the sarge?' he snarled. 'Licence and ID, bitch.'

Savannah stood. Hands on hips, eyeballing the rookie, 'Bitch, is it?'

The rookie quailed, something in Savannah's confident manner well and truly took the wind out of his sails, he gazed desperately at his partner, who said nothing. The sergeant handed Spencer's ID and licence back with a wink, and continued to watch the interaction between his junior partner and Savannah. Spencer wondered if it was the younger officer's first day on the job.

Savannah moved closer to the young cop. 'Is this the way they taught you in the academy? Is this the way you speak to a lady, who isn't in any way a suspect? Well…?' and she barked, in a voice even the diners probably heard, 'Answer me!'

'Sorry Ma'am. Sorry. I thought. I mean. You looked. I mean. You know, the tattoos and all.' He again turned a desperate gaze to his partner who stood there rocking in his size fourteen shoes, his face now battling to control his mirth.

Savannah laughed as she placed a motherly hand on the young officer's shoulder, she leaned forward, he flinched. Savannah whispered into his ear, 'Actually kiddo, it's Special Agent Savannah Steele of the FBI. Now…do you want to take my word for it? You really shouldn't you know. I could be making it all up. I could be Savannah Steele, America's most wanted.'

The sergeant finally entered the discussion. 'I heard that. You're FBI? And this one?' He pointed a finger at Spencer.

'Yep, him as well.' Savannah nodded. She turned to the young beetroot-faced patrolman.

'What's your name?'

'Umm Kevin…Ma'am. Umm, Deputy Kevin Farrell.'

'Ok, Deputy Kevin Farrell, no hard feelings.'

CHAPTER SEVENTEEN

ROCHESTER

Savannah and Spencer were both well and truly in holiday mode as they left Pearl Lake, once again deciding on the scenic route. This took them through Lake Kegonsa State Park in Wisconsin.

Their two vehicles wound their way through dramatic twists and turns with views of the magnificent lake. A burst of warm weather saw people swimming, setting up tents and unhitching trailers from their Chevrolets and Fords. This was America at play. Nature's display in the early days of summer was stunning. They passed through wetlands, old forests and rolling prairies. The large sprawling white oak trees, their width almost the same as their height dotted throughout the park. Crimson and white cone flowers added vibrancy, beautiful petals, born to parade in the light breeze.

With the wind in his hair and the contented roar of the big twin resounding in his head, Spencer found he was dwelling less and less on his past. You *can only deal with the cards you've been dealt.*

All too soon they had left nature's beauty behind and were back on the interstate and entering the city limits of Rochester City, Minnesota. It held neither the cosy small down appeal, nor the impressive skyscrapers, but its lake and the angry, incoming stormfront gave it its own majesty.

Savannah had booked ahead at a Holiday Inn near the famous Mayo Clinic. She'd figured the anonymity of one of the chain hotels might be the smartest move. Their outlaw appearance certainly raised the eyebrows of the check in clerk, but the FBI identification quickly bought an obsequious smile to his carefully shaved features.

'Have a lovely stay, ma'am, sir. Anything you need, just let me know.'

Dinner was at Nellie's on historic Third Street. The eclectic denizens of Rochester's Latin Quarter, the Montmartre of Wisconsin barely gave Spencer and Savannah a second glance.

Savannah and Spencer liberated a fine old Bordeaux before attacking two eye fillets, with green beans and dauphine potatoes.

Gazing at the menu, Spencer had a moment of panic at the eye watering prices. His salary certainly didn't run to ten-dollar steaks and fifteen-dollar bottles of red wine.

Savannah had leaned back in her chair quaffing her pre-dinner Budweiser. 'Wipe that worried look off your face, Boy Wonder. Expense account, ok? Hey, do you remember when we dined at the Brown Derby in LA and you ordered that expensive cognac and I read you the riot act? My God that was a night, wasn't it?'

Spencer stared blankly. 'Um, no, not exactly.'

Savannah pointed an accusing finger at him, and burst into laughter. 'Hell in a handbasket, it was hilarious. I was absolutely star struck when I saw Rock Hudson dining at another table, and then you told me the bad news, he was a friend of Dorothy. You could have knocked me over with a feather.

'And then of course Tokyo. Surely you remember Tokyo?'
Spencer shook his head.

'Jesus H, the fight to the death with that Yakuza prick. You killed him, and we thought the Yakuza were going to kill us; instead they damn well apologized. I'll never understand those yellow mongrels.' Savannah shook her head. 'Oh, and tell me you don't remember the gunfight at the OK Corral, when I shot that guy? That was Olympic class, that shot, and dammit, seriously, you don't remember?'

At the mention of Japan, Spencer had a brief vision of a waterfall, thundering down. Pain, an old Japanese man, fatherly, someone important. Then he remembered the words "Kokoro." *Only use the power for good.* He remembered a brick being crushed to a fine powder as he squeezed it.

Then the vision was once more cruelly wrenched away.

CHAPTER EIGHTEEN
THE FUNERALS

The old drinking establishment had been renamed The
Long Branch.

Con-Rod noticed the boys were in town. Blue Boy's old
Indian motorcycle, his pride and joy was at rest, with its cherry
red paint and the emblem of the gold Red Indian, scowling on
its tank. Next to that was Thumb Tack's Knucklehead,
rumoured to have belonged to Elvis. There was also a
collection of British speed twins, Triumphs and Nortons
mainly. Altogether, he counted around twenty motorbikes.
Most of these were the veteran members of the Black Hills
Demons, but they had a couple of nominees. Fresh faces, but
all bearded.

'Someone else can dig the God damn holes this time.' He
chuckled, a low rumbling sound, and shifted his toothpick
over to the other side of his mouth. 'The God damn nominees
can do the dirty work. They want their patch; they can damn
well earn the motherfucker.'

Slamming the door of his Jeep, Con-Rod by-passed the
saloon and made his way to the livery stable next door. In one
of the long disused horse stalls, he began to examine a
collection of old stone and wooden headstones. He and the
boys had filched these unique pieces of western history from

cemeteries across the Midwest and as far away as Arizona and
Texas. He chuckled again as he dragged out a favourite.

Here Lies Lester Moore.

`four slugs from a 44.

No, Les

no more.

DODGE CITY

1865

The next choice was a barely legible wooden sign with
roughhewn wording.

Dick Dancer

Horse Thief

Hanged

ARIZONA

1871.

Con-Rod flicked his toothpick and sucked at his teeth
before hauling the two headboards to his Jeep. Opening up
the tailgate, he threw them on top of the corpses.

'Damn. Time for a beer.' Dusting off his hands against his
jeans, he swung the old oak batwing doors aside and strode up
to the bar. Two Barrels Harper was the barkeep.

Grabbing the pewter mug of beer, he leaned back against
the bar. 'Listen up, boys. It's funeral time.' He pointed to one
of the nominees. 'Hey you. Hank, isn't it?'

A lean, hard-muscled man, clad in denim jeans, shirt and
Stetson, raised his hand. 'Yo.'

'And, now, let me see. You there, what's your name?'

'They call me the Ferret.' A thin, rat-faced man with
pronounced acne scars and teeth that resembled a demolition
derby, held up his hand.

'Ferret, Hank, grab some shovels from the livery stable and head off to boot hill. Jasper, I hope the holes been dug already.'

A man mountain with long black greasy hair, clad in jeans and his Black Hills Demons vest growled. 'Been dug for days, Con-Rod. Who we burying?'

As a mark of respect, Con-Rod removed his Stetson. 'Well boys, today we's burying Lester Moore and Dick Dancer. We gonna give em a proper Christian burial. So, I want you all up at Boot Hill. And you, Gearhead, isn't it?'

'Yeah, that's me.'

'I want you to dig another hole. It shouldn't be long before we have another customer. From south of the border, if you follow me.'

Gearhead had no idea what Con-Rod was talking about, but he knew he had to do as he was told.

'Sure thing, Con-Rod.'

Grabbing a worn bible from the scarred old black walnut bar, he strode to his Jeep. The motley crew of bikers quickly threw down their beers and made their way to the top of Main Street.

Warbonnet, Boot Hill.

'We meet here today in the sight of God to pay honour and tribute to men taken before their prime.'

CHAPTER NINETEEN

DEADWOOD

The Panhead led the way as Savannah and Spencer made their way to Deadwood. The *thump, thump* of the chopper's exhaust reverberated off the wall of Spearfish Canyon. They had travelled through the Badlands where more and more and more Harley Davidsons decked out in colourful artwork could be seen.

A lot of the riders, Spencer reckoned, were weekend warriors. Accountants and school teachers during the week and bikers on their days off. Amongst this eclectic throng were a number of outlaw riders with their tell-tale patches. Hells Angels, Comancheros, and so many more. Spencer even noticed a Japanese outlaw with the words "Sapporo MC Japan", emblazoned on his patch.

Deadwood was a town taken over by choppers of every make and model. The roar from the big twin motors was constant and deafening. Spencer and Savannah drove slowly along the main street and then headed up the hill to their motel Hickok House.

Anonymous would be the best description. Nothing fancy, Hickok House was a replica of thousands of other motels across the US: a broad carpark in front of an L shaped accommodation block. Next to reception was a compact restaurant with all the western favourites. Naturally, photos of the late Mr. Hickok were prominently on display, along with his reputed paramour, Calamity Jane.

The bored receptionist repeated like a Hare Krishna mantra, that we could view the grave of Calamity and Wild Bill, up at Boot Hill, a short walk away.

They collected their keys for adjoining rooms on the ground floor. Spencer grabbed their bags from the Plymouth.

'I'm bushed. How about we have a bit of a rest before we investigate the natives?' Savannah yawned.

Spencer was pleasantly surprised with his spacious motel room. The double bed featured a rustic brown chenille bedspread. A deep pile carpet in a chocolate brown was complimented with cream walls and a wallpaper with miniature pictures of Buffaloes, which seemed appropriate. On the dresser perched a very chic portable television. Spencer idly grabbed the cornicello from his pocket, examining it closely as he had done countless times before, admiring the ancient, filigreed silver. *Are you the key to my past?* He had a spasm of laughter. *Bloody mumbo jumbo.*

Still, the image came to him, unbidden, of having *sake* with a whole host of Japanese men in suits, around a low table. The image was gone as soon as it had come.

Thrusting it back into the pocket of his jeans, he switched on the TV and kicked his boots off. Rising from the quaint barrel chair, he grabbed the television guide from the coffee table and flopped onto the bed. Spencer had dozed off while watching a rather improbable show about a beautiful witch, residing in suburban USA. He woke with a start when his bedside phone trilled.

'Oi, Spencer, wake up. Time to bring some mayhem to Deadwood.'

Spencer was taken aback when he knocked on Savannah's door. She grinned and gave a small curtsy. She was decked out with leather trousers, a black sequined shirt and a bulky black Marlon Brando style motor bike jacket. 'How do I look?'

Spencer grinned. 'In a word, scary. The jacket's a bit big.'

'Yeah, well it's hiding you know what.'

She opened the jacket, revealing the Magnum in its quick release holster.

Spencer raised an eyebrow. 'That's it?'

'No, not exactly.' Savannah pulled up the leg of her black jeans, revealing a small matte black automatic nestling into a neat ankle holster.

'Any more?'

'Well of course there is…' Savannah pulled out a wicked looking Bowie knife from an inside jacket pocket.

The car park was crammed with Harley Davidsons, Indians and even a couple of old Henderson and Ace motorcycles. Spencer was now a bona fide enthusiast for all things on two wheels. 'Hey Savannah, just check this little beaut here.'

'Do I have to?' She yawned. 'Dammit, I think I preferred the old Spencer who wasn't interested in things mechanical. Ok it's a motorbike. So what?'

Spencer was drooling. 'This is an English HRD Vincent. Worth thousands.'

'Enough already, let's get unpacked, hop on your chopper, head into Deadwood and see if we can't liven things up.'

CHAPTER TWENTY
THE WAKE

The mourning party made their way back to the saloon. A cheerful Con-Rod flung open the batwing doors, flipping the toothpick end over end in his mouth. 'The drinks are on me, boys.'

A dozen bearded, tattooed, leather clad bikers ambled into the bar. 'I just love funerals,' a tall thin man bellowed. 'Hey there, Two Barrels, start pouring them beers. Digging graves is God damn thirsty work.'

'It's all right for you, Jimbo, I didn't see you getting your fucking hands dirty.' A powerfully built thug, wearing leather pants and vest, threw down a shovel onto the timber saloon floor and glared at Jimbo.

'You don't fucking scare me, Gearhead,' Jimbo snarled.

'Hey boys, boys. Can it. This is a solemn occasion. Show some fucking respect, ok? And just remember there's plenty more room up on the hill,' Con-Rod bellowed, shifting the toothpick from left to right, cocking his jaw out to one side. He pointed at the two bikers and scowled. 'Ok then. Gearhead, Jimbo, no more of your shit. We got some serious drinking to do. Two Barrels, keep the beers a coming, son.'

This was enough to ease tensions. Everyone knew an angry Con-Rod was a dangerous Con-Rod.

Two Barrels Harper kept the thirsty bikers topped up. He pulled Con-Rod aside. 'Who were those two stiffs really, Con-Rod?'

Con-Rod removed the toothpick a moment and gave a hearty laugh. 'Couple of Comancheros who thought they could sell some smack on our patch.'

'Silly move, they should've realized the consequences.' Two Barrels nodded.

'Anyway, Two Barrels, life goes on, well, for some perhaps. Who's at the factory?'

'Slack's there, he's been up there a while. You want I should get one of these guys to take over?'

'Nah, they've all had a bit to drink. Anyway, they need a chance to let their hair down. We're gonna have a big week next week.'

Con-Rod reached behind the bar, grabbing his Colt six shooter and holster.

Two Barrels grinned. 'Now just what are you up to, Con-Rod?'

'Well let's say Boot Hill isn't a segregated place. All races are welcome.' He tossed the toothpick out and made for the door.

The Jeep just about knew its own way to the factory. Con-Rod headed down the familiar path. He was largely oblivious to the aspen, birch and oak trees that dotted the surrounding hills. The beauty of nature was something that had passed Con-Rod by.

The Jeep rumbled to a halt alongside the apparently derelict old barn. Worn timbers, a shingled roof in poor repair, and windows with smashed panes added to the air of neglect.

As he entered the barn, some wood pigeons hastily flew out through a hole in the roof. Con-Rod opened a small wooden wall cabinet. Inside was a very modern switchboard, with a prominent red button. As he pressed the button a section of timber flooring noiselessly slid open. A hoarse voice called out. 'That you Con-Rod? About fucking time. I've been down here with these stinking wetbacks for at least six hours.'

'Sorry, Slack, we'll make it up to you. I want you to take the Jeep back to the saloon, have a beer, have a nice time. Tell Two Barrels I want someone to take over in three hours. Got it?'

'Yeah, but like I said, six fucking hours…'

'Keep your shirt on, Slack, just remember, bonus time next week.'

As Con-Rod had made his way down the steps, he gazed with satisfaction at the underground factory where twenty Mexican workers were transforming the leaf into cocaine. A quick glance told him they were running low on supplies. There were barrels of sulfuric acid, lime water, concrete and various other chemicals. The air conditioning emitted its familiar hum. The Mexicans glanced in his direction. One, he thought with satisfaction, appeared a little fearful.

Slack was holding a shotgun and he had a Colt 0.45 semi-automatic pistol in a shoulder holster. Skinny as a beanpole. He wore baggy jeans and a dirty white T shirt, a worn straw sombrero he'd taken from one of the workers who'd died suddenly on the job, was perched on his head.

Con-Rod leaned forward, whispering, 'That little cunt Pedro still whining?'

'Little prick never shuts up. Doesn't happen when you're here. As soon as you leave, he starts up. You know, "I'm hungry, when are we going to be able to go see our wives, our children?"'

'Sorted Slack. Sorted. Hey Pedro, where are you son? Come and have a chat to ole Con-Rod. We can have a powwow about your wife and kids.' He grabbed up his special tiny flask and shook himself out a new toothpick while he waited.

A young emaciated Mexican man made his way nervously from the back of the factory.

'Si, Señor Con-Rod. We were promised, mucho dinero, and only two months, then we leave. And, Señor Con-Rod, it's been over six months and no dinero.'

Con-Rod shook his head sadly. 'Really, that long? Six months you say, and no dinero. That just doesn't seem fair. What do you think, Slack?' Slack just grinned as he pushed the *sombrero* back on his head.

'No,' he echoed. 'Don't seem fair at all.'

With lightning speed Con-Rod grabbed his six-shooter, he cocked it and pointed it at the cowering Pedro, who'd wet his pants. 'No Señor, no…'

CHAPTER TWENTY-ONE
THE ONLY GAME IN TOWN

Spencer opened the throttle and roared into Deadwood's main street. A now acclimatized Savannah hung on to the sissy bar. Spencer was sure Savannah actually enjoyed the stares from the crowds packing the sidewalk. Once again, the primal roar of hundreds of Harleys rattled the windows of the old western town.

Spencer reversed into a small place close to the Number 10 Saloon.

They climbed off the machine, Spencer glanced at Savannah, 'Well, I guess it's time to make an impression.'

The House of the Rising Sun blasted out from the jukebox. Eric Burdon's rasping voice spilled out onto main street, competing with the gurgling, thumping sound of V twin motors.

Clearly the twentieth century had overtaken the Number 10. It in no way looked like the bar of the gunslinger days. Modern, wrought iron chairs and barstools gave the old saloon a slightly out of touch contemporary appearance. Behind the bar was a vast wine rack with the best vintages that Napa Valley provided. The whole feel was just a little too hip and modern. Spencer could imagine stockbroker types swigging their martinis as they discussed the world of finance.

There was of course no shortage of Wild Bill memorabilia. The chair he'd been seated at when he was shot in the back, hung from a wall. Bill's last hand of cards, the famous aces and eights were framed and had pride of place on another wall. The modern flashing lights of the garish poker machines looked rather out of place.

Savannah and Spencer peered into the crowded bar, hoping to see either Con-Rod Jackson or Tolstoy Barrington. A quick glance assured them neither man was there. Occupying a barstool with his back to them was a giant of a man, long greasy black locks and the obligatory tattoos. Even from the back he appeared menacing. Spencer figured he had to be at least six foot seven, and solid muscle. The patch on his back was loud and proud: "Black Hills Demons". Savannah tapped Spencer on the shoulder, 'Hell, Spencer. He looks like a handful even for you. How about a tactical retreat, or…?'

'Or what?' Spencer whispered.

'How about I just shoot the son of a bitch?'

'Come with me.' Spencer turned and walked out of the saloon. Savannah breathed a sigh of relief. 'Good idea, I reckon he was too tough even for you. Let's regroup and see if we can come up with a plan B.'

'I have an idea. Follow me.' They strolled a little further up the street, to the Deadwood Tobacco Company.

'What's your game, Spencer? You hate smoking.'

'Shhh, I've seen this in a movie. It's always appealed to me. May I have one of those please, and a box of matches.' Spencer pointed to a half Corona.

Spencer had breasted the counter of this iconic cigar shop; Savannah was totally mystified.

'Are you nuts? You're really going to set fire to that thing?'

'You bet.'

Spencer unwrapped the cigar, bit the end off, and lit it with a match. 'Well, here goes.'

He tentatively puffed on it. Immediately he was hit with a paroxysm of coughing. 'Jesus, and people do this for pleasure.' He leaned against the wall outside and puffed a few more times. 'Hey, I think I'm getting the hang of it. Now, follow me, girl.'

Spencer strode purposefully back into the saloon, pausing to speak to a waiter, "Tell me pal, what's the name of that big guy over there?'

Spencer pointed to the man mountain who was stuffing a plate full of fried rice into his mouth, while alternatively slurping coffee from a pewter mug.

The waiter paused. 'Um, that's… Look, mister, he's trouble.' Spencer noticed the young man's bottom lip start to tremble. 'Honest, just leave him be, ok?'

'His name?' The young waiter quickly appraised this heavily tattooed biker and his equally fearsome "Old lady" and obviously thought this may be the lessor of two evils.

'His name sir, is Trunk. Sir, please just leave him be, he hates to be interrupted when he eats.' The waiter held his hands together, as if in prayer.

'Not a worry, Sport, we come in peace.'

Spencer had another puff on his cigar, making sure it was still alight. He grinned at Savannah, and mouthed, 'Wish me luck,' as he slid onto the stool next to the fearsome "Trunk."

'G'day, mate, Spencer Marlowe from Australia. I'm the Sergeant at arms for "Satan's Warriors."'

'Fuck off.'

'Trunk, isn't it?' An unabashed Spencer moved a little closer.

Trunk turned a baleful stare onto Spencer and had another sip of his coffee. Spencer noticed a small swastika tattooed, high on his right cheekbone and the word 'Fear' artistically resembling the Ford slogan, inked below his left eye.

This time Spencer blew a cloud of blue smoke into Trunk's face.

Trunk sat motionless. He carefully placed his fork on the bar. His head swivelled. His face slowly broke into a humourless grin.

Spencer continued to smile at Trunk, he leaned forward. 'Allow me?' He then stirred the biker's coffee with his stogie, finishing the manoeuvre by placing the smouldering cigar into Trunk's fried rice. Spencer then offered a big, warm, toothy grin, as if to say, 'Aren't we having fun?'

Trunk had reached the end of his patience. With a fearsome growl, he lumbered to his feet, at the same time grabbing Spencer by his lapels, almost tearing the shirt, jerking him up to full height.

'Say your prayers, dipshit.' Trunk's face curled in a grimace, exposing a mouth with missing teeth, and the bits of fried rice with beef.

The two men faced each other like gunfighters of old. This was almost the exact spot where Wild Bill had been shot in the back all those years ago.

Trunk grinned as he moved an arm's length away. Spencer had thought the biker might have shown a little innovation, but then he figured Trunk only ever had to land one blow and it would be game over. Spencer had guessed correctly, Trunk wasn't a follower of Marquis of Queensberry. After all, he didn't have to. Nobody really wanted to fight him, and chances are he'd never had to really hone his skills. Well, not until now.

With a roar, Trunk threw a very powerful haymaker. Newton's Law of motion makes perfect sense. A body in motion tends to stay in motion. A body at rest tends to stay at rest.

Trunk's speed and power was truly very impressive; however, the speed and power can be used very effectively to the opponent's advantage. Spencer grabbed the huge fist and helped it along its way. A vicious kick to Trunk's right leg saw Trunk hurtle to the floor. He rolled over, knocking some wrought iron chairs over. The patrons had moved out of the way, forming a large circle. Money began to change hands, with the odds see-sawing rapidly.

For a big man, Trunk was very agile. He'd just bounded to his feet when Spencer administered a foot sweep. Once again Trunk was on the floor. Odds were now changing rapidly as stunned bikers tried to fathom what was happening.

Once again Trunk now breathing heavily staggered to his feet. 'Fight like a fucking man,' he screamed.

'Which man did you have in mind, Trunk darling?'

Trunk didn't appear to have a lot in his repertoire. He attempted another haymaker. Spencer grabbed Trunk's fist, smashing it into the old Oak bar. Trunk's face was white, as he held his damaged hand.

'Dear me, Trunk, that does look painful. You'll have to be more careful.'

Appearing to forget his hand, Trunk roared, and launched himself at Spencer. 440 pounds of murderous aggression, with one mission. There was an immediate hush from the crowd.

Spencer adroitly sidestepped, driving a very hard elbow into Trunk's mouth. A few remaining teeth clattered onto the hardwood floor. This time it was a scream of pain. Trunk fell, spreadeagled on the floor. Spencer brought the heel of his biker boot down hard on Trunk's already damaged right paw. Trunk howled as his hand and several fingers broke.

'Now listen up Trunk, and everybody else. My name is Spencer Marlowe. I want to have a meet with every Sergeant at Arms of every club in town. I have a proposition. And guess what, Trunk, that includes Tolstoy Barrington.'

CHAPTER TWENTY-TWO
MY HERO

Savannah batted her eyes at Spencer, giggling as she held a hand to her chest. 'Oh, my hero. Be still my beating heart.' Spencer and Savannah had unhurriedly stepped out of Number 10 and were strolling along Main Street.

Spencer shook his head. 'I actually thought I might have overdone it a bit.'

Savannah's mood immediately changed. 'Don't start that Bolshie stuff with me, Superman. Just remember who these bastards are and what they're up to. As far as I'm concerned, I would have been happy of you'd finished the schmuck off.' She then laughed out loud, punching him on his shoulder. 'Well I reckon we have their attention. What do you reckon?'

***

Spencer and Savannah posted flyers around Deadwood and Sturgis. In big bold letters the advertisement announced a free cookout for the sergeant at arms and patched members of all the motor bike clubs, along with dancers, a band and free beer.

'God damn strippers,' Savannah muttered as she glued another sign to a lamp post.

The chopper had made its way to the main thoroughfare of Sturgis. With difficulty Spencer had found a slot in between a Norton 650 Special and a café racer, Sportster Harley.

'Time for a beer,' Spencer announced as he admired their handywork. The fliers now placed all along Main Street.

They'd agreed to meet Ty and Gus at the Dungeon Bar in Main Street Sturgis. As expected, the bar was loud, dark and noisy, with two fearsome biker types at the door, both wearing white T-shirts with the word "Security" emblazoned front and back. One of them held a hand up. 'Excuse me sir.' Spencer paused, immediately tensing. The bouncer was if anything, scrupulously polite, 'Marlowe, isn't it?'

Spencer nodded coolly, remembering to maintain his tough guy persona. 'Who wants to know?' At the same time, he was surprised his face was known already.

'We heard what happened between you and Trunk, at Number 10. We just wanted to warn you, we don't want no trouble here, ok?'

Spencer noticed the words were uttered with a smile.

'Don't worry mate, we come in peace, fair dinkum.'

Savannah and Spencer made their way downstairs to the murky Dungeon Bar. It was loud and messy. Savannah glared at the memorabilia hanging from the ceiling. Spencer shook his head and laughed. From every available pillar, post and ceiling space hung a variety of used women's bras. It appeared all of the bras' original owners had been exceptionally well endowed. Along with the bras were literally thousands of used mainly one dollar bank notes, all autographed by previous patrons.

I Can't Get No Satisfaction was blasting from the big chrome and bling jukebox.

They pushed their way through the biker throng to the courtyard bar at the rear.

The sudden burst of sunshine made them momentarily blink. Against one narrow courtyard wall was a bar with a collection of rowdy bikers, drinking beer and talking motorcycles. The bar was roughhewn from old railway sleepers. The timber planked wall featured a long banner advertising Budweiser Beer. Pinned to the wall were endless photos of Harley Davidsons and their owners, their old ladies often posed on their machines, unrealistically clad in very un-motorbike bikinis or sexy lingerie. At the rear of the courtyard sat the inevitable pool table. Four leather clad ladies, smoking and nursing cold Budweisers were rowdily playing eight ball.

Spencer nodded to Savannah. 'Just look at those two desperadoes.'

They spied Ty and Gus hunched at a table, earnestly locked in conversation. Both looked big, mean and tough, clad in denim and black waistcoats. They appeared to be men who lived and breathed motorcycles. Gus and Ty smiled and raised glasses when Spencer waved, 'Yo, Spencer, Savannah, pull up a chair.'

Spencer and Savannah grabbed two bentwood chairs and made themselves comfortable. There was a round of vigorous handshakes and back patting as they finished recounting the fate of poor Trunk at the Number 10.

Spencer winked at Savannah. 'Now you're officially a biker old lady, how about you do your stuff?'

'Exactly what stuff?' she enquired coldly.

'Go and get me a beer, girl, and be quick about it.'

Savannah administered a short hard kick at his shin.

Spencer yelped. 'Hey, that bloody well hurt.'

Savannah leaned forward, whispering, 'Let's not get too deep into character, Spencer.'

Spencer rubbed his ankle and laughed, 'Sooo sorry girl, but we do have to play the part. It would simply look all wrong if I bought the beers.' He smiled sweetly. 'Please may I have a beer?'

Savannah scowled. 'I'm not sure I like this game.' She noisily pushed her chair back and stomped to the bar.

The next hour was spent going over the details for the big event. Spencer had picked up a decent serve of cash from Ramirez, who was envisaging a river of gold from the outlaw biker gangs. Dale had spared no expense in making the sting as authentic as possible. The hall had been wired and miked up by the FBI techs. Food and drinks were being organized. A popular rock and roll band, Dexter's Comets, were arriving from Rapid City.

Although the Black Hills Demons lorded over this section of the country, they were small in comparison to the other big biker gangs arriving here. Gus and Ty assured them that once word got around about Spencer's antics, they'd be approached by people from the Comancheros, Desperadoes, even the Hells Angels. They'd all be invited to the cookout, they'd all incriminate themselves in a place wired to the gills with microphones, and they'd all be brought down in one fell swoop by Dale.

'So long as we get the leadership of all these God damn dealers,' Savannah said, and they drank to that.

'Where is Dale, anyhow?' Spencer asked.

'They won't be out for several more days yet,' Gus said. 'Don't want any of the bikers to stumble onto the sting. The less conspicuous law around here the better.'

The conversation had now turned to motorbikes.

'Spencer that chopper of yours is one mean machine, how many cubes did you say it has?' Ty was stretched out, clearly in his element and at peace with the world.

Both Ty and Gus loved their motorcycles. Savannah was rolling her eyes. 'Hey how about we talk about something interesting. Guns perhaps?' she suggested hopefully.

Motor bikes continued as a discussion point.

'Hey Spencer, mine has an electric start, none of that God damn kicker stuff.' Ty leaned back in his chair, a smug look on his face.

Gus chipped in, 'Ty, your Electra-Glide is an old man's bike. I mean, just look at the size of the saddle. Just built for a fat old guy.'

Before Tyrone could answer Savannah jumped up. 'Enough already, I've had enough of motorcycles. I'm going to play pool with the ladies.'

Savannah sauntered over to the leather clad chicks at the pool table.

'Hi girls, Savannah from Chicago. Can I join in?'

Introductions were made. A petite, bubbly blonde handed Savannah a pool cue. 'Hey I noticed you when you came in. The tall guy, he's yours? He's super cute. My name's Charlene.'

Savannah grinned. 'Yep, he's mine, all mine. Hands off ok?'

Spencer received several sidelong looks by these girls, but they all agreed to keep off her property.

The others chimed in, 'Trixie from California.' She was a tall languid blonde in jeans T shirt and a skulls and eagles World War Two Nazi visor hat.

'Cheryl, Arkansas,' declared a short stocky girl, who offered a quick smile as she leant over the table, making a shot. 'Eight ball, top pocket,' she announced confidently.

There was a loud crack as the black and white shot unerringly into its home.

'God damn, that Cheryl, she's one hustler. I tell ya. Mickey, Albuquerque, New Mexico.'

Mickey wore the tightest jeans Savannah had ever seen. She had a very low-cut top, with a very impressive cleavage. Every time she bent over the table, whistles of approval rang out from guys at the bar, watching the old ladies play.

Cheryl won that round. They had just set the balls up for the next match when a scruffy biker, with weightlifters' arms and chest strode up to the table. 'Trixie, babe, I want some dollars.'

'Johnno, I've got none to spare, you know that.'

Johnno's face morphed into a snarl. He knew his biker buddies were watching the exchange, some already making snide remarks. 'I think we know who wears the pants here.' Yelled one. A big beefy guy with an Outlaws patch and a collection of vibrant tattoos howled. 'Hey, Johnno,' one yelled, 'She got you pegged.'

The big biker grabbed the unfortunate Trixie by the arm and bent it painfully behind her back.' Money, bitch. Now.'

Spencer nodded at Ty and Gus. 'Christ, this's all we need. This guy's going to be lucky if he comes out of this alive.'

Spencer had watched as Savannah's face became a hard mask, her mouth a thin line.

'Let her go dipshit. And I mean now,' Savannah snarled.

Johnno did indeed let the unfortunate Trixie go. He turned on Savannah, grabbing her by the lapels of her jacket. 'Watch your fucking tongue. I don't care who you are or who's old lady you are, I'll kick the fucking shit outta ya.'

His sweaty face was inches from Savannah, breathing foul nicotine and beer fumes. A solid chunk of a man, everything about him suggested manual labour. Thick, hairy, tattooed arms a big head with no apparent neck and a stomach, starting to spread.

Savannah's first thoughts were, *how did such a plug ugly brute like Johnno score a lady like Trixie?*

'Oh, dear Johnno you really shouldn't have,' she murmured.

Savannah had been holding a number one, yellow and white pool ball in her hand. She kneed the unfortunate biker in the crutch. He gasped for breath, his mouth open. She thrust the pool ball into it. He fell to the floor, wheezing. His face turned blue as he struggled for air.

Trixie came to his aid, prising the ball out of his mouth. He sat leaning against the stout wooden leg of the pool table, his breath coming in short heavy gasps.

'Are you alright, baby?' Trixie cooed. She then turned in fury at Savannah. 'You bitch, you mighta killed him.' She strode up to the now stunned Savannah. 'You're lucky I don't scratch your fucking eyes out.'

Savannah threw her hands up in the air and strode back to sit with Spencer, Ty and Gus. 'Jesus H Christ!' she exclaimed.

'Can you believe it? They damn well deserve each other. Let him beat her to a pulp. See if I care. Give me a bloody beer.'

CHAPTER TWENTY-THREE

DINNER IN DEADWOOD

Spencer and Savannah rode back to Deadwood, both locked in thought. What was the next move?

'Early dinner at Number 10, and see what happening,' Spencer yelled into Savannah's ear, the roar of the chopper making conversation difficult.

Spencer reversed the Harley into a waiting slot at the front of the tavern. They both cast a wary eye over the bustling crowd of hardcore bikers and assorted weekend warriors.

As they entered the saloon, Spencer wondered if it was his imagination, but it seemed as if a hush fell over the bar. He felt like Wild Bill himself, as if he was the famous gunslinger about to gun down some errant cowboys. Spencer and Savannah glanced at the stool where the unlovable Trunk had been sitting. The chair was empty.

Grabbing two of the heavy wrought iron chairs they took a seat at one of the fashionable timber and black iron tables.

The same nervous young waiter from before approached with two menus. Tall and thin with a riot of acne, his hair was cut in the fashionable Beatle style. Spencer winked at Savannah. He immediately felt sorry for the lad. His hands were visibly shaking as he handed over the cards with the bill of fare.

'What's your name, sport?'

'S-S-Simon, Mister Marlowe.'

'Simon, mate, we come in peace, truly.'

Simon appeared to have a little bit of courage 'W-w-well sir, that's what you said last time.'

'Simon, old son. No trouble tonight. Guaranteed. Two steaks and two cold Budweisers. Ok?'

'Yes sir, Mister Marlowe.' Simon appeared visibly relieved. 'Oh, and Mister Marlowe, I have a message for you.' He pulled a piece of paper from his top pocket, and handed it to Spencer.

Spencer showed the scrap of paper to Savannah.

"Phone me. I want a meet. Tolstoy". Under that was a hastily scrawled phone number.

Savannah grinned. 'You going to call?'

'You bet, but steaks first.'

***

The sky had miraculously changed from tar black to cocktail blue. Spencer and Savannah had arranged to see Tolstoy Barrington in his self-described "humble shack" in Spearfish Canyon. The racket of the V-twin Panhead motor reverberated off the walls of the canyon. Once again the beauty of the Black Hills seemed to be at odds with the brutality waiting to strike.

Spencer had phoned Tolstoy after dinner. They had agreed to meet at 10 the next morning.

Having spent a restless night tossing and turning, Dale's warnings about Barrington played on Spencer's mind. Savannah, on the other hand, slept like a baby.

'I think this is it,' Spencer yelled to Savannah.

Tolstoy's "humble shack" sprawled alongside the river, it's designer roughhewn log construction and shingled roof with its stables and outbuildings was impressive to say the least. It reminded Spencer of the Ponderosa, the home of the Cartwright family in the TV series Bonanza he'd watched with Savannah and Inez.

Spencer idled the chopper up to the front of the house and kicked the stand down, parking next to a Jeep Wagoneer. 'Humble shack my arse.'

Savannah was now adept at climbing off the Harley without scorching herself on the exhaust pipes. She immediately scanned the area looking for hidden threats.

In keeping with the rest of the house the front door was sturdy panelled oak, varnished to a mirror finish, an incongruous Xmas wreath pinned to the top, Spencer imagined leftover from December.

Spencer winked at Savannah. 'Here goes.' He rapped noisily on the solid timber.

A small wood panel slid open. Spencer smiled at the baleful eye, peering at them, the eye's owner obviously trying to figure if they were friend or foe.

'We come in peace, brother,' Spencer boomed. 'And…bearing gifts.'

The door was flung open. Spencer observed a hulking biker with a full beard. A six gun was ominously holstered at his waist. Gun aside, the big biker looked tough, but slow moving. It was habit ingrained that Spencer automatically evaluated potential trouble; he noticed the beginnings of a paunch, the man was left-handed, so that would be the direction a punch would emanate from. Mainly he saw confidence: this man rarely was confronted with serious opposition, Spencer figured. He also saw complacency. In this man's world there were no threats.

'Who is it, Con-Rod?' a voice from within yelled.

'Yeah, Tolstoy, it's them. Ok, you can come in,' growled the surly Con-Rod. He grabbed the toothpick out of his mouth and scowled, then rolled it between his fingers. Eventually it found its way back into his mouth, where it stayed in motion the entire time. Spencer thought it made the biker look ridiculous, his mouth twisting this way and that, one sneer transforming immediately into another.

Savannah and Spencer warily entered the spacious domain of Tolstoy Barrington. Spencer took in the vast living room with its magnificent timber finishings and the picture window overlooking the jewel blue stream that was Spearfish Creek, as it curved gently through the forest, happily hopping over rocks. Altogether as pretty a scene as one could imagine.

Spencer figured Savannah was probably oblivious to the beauty of nature and would certainly be evaluating the two men and would secretly be itching to find an excuse to grab the magnum concealed under her jacket, in her spring-loaded shoulder holster. As always Spencer was more concerned about a volatile Agent Steele than the possible threat from two complacent bikers.

Tolstoy appeared at ease sprawled on a wide leather and timber easy chair. His feet encased in biker boots and resting on a large oak coffee table.

He nodded, but didn't get to his feet. 'Frisk 'em, Con-Rod.'

Con-Rod leered as he went to pat Savannah down, the toothpick seeming about to drop out of his mouth onto her face for a moment.

She growled, 'Touch me, you son of a bitch, and your Con will separated from your Rod. Comprende?'

Con-Rod was clearly taken aback. Something in Savannah's voice appeared to make him pause.

'Tolstoy?'

Tolstoy laughed. 'I think she's got you worried.' Tolstoy's laughter seemed to defuse the situation.

Spencer chuckled. 'I tell you what, sunshine, how about you frisk me twice, and leave the lady alone. Believe me son, she doesn't take prisoners.'

Con-Rod ran expert hands over Spencer. 'He's clean, Tolstoy.'

'All right, have a seat. Coffee?'

Spencer and Savannah sat together on a small two-seater leather divan.

Spencer shook his head. 'No, let's just get down to business.' With that he pulled a clear packet of white powder out of his jacket pocket and threw it to Tolstoy. 'Like I said, a present for you.'

Tolstoy caught the plastic packet with one hand, one eyebrow was raised. 'Is this what I think it is?'

Spencer nodded.

Tolstoy opened the packet, had a sniff, dipped an exploratory finger in and licked it.

'Very good. You have my attention.'

Spencer then outlined the business model he and Ramirez had formulated. Tolstoy listened, saying little.

Rising to his feet, Spencer expanded the plan, 'So in essence every biker gang will have one state of the union as their own territory. In your case the Black Hills Demons will have both South and North Dakota. It'll be your responsibility to maintain order on your own patch. If any outsiders try and muscle in, that's your problem not ours. I guess you can handle that?'

Con-Rod smirked around his toothpick. 'Yeah well we just sorted out a…'

Tolstoy cut in, 'Shut it Con-Rod, ok?'

Spencer glanced at Savannah, she nodded imperceptibly.

Tolstoy grunted. 'So, you can guarantee virtually unlimited smack of this quality for a thousand dollars a kilo? How the hell can you do that? Where is Ramirez getting it from? Sonofabitch, how the fuck does he do it?'

Spencer sat back down. 'That's none of your business. All you need to know is the supply will keep coming.'

Con-Rod stomped over to Spencer. 'You're a cocky prick, aren't you? I don't think you're so tough.' He took that toothpick and flicked it directly past Spencer's ear with expert aim. Still, he now seemed naked without it. His mouth twisted and grimaced like it was still there.

'Shut the fuck up, Con-Rod,' Tolstoy barked. 'You know what he did to Trunk. Anyway, this is business, it's not about who can kill who, ok? "Ad Meliora" eh Spencer?'

Spencer grinned. 'Yes indeed, "Toward better things."'

Bloody hell, where did that come from? I know some Latin?

Tolstoy roared with laughter. 'A man after my own heart. You speak Latin, Huh?'

'A little.'

Savannah gazed at him in awe. 'Jesus, here we go again. I didn't know you spoke that crap.' Spencer shrugged; he didn't know himself. He felt in his pocket for the reassuring outline of the cornicello.

CHAPTER TWENTY-FOUR
FAMILY TIES

'Jesus, I don't believe it.' Tolstoy Barrington screwed up the telegram and threw it unerringly into a wicker wastepaper basket.

'What is it you don't believe?' Con-Rod enquired.

'I extended an invitation to my sister in Illinois to let her son Elmer Budd spend a couple of weeks with me. Apparently, the little bastard has been going off the rails, you know, drinking, living it up, chasing the chicks, that sort of thing. Christ, I never thought she'd take me up on it.'

Con-Rod raised an eyebrow. 'Sounds ok to me. Pretty normal, in fact.'

Tolstoy shook his head. 'Yeah well, what do you do? Anyway, we'll have to watch over the little prick and make sure he doesn't get into trouble. And…and that means he can't know about our business. So just pull your head in and make sure he doesn't get any ideas, ok?'

Con-Rod took a healthy swig of his Budweiser and broke into laughter 'Elmer Budd, you're kidding me. And will the wascally wabbit be coming along as well?'

'What the fuck are you talking about?'

Con-Rod wiped a hand across his mouth 'You know, Elmer Budd and Bugs Bunny?'

'You idiot.' Tolstoy grinned. 'That's Elmer Fudd, not Budd. But yep, it's sorta close enough. Why in hell would you call a kid Elmer anyway?'

Con-Rod just shrugged. Although he didn't want more going on, not with the Sturgis Rally, the lab underneath Warbonnet, and this new Australian prick, there was nothing to be done about it.

'I gotta go pick up the kid,' Tolstoy said.

Con-Rod blanched, his toothpick falling to the floor. 'But—'

'Hang onto your balls. I'll be back with the little prick before this whole deal kicks off.'

CHAPTER TWENTY-FIVE

THE BOYS ARE BACK IN TOWN

The old church hall was both dilapidated and weather beaten. Its ancient timbers, carved out of Black Hills oak and spruce, would have witnessed weddings, wakes and hoedowns. It stood forlorn and forgotten in a clearing nestled in a meadow. The beautiful small valley, with sky-punching mountains in the background, was home to the pollen rich black-eyed Susans and the blanket flower with its yellow ray petals.

FBI tradesmen had hurriedly fitted the hall out with everything required for the big night. Power had been reconnected, the spacious hall had been swept, dusted and polished.

The carpark that would have hosted horse and buggies and probably covered wagons now accommodated a black Lincoln with Chicago plates, a Jeep Wagoneer and three Harley Davidsons.

Spencer, Savannah, Tyrone and Gus had rolled up on their motorcycles moments after Ramirez, Hugo and Jerry arrived. Minutes later Tolstoy and Con-Rod had slowly entered the car park in their Jeep.

The men gazed warily at each other, hard faces, and suspicious glances.

Spencer clapped Hugo on the shoulder. 'Jesus, mate, you scrub up a treat now you're out of your faggot city clobber. What do you reckon Savannah, you'd never guess he was a city slicker would you?'

Hugo snarled. 'You don't scare me Marlowe. One more…'

Hugo's hand was just snaking to his jacket pocket when Ramirez barked, 'Hugo, fucking behave yourself, Marlowe was just "taking the piss".' He grinned. 'That's what you Aussies call it, right?'

'Got it one, Enrique.' Spencer turned his gaze to Hugo and held out his hand. 'Come on, sport I was just having a lend, as we say back home.'

Hugo sulkily grasped Spencer's hand.

'Moving right along, how about we move on into the hall and Enrique you can see where some of your money has been spent. Before we go any further, I'd like to introduce everyone to my boys Gus and Ty and…'

Jerry had been silent up until now. 'And just who the fuck are you?' He pointed at Savannah.

'And…' Spencer glared at Jerry. 'That's Savannah. She's with me. She's one of my team. Get it?'

The rest of the introductions were made, Tolstoy and Ramirez had been warily sizing each other up. Enrique offered his hand. 'I've heard of you, Tolstoy. I believe you run a tight ship.'

'Yep, Enrique, nothing goes down in South Dakota without my say so. I've heard things about your Chicago operation. So far, I don't have a problem with what Marlowe's suggested.'

'Great.' Spencer smiled. 'This is a regular love in, isn't it? Come inside, have a beer.'

Decked out with bunting and lights, the hall looked like it was preparing for fourth of July. Wooden chairs and tables were placed neatly around the sun dappled hall, its tall arched windows, with their aged glass panes afforded a splendid view of some ancient aspen, birch and oak trees and Iron Mountain in the distance.

Ramirez wandered around the hall, fingering tablecloths, gazing at the stacks of glasses, cutlery and all the equipment needed for the big night.

'Dios mio, Spencer, you've done one hell of a lot in a short time. I thought this place was a dump when we rolled up. Everything is here, the stage for the band, the kitchen…hell, all this for one night?'

'Yep, Enrique, Tolstoy, just one night, but it needs to be impressive, we don't want the bikers to think they're dealing with amateurs.'

Spencer had a table placed under a brooding picture of Abraham Lincoln. Spaced between the windows were similar pictures of past presidents and a striking picture of the Lakota leader Sitting Bull.

What Ramirez and Tolstoy didn't realize was behind each of these venerable old photos, hidden sensitive microphones were already listening and recording.

Somewhere a tape deck rolled and the conversation was kept for posterity.

'Excuse me boys, beer time.' Spencer stepped into the spacious kitchen at the rear of the hall, where Dale's men had installed a commercial refrigerator and a modern stove. He returned to the table with some cold beers.

'Ok, boys and girls, this week Saturday, all the boys will be here. Steak, and beer, strippers and a band. I tell you these biker dudes will be eating out of our hands.'

The next hour involved several more beers, and a discussion about just how much money was waiting to be made when every state of the union was flooded with cheap heroin, distributed by willing and able outlaw biker gangs.

Tolstoy gave his blessing to host such a prestigious summit here in his territory before taking his leave early. He had a family matter to attend to out of state. He left Con-Rod to represent him, but the biker only stared down the presidents in their portraits, one after another. He assured a twitchy Savannah and a less outwardly affected Spencer that he'd be back for their Saturday get-together. Hugo and Jerry took their turns scowling and sulking, and Spencer kept their heads full of all the cash they were about to rake in. They were going to be swimming in it.

'God damn right,' Con-Rod said, raising a glass. They all toasted. Con-Rod threw the glass up in the air, drew, and blasted his beer mug to smithereens.

CHAPTER TWENTY-SIX

ELMER'S EDUCATION

'Elmer, you are going to stay with your uncle for a week and that's the end of it.'

'Jesus, Sir, I'm going to Hicksville to stay with an uncle I've only met once in my life. For God's sake, he lives in Ma and Pa Kettle country.'

Mister Budd thumped the table and barked, 'Listen to me you ungrateful little whelp, since I bought you the Chevrolet, you've done nothing but cause me problems. I've got standing in this community and all you've done is bring shame and embarrassment to me and your mother.'

Mister Budd was a large florid man. Everything about him screamed success, from his carefully crafted Brooks Brothers clothes, the classy Florsheim brogues, polished to a dull sheen and the gold Patek Philippe watch on his wrist.

Mister Budd had started his trucking company with one old Kenworth thirty years earlier. He had fought off rivals, stood up to the mob-controlled Teamsters Union and gradually, piece by piece, had built up a company sprawling across the United States and Canada. His simple catchy logo, "Want it yesterday? Budd's the name. Don't forget it" was now seen on thousands of Kenworths and Internationals as they plied the interstates across the nation.

'That's right, dear.' Mrs. Budd sat primly on a brocade divan, a bone China Wedgewood teacup held daintily in one hand. The home had been decorated expensively; a mixture of endearingly vibrant colours imposed an air of trendy sophistication.

Mister Budd didn't care for tea, but Mrs. Budd had insisted that beverage was drunk in the best homes. 'Just the other day, Pearl was making snide remarks at my bridge club. She pretended to be concerned about Elmer's welfare, but seriously Morgan she was just looking for an excuse to bring up Elmer's last little run in with the police. Honestly, darling, I was so embarrassed.'

Elmer packed his bags in a huff that night. He muttered profanities and cursed his bad luck, and had no idea how wrong he was about the future. From time to time, he glanced out at the Chevy his parents had bought him, the source of his misfortune. To make matters worse, he wasn't even taking his pride and joy out to the boonies to be with his uncle.

Ordinarily the very sight of his sleek Chevy Impala convertible would bring a smile to his face. He felt like king of the walk every time he fired up the 348 cubic inch V8, but not today. All he felt was doom and gloom and a sense of injustice. Yes, he'd been busted by the cops because he had a bit of weed. Didn't everybody smoke a joint now and then? He remembered his discomfort when his father had berated him over the incident. Fortunately, Mister Budd's influence had quickly seen the charges dropped. Then there was the incident with one of the cheerleaders. How the hell was he to know the little whore was only fifteen? Once again, his father had come to his aid. This time there was perhaps a little nudge, nudge, wink wink. His Dad had chuckled as they had left the station house. 'Your mother might not see the funny side son, but hell, boys will be boys. For Christ's sake, just be more careful. These little tarts are just waiting to get their claws into Budd money.'

Uncle Lester, a square name if Elmer had ever heard one, showed up promptly at seven thirty the next morning. Elmer expected a thin, severe, bald man in a priest's robes with the white collar. Spectacles. Driving a Model T, for Christ's sake. The type of man who ate gruel for all three meals and wouldn't know fun if it bit him on the face.

Elmer really was in a foul mood, and not just because he was forced to wake up before nine. He was going to live in a windswept Puritanical Hell while Uncle Lester quoted Chick Tracts at him. No booze, no girls, no weed, no joyriding.

The man who stepped into the entryway *loomed*. He stood six foot two, with a Stetson covering black hair, and an impeccably groomed beard. His beefy frame looked just wrong in the brown suit coat and workman's khaki pants. These were tucked into tall cowboy boots.

Elmer stood miserably with his mother and father, all three of them staring up at Uncle Lester.

'Lester,' Elmer's mother said.

He tipped his hat, saying, 'It's been too long, Eleanor,' before enveloping her in a large hug. He then grasped his father's hand in a powerful handshake. Elmer noted his father's wince with pleasure.

"This is young Elmer, is it?"

'I'm afraid so,' Mrs. Budd said, and elbowed him.

'Sir,' Elmer said despondently.

'I've heard all about you, son,' Uncle Lester said severely, and turned his attention to Mr. and Mrs. Budd. 'Don't you worry yourselves. I'll have our young man straightened out in no time.' Eying Elmer cooly, he cocked a thumb towards the window. Outside sat a Chevy Task Force, a truck that looked like the unfortunate love child of a Bel-air and a real pickup. It was rusted and beaten up, at least a decade old. 'Let's get your bags in the truck and hit the road. We'll be driving all night unless we only stop for lunch and dinner.'

Elmer peered at his parents for some last second reprieve. They only stared back stone-faced, all unwavering resolution and not a hint of pity.

And then his bags were in the truck. And then he was staring at the house, watching Uncle Lester charm his parents.

His father came up beside the truck, and Elmer rolled the window down. 'Have a good time, son, but stay out of trouble. I don't know your Uncle Lester real well, but I imagine coming from out in the sticks he'd be a decent God fearing man, and most certainly wouldn't take kindly to you whoring around with the local gals, ok?'

Elmer just nodded numbly.

And then the truck was rolling. And then his old life as he knew it was over. A whole lot of Chicago disappeared in the rear-view before Uncle Lester spoke up.

'What do they call you, son?'

He had been too lost in his own thoughts to respond with anything but, 'Huh?'

'Nobody with any self-respect goes by Elmer. What's your handle?'

'Uh… Buzz. Sir.'

'Buzz. That's decent. It'll do.'

They headed South on West Fox Hill Drive towards Alsace Circle and then turned right onto Cherbourg Drive. Each mile taking him further from civilization and into hayseed country, as he saw it. Uncle Lester pressed the buttons on his radio and turned the volume at full blast. Mick Jagger out front of the Rolling Stones was singing about *The Last Time*.

Buzz goggled at the man. It got even stranger when his uncle pulled the truck over, removed his suit jacket, and revealed a t-shirt with the sleeves ripped off, and tattoos up and down each beefy arm. The Stetson went next, and he shook out his shoulder-length hair.

He even walked different, more relaxed and with his shoulders thrown back. The walk of a man who owned everything he looked at.

'You'll call me Uncle, or Uncle Tolstoy, got me? None of this Uncle Lester nonsense."

Buzz gaped for a solid few seconds before he realized he looked the fool. 'Yes sir, uh, right…Uncle.'

'How d'ya feel about Sioux Falls, Buzz?' Then he laughed, head thrown back. 'Who gives a shit how you feel? Your pops gave me an envelope with five hundred bucks in it. I figure we can find us a little fun with that kind of money, don't you? There's a titty bar I know. Girls there love me.'

CHAPTER TWENTY-SEVEN

EVERYTHING FALLS INTO PLACE

Spencer, Gus, Ty, and Savannah occupied a booth in the One-Eyed Jack's Saloon on Main Street Sturgis. Nothing fancy here: solid oak tables and chairs, a beer-stained hardwood floor and long mirror stretching across the room with a rebel flag etched into the glass.

'Well boys and girls, everything is falling beautifully into place. Apparently, the mike in the hall is picking up the voices nicely.' Spencer gazed at his comrades, a smile on his face. At this point he just couldn't see a problem. 'The band will arrive in a week's time. All of the gang leaders are champing at the bit. Apparently, Ramirez's reputation is pretty darn solid. When this wraps up, we should have all the main players behind bars, looking at lengthy jail sentences. What could go wrong?'

Gus took a swig of his beer, and burped indelicately. 'Let's just run through the end game Spencer. We wait until Dale Fletcher, and how many Feds?'

'Ok, guys and gals. We wait until Dale turns up. There are four agents in his Chevrolet and another five in the prisoner transport bus. As soon as Dale turns up with his men, we're going to arrest Tolstoy, Ramirez, Hugo, Jerry and let's not forget that piece of work, Con-rod.'

Ty pointed a finger at Spencer. 'You don't think some of the bikers might get a little excited? You know, take the law into their own hands? These guys don't much like the law, federal or otherwise.'

Savannah rolled her eyes 'This isn't amateur hour fellas. At least four feds are going to patrol the perimeter, and they're armed with Thompsons. I've suggested to Dale, if the natives get restless, the guys fire some rounds into the air from the Tommy guns. Let me tell you, if push comes to shove, four sub machine guns firing rounds at 500 per minute are going to pull bikers into line. Spencer is going to grab the mic from the band and tell everyone the event is completely surrounded, and if they don't want to get arrested, they should climb onto their Hogs and disappear. I'm going to ask Dale to give up on the idea of grabbing the chief honcho's of all the other gangs, I had no idea this Sturgis event was so huge. If we try and arrest the heads of Comanchero's, the Desperadoes and the others it could end up being a huge firefight with a lot of innocents in the crossfire. The death toll could be enormous.'

Ty grinned 'Good idea Savannah. Dale gets a bit carried away. I have to admit I'd rather not take on 1000 unhappy bikers. I'm more than happy with what we have happening.'

'I'm with you, pal,' Gus raised his glass.

They had finished a dinner of massive, perfectly seasoned T bone steaks, juicy and seared brown on the outside, accompanied by a mountain of crisp fries along with a few icy beers. Clearly Ty and Gus were very relaxed, they saw the whole operation as being a slam dunk. No dramas, a bit of fun, almost a holiday. They would finish the op, climb on to their machines and make their way back to the windy city.

The night wound up on a happy note as Ty and Gus drained the last of their beers and jumped onto their Harleys, roaring off down Main Street to their hotel.

Even Spencer and Savannah felt like they were on holiday. They were enjoying the laid-back biker lifestyle. They'd spent the week mingling with all the bikers who'd amassed in huge numbers in Sturgis, Deadwood and every town and hamlet in the county.

'Well, Savannah, we should have all this wrapped up in no time and you can be back with Inez and Capone and all will be right with the world.'

Savannah and Spencer were both nursing Budweisers and relaxing in the Dungeon Bar. It seemed as if they had now attained some sort of rockstar status. Spencer's handling of Trunk and Savannah's taking down of the biker Johnno had spread like wildfire. Hulking bikers would buy them drinks, while their old ladies would shamelessly flirt with Spencer. A growl from Savannah would send them hurriedly on their way.

'Savannah,' Spencer would remonstrate, 'that girl was only being nice. Let's not start World War Three. And anyway, I am quite capable of looking after myself.'

'Nice, nice. Jesus H, Spencer, that tart had one thing on her mind. And as I recall you are spoken for.'

Spencer shook his head. Once again he felt his hand grasp the cornicello. A fleeting vision of a Japanese lady would flit through his mind. The vision never paused; it was like a movie on a fast wind. 'I'm at a loss, I still have no memory of anything. I must admit, deep down I believe you're right. There is simply no way there isn't a life somewhere that I was part of. My God, I would just like to remember. There has to be more. Loved ones, children even. I mean, dammit someone out there must be searching for me, wondering.'

Savannah took a long pull on her beer, finishing it with one big gulp. 'When we were in LA, Mexico and before that, New York and Japan, I always had the impression you knew more but just weren't telling. But this time I actually believe you have no memory. The question is…?'

Spencer grinned. 'Hold on I'll go and grab a couple more beers. I want to hear this.'

Spencer padded up to the bar and bought two more tankards of the foaming ale. He glanced momentarily at the mirror running the full length of the rough-hewn plank bar. Momentarily he had a fleeting vision of being in another time, another place. He remembered toasting his image. He remembered there was danger, uncertainty. Another country, hot, tropical. Again, the image disappeared. This time he saw a tall man covered in outlandish tattoos. He scanned the noisy saloon filled with rough, tough men and their women, also covered in tatts, mini-skirts and revealing tops. He glanced back at Savannah, comfortable now with her new identity as a biker chick. In this bizarre world filled with danger and uncertainty he saw Savannah and Inez being his anchor, his family. Whatever his future held he knew absolutely these two ladies meant everything to him. Heaven help those who might take them from him. 'Ok girl. And the question is?'

Spencer plonked down heavily spilling a few drops of beer.

Savannah grabbed her tankard and took a healthy swig 'OHHH That's good.' She burped noisily into her hand. 'Yeah, now here's the thing. Here's the thing,' she repeated, stabbing a finger in his direction, 'just what are you going to do when this business winds up? You're a contract guy. Dale's a lovely man, but he's going to simply cut you loose when this is over. What then big boy?'

Spencer stared, trying to think of something to say, 'I…I…I don't know. I just thought, you know. I thought…'

'Spencer, Spencer.' She put a hand over his. 'You are very important to both Inez and I, and…and whatever happens you'll always have a home with us, but sooner or later, well, sooner or later you're going to…I guess, leave the nest. You're going to have to find a job. I mean a real job. I mean what can you do. Hell, I know damn well you can fight. Can't shoot mind you. But what else can you do? I mean what was your regular job?'

'I have absolutely no idea. Nothing, I mean nothing springs to mind. I might have been a tradesman, you know, plumber, electrician that sort of thing?'

Savannah shook her head. 'Enough already. Move on. Hell, knowing you, you'll probably just disappear again and then eventually turn up like a bad penny. Now remember, tomorrow we have to scoot out again to see that moron Tolstoy at his ranchero to run over some stuff for the big night.' They left the Dungeon, waving a goodbye to the bikers and their ole ladies.

The evening in Sturgis was noisy with Harleys burning up the street. Brightly coloured bunting splashed their messages across the Sturgis main drag. Street vendors yelling their spiel hawked hot dogs and tacos. Countless hastily erected stalls spruiked lurid T-shirts screaming the Harley Davidson message. Everywhere the conversations seemed to be about Panheads, Knuckleheads, the upcoming Shovelhead model, cams, and pistons. And of course, babes. Most of the conversation would be meaningless to those who weren't motorcycle fans, but there weren't any such people in Sturgis in motorcycle week. Sturgis was simply a heady mix of two wheeled horsepower, beer, whisky and babes. The many bars and clubs were doing a roaring trade in Harley Davidson week. Relaxed police turned a blind eye to the mostly law-abiding bikers. Climbing aboard the chopper, Savannah threw a leg over and grabbed Spencer around the waist. 'Let her rip, big boy, let her rip. Wrap it on.'

Spencer turned on the power, the V twin motor howled its exuberant message. The Harley went up on one wheel, bikers and their women cheered as the Panhead powered up the street. Savannah laughed as she clung on to Spencer. He smiled to himself remembering Savannah's initial distrust of the powerful machine.

CHAPTER TWENTY-EIGHT
I REMEMBER YOU

Bacon, eggs, flapjacks with maple syrup and brewed coffee. Breakfast, consumed with gusto at the Buffalo Bodega Casino and Steakhouse on Main Street Deadwood. Spencer Marlowe burped and pushed his plate aside, reclining in his Western saloon bentwood chair watching the diehards pour nickels, dimes and quarters into the flashy, noisy one-armed bandits.

Eight am and the casino was pumping. It seemed when bikers weren't on their bikes or drinking beer, they enjoyed five card stud, blackjack and poker machines. Spencer wondered how many of the patrons knew Wild Bill had met his end playing poker ninety years earlier in the Number 10 Saloon, a little further down the street in Deadwood, still clutching aces and eights when the coward Jack McCall shot him in the back.

'Ok, what's the plan for the day?' Savannah had just phoned Inez. She strode across the beer-soaked gaming floor before slouching onto the wide swivel chair, motioning the waiter to bring more coffee.

'Tolstoy is becoming anxious to receive his quota of smack from Ramirez. So, we'll pay him a friendly visit. He wants to go over the final details of what's going down. I tell you kid, it's all over bar the shouting. Another successful mission by Agent Smart and 99.'

Savannah paused, coffee cup in midair. 'Who? Who or what is Agent Smart and 99?'

Spencer shook his head. 'I have no idea, it just flashed through my mind. I've no idea where it came from. I just had this image of…of these two secret agents, it's…I think it's a TV show, but it's gone. Every time I think my memories returning it just seems to hit a brick wall.'

Savannah eyed him strangely. 'Well, it's been months now, and no improvement.'

CHAPTER TWENTY-NINE

THE BEST LAID PLANS

Con-Rod opened the door to Tolstoy's place. 'This will be your nephew, I reckon. Hell, he ain't so little. He's a big son of a bitch.'

The kid was bleary-eyed from waking up at the crack of dawn, but grew instantly alert.

Tolstoy gave a mighty yawn. 'Need me some God damn coffee. Con-Rod, this is Buzz. Buzz, this fine upstanding gentleman over there is Leopold Jackson, known as Con-Rod. You'll call him Con-Rod or Con.'

'Eh, it's, uh… nice to meet you, sir.'

'I think he's shy.' Tolstoy grinned at Con-Rod and rolled his eyes, mouthing, 'Be nice.'

Tolstoy shouldered past his second in command. 'Coffee!' Inside, one of the biker babes who Con-Rod had over last night sprang to life and started banging around in the kitchen. 'Everybody better be decent in here! There's a kid with us.' The sounds in the kitchen changed to scrambling.

Con-Rod retrieved a toothpick and slotted it into his usual spot. 'Good ta meet ya, Buzz, come in, come in.'

Buzz hesitantly stepped inside and nodded at Con-Rod, his eyes momentarily focusing on the holstered six shooter. He held out his hand.

Elmer nodded towards Con-Rod. 'Nice to meet you, sir.'

Con-Rod grabbed the young man's hand in a firm grip. 'That's enough of the "sir" crap. Hereabouts I'm known as Tolstoy. You call him Con-Rod.'

Buzz caught sight of one of the biker babes strolling through the house wearing an oversized t-shirt and possibly nothing else. Headed for the kitchen, blonde hair bouncing.

'I'm sure you're going to have a nice time,' Tolstoy said, grinning. 'Your room is all ready.'

'Yeah,' Buzz said. 'A nice time.'

***

'Buzz.' Tolstoy entered his nephew's room a few days later without knocking. Not that Buzz would complain, ever. This was his uncle's house and guns were everywhere. 'Listen boy, I have a business meeting this morning. Confidential, if you know what I mean?' He gave Buzz a wink. Actually, Buzz had no idea. In fact, he had absolutely no idea what business his uncle was in. Buzz didn't care. Life didn't get any better than this.

'Righto Uncle, I'll stay out of your way.'

The boy had a stack of motorcycle magazines he was leafing through. Tolstoy smiled at the sight of his nephew admiring the photos of custom motorcycles. He wasn't entirely sure whether it was the bikes that held his attention or the curvy, busty, scantily clad ladies who were draped over them.

Buzz was enjoying his sojourn with his uncle. Perhaps enjoying wasn't the right word. It was a young testosterone fuelled man's dream. Tolstoy was everything his father was not.

There was always beer in the fridge, marijuana on the coffee table and it seemed to be one endless party. His uncle or his henchman Con-Rod didn't appear to have a regular job. Rough looking biker types came and went. There was a very agreeable bevy of young ladies who also came and went. Buzz was astounded, when he would leave his room upstairs, make his way down the carved oak spiral staircase for breakfast and stumble into the large sunny kitchen-cum-dining room where he would be confronted by laughter and the tantalizing odour of frying bacon and find yet more buxom young ladies often clad only in knickers and sometimes not even those. Mealtimes with his mother and father seemed a distant memory. First, they would thank the Lord for every God damn thing. His father would pontificate about business and his mother would gossip about her church group.

Tolstoy seemed to enjoy watching his nephew, who initially was tongue tied and embarrassed, but quickly got into the swing. These agreeable females were more than happy to bestow their favours on the handsome young football jock. Buzz had learned more about sex since he had arrived in South Dakota than his years in Chicago. Sex had been very available in his hometown, but the ladies at his uncle's house were very experienced and not at all like the fresh-faced young innocents he had routinely deflowered in the back of his Chevy.

If only Con-Rod wasn't a prick. That guy and his toothpick were loud, mean, smelly, and violent. When Uncle Tolstoy clapped a hand on your shoulder he was companionable; when Con-Rod did it your shoulder hurt the whole day. And he yelled: at the other bikers, at the girls. He was just a dick.

'Hey Buzz, I'm not sure you should tell your ma and pa about playtime with your Uncle Tolstoy.' Buzz was inclined to agree. As far as Buzz was concerned this was as good as it gets.

Buzz had just spent an enlightening hour with a young lady who said she was from San Francisco. She had driven him to new heights of sexual tension. When eventually they climaxed simultaneously, he felt like he had just finished a marathon session as a quarterback in the Super Bowl. He laid back on his bed and watched languorously as she pulled on jeans and a loose T shirt over the most stupendous breasts he had ever seen. Just as he felt another surge of arousal he heard the familiar sound of a Harley V twin pulling up to the front door. He raised himself up, pulled back the drapes and peered below. He saw two vaguely familiar figures.

'Esther, that was wonderful.'

'Actually, it's Ingrid. But I don't mind. You're sweet. We might do it all again sometime.'

After Ingrid exited the room, Buzz heard the sound of voices as the bike riding couple entered downstairs. He heard his uncle greeting them. Buzz slipped on some shorts and a T shirt and padded to the balcony. He stood in the shadows unnoticed. Watching.

CHAPTER THIRTY

JUST ANOTHER DAY IN THE OFFICE

Tolstoy had greeted Savannah and Spencer like old friends. Plans were discussed, coffee and cookies were served. Their business arrangements were complete. Tolstoy was firmly of the belief the two affable bikers were going to be instrumental in bestowing great wealth upon him. All was right in the world.

After handshakes all round Spencer and Savannah headed back to Deadwood, once again enthralled by the majesty of Spearfish Canyon.

Buzz slowly strolled down the staircase; his bare feet cold on the hardwood steps.

'Uncle,' he said hesitantly.

Tolstoy glanced at the boy who he had become quite fond of. 'Yeah Buzz?'

'Who were those two people?'

'Like I said before, business acquaintances. Why the interest?'

'Well…I'm not sure, but they, or maybe just the lady, may be FBI.'

Buzz haltingly told his uncle about the incident with Savannah and Spencer. Tolstoy listened with interest, not knowing exactly what to think. 'Did either of them show you any ID?'

'No Uncle, but none of us doubted for a minute that the lady wasn't what she said she was. The man, well, I don't know. He certainly wasn't American. I mean he sure didn't…Uncle, I don't really have a clue. But does it matter. I mean if she's FBI, what would that mean?'

It had already filtered through to Buzz that maybe his uncle and the affable Con-Rod were not exactly on the right side of the law.

Tolstoy smiled. 'Nah, it's not really important. It's just sort of odd, you know what I mean?'

Buzz stretched and yawned. 'Is it ok with you if I head into Deadwood? I'm meeting some guys to shoot a little pool.'

Tolstoy waited until the Chev disappeared out of the drive. He wandered into the garage where Con-Rod was servicing one of the Harley Davidsons.

'We gotta talk.'

The garage was a barnlike structure with a collection of American automobiles in various states of repair. A classic Cord straight eight convertible was on a hoist waiting a minor repair job. In a corner was a 1930, sixteen-cylinder Cadillac covered with a dust sheet. Vintage motorcycles were lined up against a wall. An American Ace and a Henderson. Pride of place was a British Brough Superior. The walls were adorned with advertising banners for motor oils and motorcycles and American muscle cars. Tolstoy grabbed an old steamer chair, dusting it off with a rag before he plopped into it. 'I tell you, Con-Rod, this throws a fucking spanner into the works. Could the bitch be FBI? She sure doesn't look like law.'

Con-Rod stood up and wiped his hands on an oily rag. He leaned against a timber work bench. 'Yeah, ok, and what about this prick Marlowe? That doesn't make sense. There's no way in the world he's FBI. He says he's Australian and I believe him. And what about those two fuckers that are with them? What was it? Gus…and Ty? Could they be cops of some kind? Oh, and while we're on the subject, what about fucking Ramirez? Christ, where do you finish?'

Tolstoy gloomily rubbed his chin. 'Alright let's look at what we got. Ramirez, he's fucking kosher. And so's his offsiders. No doubt. No fucking doubt. Marlowe, question mark. And Miss Savannah Steele, she's the issue. I'm going to check with some people I know in Chicago. They may know something. Con-Rod, say something. Cat got your tongue?'

Con-Rod stood and paced the floor. He shuffled over to the work bench and placed the screwdriver into its rack on the wall. 'Jesus, I don't fucking believe it. Ain't it a small world…I tell you…'

Tolstoy leaned back in his steamer chair; his hands interlaced behind his head.

'I guess at some point you're going to let me in on it?'

Con-Rod grinned. 'You're not gonna believe this, Tolstoy.'

'Yeah, you said that already. Gotcha, I'm not gonna believe it. Now for fuck's sake, out with it.'

Con-Rod shook his head. 'I tell you if this don't beat all. Tolstoy, do you remember my cousin's buddy from Alabama?'

Tolstoy rolled his eyes, 'That Southern cracker, what was his name again?'

'Billy Bob Jackson, his daddy was married to…'

'For fuck's sake, Con-Rod, I don't care who was married to who. He was probably married to his God damn sister, for all I know.'

'Do you remember he came to Sturgis with his buddies? And he looked me up. We had a few drinks, a few games of pool?'

'Go on.'

'You might remember he was with his cousin Jim Bob, and his cousin…I think his name was Earl?'

'There must be a shorter version of this story, surely?'

'No, listen, listen. Don't you remember they were telling us this story about their trip to LA?'

Tolstoy stared hard, 'Yeah. I remember. Refresh my memory.'

'The boys were at a shooting range… shit, I don't remember the name.'

Tolstoy jumped up. 'By Christ, I do remember. It was the Southern Belle. A fucking FBI bitch pistol whipped Jim Bob, and the big guy with her belted Billy Bob. Took their fucking guns as well. Jim Bob wouldn't stop going on about how he was going to find that FBI cunt and get his revenge. Fuck me. I don't believe it.'

'Small fucking world,' Con-Rod said, holding his toothpick between thumb and forefinger. 'Well, well well.'

'And, I remember Jim Bob saying the tall dude had an accent, he thought he might have been a limey. He reckoned the son of a bitch couldn't shoot worth a damn and that's what started the argument.'

'That's Marlowe for sure.'

CHAPTER THIRTY-ONE

THE PLOT THICKENS

Four grim-faced men were listening closely as Tolstoy and Con-Rod poured out the unpalatable details about their would-be business partners.

Hugo sprung to his feet. 'I just knew that son of a bitch Marlowe was a fucking plant. I fucking knew it.'

'Shut up Hugo,' Ramirez snarled. 'You had no idea. You didn't like him because he made you look silly. Well, sillier than you really are. The question is, what exactly are we going to do about it?'

Jerry reclined in one of the plush fake Rococo style plush velvet chairs, he tapped ash from a long panatela into a porcelain ashtray. 'Well,' he drawled, 'I would have thought it was fairly simple. We ice the lot. Marlowe, Miss "Aren't I so tough" Savannah Steele and those other two feds, Ty and Gus. They just disappear, never to be seen again.'

Ramirez studied the men before him. He understood Hugo and Jerry's desire to mete out a probably painful death. He had some fairly creative ideas on that subject himself. He had been sitting behind another Rococo imitation, a broad teak desk. Ramirez strolled over to the window and gazed down on the street below.

He had a rare feeling of regret. He'd rather liked Spencer, admiring his brash confidence. The way he dealt with Hugo and Jerry he thought was most impressive. He'd had visions of them continuing with a long and lucrative partnership Tolstoy and Con-Rod had obviously uncovered the truth, and there was certainly no doubt he was dealing with the FBI. Ramirez was confused about Marlowe. His accent and foreignness meant it was unlikely he was a homegrown lawman, but he figured there was an association or connection with the late Australian thug Peter Gordon. So, it figured Marlowe was probably connected to some God damn Aussie crime fighting outfit.

And now Ramirez would see him dead.

***

It had been a long couple of days, and fraught. Each one of the major biker gangs was just as dangerous as Tolstoy and his Black Hills Demons. All of them had their own underworld element, and all four of them were eager to get in on the deal Savannah and Spencer were offering. They were also wary of a potential double cross.

Spencer used Ty and Gus to even out the numbers and provide a semblance of security while Dale and his people arranged the sting. For two of those meetings, it had meant Spencer going in there with only Savannah as backup. Gus and Ty needed to be poised to cut a swath of destruction if things went bad. Luckily they had access to Savannah's arsenal of weaponry.

Even more luckily, they hadn't needed to use any of it.

By the end of the tete-a-tete with the Comancheros, the Hells Angels, the Outlaws and the Desperadoes, Spencer had broken two arms and rendered three men unconscious. Savannah had come within inches of of blowing four different mens' heads off. There'd been a lot of speculation about Spencer until he separated the shoulder of a three-hundred-pound bearded biker called Grizz.

It seemed like taking down Trunk, and then Grizz, was the trigger that ended that speculation.

The different biker gangs listened to Spencer's jovial speeches and grandiose claims, and they started talking plans. Each of the four major gangs were in contact with smaller ones, and intended to invite them to join in this distribution network. They pulled up maps and outlined territories. More fights nearly broke out. Some ended in rumbled laughter, and others ended in grudging assent.

'When's Dale and the cavalry show up?' he asked after they were done with the Desperadoes.

'The problem is evidence,' Savannah said. 'Gus and Ty were only able to get so much out of the first three meetings. They couldn't get close enough with the microphones.' Situation as it was, Dale could only get a dozen heavily armed men.

Spencer arched an eyebrow. 'We're going to have something like a hundred-armed bikers at this party. What's the hold up?'

'Hold your God damn horses, Spencer. This last meeting was the one. We're on audio talking about the nationwide distribution network. The leader mentioned Ramirez and drugs in the same sentence, and threatened to kill anyone who messed this up.'

He stared at her.

'What?'

'I was there. I recall.'

'Well Dale damn sure wasn't! And the people who authorize the God damn artillery weren't there. Now that we have it on tape, we can send that tape into the nearest office and get authorization. Then they can send every FBI resource in the continental US to round em up.'

'Ah,' he said, grinning. 'Makes sense.'

Walking the knife's edge of death four different times in three days was hungry work. Savannah and Spencer stopped by the Buffalo Bodega to grab a quick sandwich and a coffee. They were idly watching four guys noisily playing pool. It was clear money was changing hands. The star player was a buzz cut college type who may well have been a hustler. Deft and precise, the balls shot off the end of his cue with a crack that resounded across the room. The kid was good. Nominating pockets and sending the coloured balls unerringly to their destination. The two biker types on the losing side appeared to be getting quite annoyed.

Savannah took a sip of her coffee. 'I tell you, the kid's not too bad. He looks familiar, what do you reckon?'

Spencer stared hard. 'Yep, he's good alright. And yes, he looks familiar. But I guess he looks a bit like a million other college kids.'

'Hey boy,' one of the bikers with a Texan Comanchero patch said with an unmistakable air of malice. 'I think you might be one of those big city hustler types, gonna take us dumb crackers for a few bucks. What do you reckon, Ethan?'

Ethan scowled, crunching an already homely face into something downright wretched. 'Yes sirree, Hurt, I reckon you may be right.' Ethan was short, squat with a weightlifter's chest and massive tattooed arms. Hurt was just big. Everything about him was big. He was tall, his huge shoulders appeared almost grotesque. He looked like he could bench press a Sherman Tank.

The college boy seemed oblivious to the air of menace, 'Guys just lucky. You know how it is. You win some, you lose some.' His pool partner, a skinny kid in blue jeans white t-shirt and sneakers gazed nervously at the two opponents. 'Buzz, I gotta get going. How about we finish up?'

Buzz grinned at his pal. 'Sure thing, Dan. Ok, guys you owe us twenty bucks apiece.'

Hurt carefully placed his cue on the blue felt and strolled up to Buzz, standing face to face. 'I tell you what, you college faggot, you give me and my buddy here fifty bucks apiece, and you both get to walk outta here. Believe me, that's a bargain, cos otherwise, well, let's just say your boyfriends' ain't gonna recognize ya. Got it?'

It seemed the penny finally dropped and Buzz realized he was in trouble.

'Listen guys, we beat you fair and square, but if you're not going to pay, well there's not much I can do about it. So…'

Hurt grabbed Buzz by his shirt, pulling him closer. 'You don't seem to be getting the message boy. It's fifty bucks apiece and you walk…otherwise?'

Sweat was running down Buzz's face. Ethan had now moved into place next to the terrified Dan, who spoke up. 'Buzz, let's just pay 'em? Only I ain't got fifty.'

Spencer and Savannah had been watching with interest. Spencer scratched his head and sighed 'I guess I better step in and help the lads. What do you reckon?'

Savannah chuckled. 'Yep, go for it, Superman. Do you think you need a hand?'

'Nah.'

Spencer ambled up to the table. 'Guys, guys. We do seem to be a bit short of brotherly love here.'

Hurt let go of Buzz and swung round, eyeballing Spencer. 'Fuck off. None of your fucking business. Fuck off.'

'Nice dialogue. Hurt, is it?' Spencer chuckled.

Hurt made a grab for Spencer's throat. With lightning speed, Spencer clamped onto the offending hand and squeezed. Hurt cried out. The horrible sound of the fourteen finger bones snapping could be heard clearly. The noisy bar had fallen quiet as tough bikers, their old ladies and locals gazed open mouthed at the drama unfolding.

'You must not've been at the meet n' greet, eh Sunshine?' he whispered.

Ethan watched stunned as his buddy dropped to his knees, his hand now a bloody mess. Ethan grabbed the pool cue by the pointy end.

Savannah watched the proceedings with interest, happy to stay out of the stoush, until Ethan grabbed the pool cue. She reached into her biker boot and grabbed her Walther PPK semi-automatic. A mere 6.1 inches long with a 0.32 round. She stepped forward and as Ethan brought the cue back, ready to strike, she grabbed it with one hand and thrust the Walther firmly into Ethan's neck. 'Butt out, cherub.'

Ethan turned slowly, placing the pool cue on the table, he leaned with two hands on the burnished walnut surround of the table. 'You don't scare me, slut.'

'I don't scare him,' Savannah called out to Spencer.

Spencer had appeared to be in a trance-like state as the biker's hand had been crushed. 'What, um, oh right, not scared, huh?'

Savannah lowered the Walther. Ethan grinned, winking at his buddies. Savannah slammed the steel butt of the Walther down hard on Ethan's right hand. There were now two bikers with shattered appendages.

'You fucking bitch!' Ethan howled as he grabbed his bloody hand.

'Well guys, that's it. Time to go.' Spencer leaned against the pool table. Hurt leaned against a pillar, his face white, his damaged hand thrust under an armpit. 'Before you go, pay the boys, ok?'

CHAPTER THIRTY-TWO
PARTY NIGHT

Dexter's Comets tour bus cruised noisily along the main street of Sturgis. Their latest hit single *My Girl Don't Play Around No More*, blasting from speakers mounted on the roof.

'Well big boy, tonight's the night. Keep your fingers crossed.' Savannah waved at the long-haired girl driving the bus.

***

'Put the lights on high beam, Murray. It's as dark as.'

Agent Murray Blanche drove Dale's Impala through Spearfish Canyon. 'How far now, Dale?' Newcomer Agent Don Bruce murmured from the back seat.

'We'll hit Deadwood in about fifteen minutes, then it's a further ten miles to Sturgis. Everyone happy?'

The Impala Wagon lead the charge, closely followed by the drab grey prison bus that was meant to have a number of unhappy villains chained on their way to a secure Federal prison.

The lights of the Chevrolet cut through the blackness like a knife slicing butter.

'Jesus, Murray, watch out!' A massive, bleary-eyed bison stared owlishly at the Chevy; seemingly unaware he was about to become hamburger.

Murray didn't have time to hit the brakes. The blue Impala Station Wagon cannoned into the bison at 60 miles per hour. Steam erupted from the radiator, which looked like the Old Faithful geyser at Yellowstone. The front end of the Impala now destroyed. The four agents braced themselves, knowing what was about to happen. The ungainly Crown Clark super coach fitted with solid steel seats and shackles slammed into the back of the Chevrolet Impala Station wagon. The shattered Chev bounced over the corpse of the bison. The twin headlight beams bounced off the walls of the canyon. These vehicles were going nowhere.

CHAPTER THIRTY-THREE

THE BEST LAID PLANS

'Something's gone wrong.' Savannah checked her watch. 'Dale and the boys should have been here by now.'

'There's nothing for it, we'll have to go and join the clam fest. We've got Ty and Gus. What could go wrong?'

Savannah checked the trunk of the Plymouth, a taut smile on her face as she checked its lethal contents.

Spencer climbed aboard the Harley, grinning as he revved the motor. They headed off to the shindig, Savannah leading the way in the Plymouth.

Dexter's Comets blasted out a slow version of the Chuck Berry song *Little Queenie* as Spencer kicked the stand down of the Harley and climbed off the machine. The car park was in darkness. A sea of motorcycles, lay before them. Harley Davidsons, Indians and a few British speed twins ridden by diehard enthusiasts, nestled amongst the American iron. Triumph, Norton, and BSA. Polished chrome gleamed in the moon light.

A number of men bearing the patch of the Black Hills Demons strolled menacingly around the parking area. Spencer figured they were security to watch over the expensive machines.

Savannah found a slot nearby; she gave him a wave as she locked the Plymouth.

'Ty and Gus said they'd meet us just inside.' Savannah reached down to one of her biker boots. 'Just a little uncomfortable.' She grimaced.

'Really? Now I wonder why?' Spencer grinned.

'Well…you know me. Better safe than sorry.' Savannah slid out a vicious looking stiletto from its sheath.

***

'How about we split up? If you see Gus and Ty, ask them to meet up in the carpark and we'll figure out what to do.' Spencer was worried. *Where the hell are Dale and his men?*

'We're just going to have to cool it until the cavalry turns up,' Savannah agreed.

'Try not to shoot anyone,' Spencer whispered to Savannah's retreating back. She responded with a thumbs up.

Savannah pushed through the line of people waiting to enter. The two doormen, both with Hells Angels New Mexico patches, waved her through.

The room was mesmerizing black. Strobe lights jarred the senses. Two scantily clad girls twisted and bumped to either side of the stage. Bikers stuffed banknotes into their G-strings. Dexter, the beanpole leader of the Comets, leapt and writhed like a dervish. Twin spotlights highlighted his lean cadaverous features. Artfully applied makeup gave his eyes a ghoulish appearance. The Comet's lead guitarist was on one knee, Fender Strat screaming and wailing. Marijuana smoke twirled silver blue above the dancers' heads. The floor was packed with sweating figures moving to the music.

Savannah paused, waiting for her eyes to adjust. Almost immediately she felt it. Tension. Something wasn't right. Over to her left she could make out Con-Rod, casually heading in her direction. Over on the left Jerry and Hugo looking decidedly out of place in their new biker gear, both slowly moving towards her.

Savannah knew this was trouble. She could hardly grab her revolver and start shooting.

Time to go, I think.

'Hello, darling.' She felt a tap on her shoulder.

'One false move, bitch, and I pull the trigger.' Tolstoy Barrington shoved the snub nosed 0.38 hard into Savannah's waist. 'Next to the stage, there's a door. Now move it.'

Con-Rod had now stood on the other side. She felt the barrel of another gun.

'You and I are gonna have such fun together.' Con-Rod leered.

The dancers paid no attention as the trio made their way to the stage door.

Hugo opened the door and Tolstoy shoved her, hard. She sprawled across the floor, landing hard on one elbow. She would have gone for the Magnum, but the barrel of a pistol appeared before her eyes like magic. The next thing she noticed was Ramirez, reclining on a tattered green satin armchair, a fat cigar in his hand. Finally, her eyes locked on Tyrone Brookman, tied to a chair, either unconscious or dead. A crude bandage leaking blood had been wrapped haphazardly around his head.

'What have you done to him? 'Savannah demanded.

'He'll live.' Ramirez puffed on his cigar.

'Not for fucking long.' Hugo grinned.

'Where's that Aussie prick? Bitch.' Tolstoy hauled Savannah to her feet and shoved her roughly onto a dirty steamer chair.

***

Spencer was dodging club-going traffic and heading toward the sprawling carpark. The place was a jumbled mass of choppers, and absolutely no Impala belonging to Dale. He'd made it halfway through before his instincts kicked in and he dodged a shoulder check.

'Oh sorry muh—' the biker started, but seemed confused not to have slammed into Spencer. He and the biker just behind him frowned in confusion.

'Not how the plan was meant to go?' Spencer asked amiably. 'Did I bugger it up?'

He caught the glint of a knife and raised his hands before backing away. When he saw his opportunity, he chopped at the biker's wrist. A grunt and the knife went clattering out of the man's hand. He staggered back with a grunt of pain. His buddy looked to be raising a firearm, so Spencer kicked the first biker directly in the chest. Hunched over as he was clutching his wrist, he went flying back into his friend. Both of them fell in a heap, and Spencer kicked the gun away behind him.

'You Trunk's mates? Or buddies with that Grizz bloke?' Spencer slowly advanced on the two as they clambered over one another to try to get to their feet. 'Or wait, that other one who went after me with a broken beer bottle. The one with

175

the really bad tattoo and the two broken arms. You friends with him?'

He couldn't see any patches on these ones, and that was odd.

'You know, it's tough to tell with all the hands, arms, and balls I've busted this last week,' he lamented.

The second, smaller man growled at the first, 'Get—'

Spencer snapped a kick at the inside of the front man's kneecap and he heard the loud snap. The man shouted, and his insistent buddy immediately thought better of messing with the guy responsible for all the broken bones. He helped his would-be accomplice limp back to their bikes.

'All right then, nice chat!' he called, and bent to pick up the abandoned gun. 'Wouldn't do to have some kid just happen upon it… in the middle of the night… in the middle of a gigantic biker rally.' He chuckled to himself to hide the sinking feeling.

What the hell was going on?

CHAPTER THIRTY-FOUR
BUZZ

Spencer hesitated at the front of the hall, he noticed a familiar Jeep Wagoneer drive past and stop behind the back of the venue. Then came the distinctive *thump thump* of a Harley V twin.

Gus waved as he slammed to a halt next to Spencer, squeezing the bike between a long row of Harley Davidsons. He kicked the stand down and uncoiled himself from the Panhead chopper.

'What's happening, buddy?' Gus shook Spencer's hand.

Spencer explained that Dale and his crew hadn't arrived, and that two bikers had just tried to assault him. He left out the knife and gun just in case those two had been friends of one of the bikers he'd put in the hospital.

'Ty was supposed to meet me in the car park. I can't see him. It's not like him to be late.'

'Mr Marlowe.'

'You know my name?' Spencer spun around, recognizing the hustler pool player from earlier.

'You helped me and my buddy when those bikers were going to beat the hell out of us.' The kid gave him a smile that was half gratitude, half sheepish.

'Yeah sure. Good to see you, but we're a little busy at the moment.'

'That's what I want to talk about.' The kid gazed nervously about. 'You probably don't remember me.'

'Should I?' Spencer hiked his shoulders.

'Do you remember back in Chicago? Me and my buddies were drunk. We were in my Chevy; you and the lady were on your chopper…'

'Oh yeah. Savannah thought you looked familiar. But look, like I said we're kinda busy…'

'Tolstoy is my uncle,' the kid blurted out.

'Really?' Spencer looked sideways at Gus. 'And you're telling me this. Why?'

'Mr Marlowe, I think the lady is in trouble, and…and…hell. This's a mess. I think she's being held in a room behind the stage.'

'How in hell do you know that?' Spencer barked.

'This is awful, I was watching the lady when I was in the hall. My uncle and Con-Rod sorta steered her over to the back room. And… I think they might be criminals. I mean, they're definitely criminals. I just don't…' He faltered, and didn't seem to know how to finish that sentence.

'All right, all right. We'll take care of it.'

'I think she's beautiful. Actually, I was going to ask her to dance. I know she's older than me but… are they gonna hurt her?'

'Great, kid, great.' Spencer glance sideways at Gus, who shrugged.

'Well, I was watching her and I saw Con-Rod and Uncle Tolstoy go up to her. I reckon Con-Rod had a gun. Then they all sorta marched to the room at the back. I'd already seen them grab another guy, a biker and take him to the room. I figured he must have been some sort of troublemaker, but he didn't seem drunk or high or…'

'Shit, that'd have to be Ty,' Gus said to Spencer.

The kid introduced himself as Elmer Budd, known as Buzz. He then explained that he had inadvertently told his uncle about Savannah being an FBI agent.

'Mr Marlowe, I sort of got the idea pretty quickly that my uncle was a crook, but it took a while before I could put the pieces together.'

Just then the Jeep Wagoneer appeared from behind the hall and roared down the slip road onto the blacktop. The Jeep was followed by a Dodge van, with the distinctive Black Hills Demons logo painted on the side, a laughing skeleton, wearing a top hat, sitting astride an elongated chopper with ridiculously extended front forks. Spencer recognized the driver of the van as Con-Rod. Buzz noticed also, and seemed to shrink behind Gus and Spencer.

'Con-Rod…' Buzz muttered darkly, and shivered.

'Yeah.'

'Guy scares me.'

'So, what's the go, Spencer?' Gus also had recognized the driver.

'Buzz, where's your uncle taking them, hey?'

'I think I know.' Buzz's face was white.

Spencer didn't know this kid from Adam, but his gut told him the kid was straight.

'Let's have it, Buzz.'

'My uncle owns a ghost town called Warbonnet. It's a sort of home for all the Black Hills Demons. They have a jail, a saloon, a courthouse, everything. I reckon they're taking the lady there.'

'What's the bet they've snatched Ty as well and he's probably with them. In the back of that stupid Dodge van, I reckon. This has turned to shit. Where the hell is the fucking cavalry?' Gus's face was grim.

Spencer realized the hall was now enemy territory.

'There's... this other thing.' Either the kid felt more comfortable in the presence of law enforcement, or Con-Rod scared him that badly. Spencer understood that much; most of these blokes were bad as bad could get.

'Ok, let's hear it.' Spencer smiled at the boy.

'I overheard Uncle Tolstoy talking to Con-Rod. There's something, it sounds like it's an old barn, or something like that. It's near Warbonnet.'

'Go on.' Spencer glanced sideways at Gus.

'It sounds awful. It sounds like a sort of slave factory. I think it's probably underground. I'm not sure what goes on there. I think it may be drugs.'

Spencer thought for a minute. 'Buzz, the Black Hills Demons know who you are, right?'

'Yeah sure, I've met most of them.'

'Well how about you go back into the hall and see if you can find out what's going on? Ask where Con-rod and your uncle are. Can you do that?'

'I guess so.'

'At the same time, go into the back room and see if Savannah or our friend are prisoner, tied up, or whatever.'

'Hang on, Spencer. If Ty and Savannah are being held prisoner in the back room it's unlikely they'd let the lad in.' Gus frowned.

'Sure, but my guess is they have already been taken to this Warbonnet place. Buzz, please go and have a look and make a point of asking where your uncle and Con-rod are.'

Buzz vibrated nervous energy. 'Sir? Mr Marlowe?'

'Is there a problem?' Spencer stared at the boy.

'Am I going to be in trouble? I mean with the cops, or the FBI? I had no idea that my uncle was bad. It's only in the last week or so that I started to get an idea of what was going on.'

Gus put his hand on the boy's shoulder. 'Listen son, you're not in any trouble, in fact help us and you'll probably get a medal. Bu…?'

'I thought there might be a but.'

'The but is, that your uncle is not going to be happy if he finds out that you've helped us. Family or no family, he'll…' Spencer looked grim.

'Yeah, I know. I'll be dead meat, won't I?'

'Unfortunately, you're caught between a rock and a hard place. But the FBI are not going to let go of your uncle or his comrades and sadly you don't have a lot of options. You're not going to play an active part but already you have committed the cardinal sin of being a snitch, and there's no going back.' Spencer stared hard at the boy.

'Well actually I want to play an active part, and the fact is you need me.' Buzz's jaw was clenched.

Gus turned to Spencer. 'He's right.'

'Sure I am. You need me to go and find out what's happened to the other agent and…what is the lady's name? Is it really Savannah, or is that just a cover?'

'No, it's really Savannah.' Spencer told him.

'I guess she's your old lady, huh?'

'No, she's not. We're working together, but she's also my friend.' *The fact is she's my only friend.*

'I think she's gorgeous. I know I'm younger than her, but I'm pretty mature. Do you reckon…do you reckon I'd have a chance. What do you think Mr Marlowe?'

'Yeah Spencer, what do you think?' Gus waggled his eyebrows at Spencer. Savannah's relationship with Inez had been the talk of the FBI, when the story got out.

'Actually Buzz, Savannah is spoken for. I'm sorry, but you have Buckley's.'

'Buckley's?' Buzz glanced at Gus, who shrugged.

'Sorry Buzz, that's an Australian expression. It means you don't have a snowball's chance in hell. Get over it boy. Move on. Find a college beauty queen.' Spencer kept his tone gentle, but ended up grinning at the kid's insistence.

'Well, whoever he is, he's one lucky son of a bitch.' Buzz frowned.

'Yep, he's one lucky son of a bitch.' Gus parroted with a knowing smile.

CHAPTER THIRTY-FIVE
ACTION STATIONS

Buzz trotted off confidently into the hall to ask questions. Spencer felt uneasy letting the lad be thrown into such danger. He'd now absolutely accepted Buzz was firmly on their side. All they could do now was wait.

Minutes ticked by. Spencer and Gus were feeling a little uncomfortable standing in the carpark. A Demons member sauntered over and squatted to admire Spencer's machine. 'Hey, Bro, this is one cool cycle. How many cubes?'

Spencer remembered the Aussie description "built like a brick shithouse." This guy was massive with tattooed arms like tree trunks. His head was shaved with only a tiny rat's tail. Inked across his forehead was the word "Killer." *Not very subtle.*

Spencer grinned. 'Enough. She goes like a bat outta hell.' He couldn't remember what the engine size was.

'She's bored out to 80 cubes.' Gus winked at Spencer as he answered the question. 'And man, she's got the wildest cam.'

What the hell's a bloody cam? Spencer was grateful for Gus's intervention; he knew he was expected to know all of the technical stuff.

'Stay upright, bro.' The biker jumped to his feet. 'Waal, my shift is about over. I'm gonna find me some sweet babe and some grass.'

'Whoa, I wouldn't like to meet him in a dark alley.' Gus stared at the biker as he headed towards the hall.

'He's the least of our worries. Hang on. Look who's here.' Spencer spotted Buzz running full tilt towards them. 'Mr Marlowe, things aren't looking so good. I haven't been told specifically, but it sounds like Savannah and the guy with her have been taken to Warbonnet. And…and my uncle, Con-Rod and some of the others have gone as well. And…'

'And? There's more?' Spencer asked.

'I think so, I don't know how important it is.'

'Let's hear it Buzz, and let me tell you, I'm very grateful for what you have done for us so far.' Spencer gave Buzz a thumbs up.

'Well, there's this other dude. He's some big shot from Chicago. My uncle didn't say much, but I think he's maybe a new partner. I don't know but he arrived in a big flash Lincoln Town car, with two other guys. Mean looking suckers.'

Spencer glanced at Gus. 'That's Ramirez, sure as eggs.'

'Yep, and the two others are obviously Hugo and Jerry.'

'Yeah, that's them. Hugo and Jerry. I heard the names!' Buzz exclaimed. 'Well, here's the thing. I think the bigshot and his buddies have all gone to Warbonnet.'

'How do we find this place, Warbonnet?' Gus asked.

'I can show you. It's tucked away in the Black Hills. It's on an old dirt road.'

'Hey, hold on.' Spencer interrupted 'You can't come, things are likely to get messy. We can't risk you getting hurt.'

Buzz puffed out his chest and glanced between them. 'Tough titties, Mr Marlowe, you won't find it without my help.'

'The kid's right. I haven't got a clue how to find this place. You?' Gus glanced at Spencer. 'But this is where it gets a little iffy. I've got a 0.38 and a spare box of slugs. What about you, Marlowe? You carrying?'

'Actually no. But…'

'But?' Gus's eyes narrowed.

'Follow me, Gus. I have a surprise.'

'Me too?' Buzz piped up.

'Yes, dammit, you too.'

'Groovy.' Buzz pumped the air.

'This better be good,' Gus mumbled.

They picked their way through the mass of motor bikes, to a small, gravelled section where a number of cars were parked. Spencer stopped next to a vivid red Plymouth.

'Hey, that's Savannah's automobile. You have a key?' Gus enquired.

Spencer grinned, kneeling down he ran his hand under the front fender. He stood up with a small metal box in his hand. 'You bet.' He slid open the lid of the magnetic box and held up a pair of keys.

'Great, it's certainly going to be a lot quieter taking the vehicle, but we still only have my 0.38. Not good odds.'

'I guess you don't know Special Agent Steele that well, huh?'

'By reputation. She's one tough lady, but…'

Spencer opened the trunk.

'That she is, Gus. She's one tough lady and she came prepared. Cast your peepers on this little lot.'

Gus gasped when he saw what was so neatly stacked in the cavernous trunk of the Plymouth.

'Holy mother of God. That box there.' Gus pointed.

'Yep, M26 grenades, I think I remember Savannah said.'

'God dammit, I don't believe it.' Gus leaned in and grabbed a weapon. 'How the hell did she get authorization for this?' Gus gingerly held up a wicked looking automatic assault rifle.

Spencer shrugged, wondering the same thing. At that moment, as if to answer the question, he had a flash of memory: that of Savannah picking up a kilo of drugs and chuckling over the shock on his face. She had… smuggled it across the border into Mexico? To entice a drug lord, he thought.

'She's umm, very resourceful. What exactly is it, anyway?'

Gus shook his head, smiling broadly. 'This, chum, is an M60 machine gun, it fires around 500 rounds a minute. This baby is accurate up to about a thousand yards or more. Jesus, we could just about start a frigging war.'

'Hey, how cool is this? It's sure better than my 0.22 rifle I have at home,' Buzz exclaimed.

'This is amazing. Look, four semi-automatic Colt 0.45 pistols and a couple of sawn offs, oh and look, there are two M14's as well.'

'M14?' Spencer asked.

'Yep, M14. This is the rifle currently being used by the military. It has a twenty-round magazine. And look, there's boxes of shells for them. It's pretty darned accurate. Jesus, honestly, she's thought of everything. And look. Love this.' Gus held up a shotgun. 'I don't think this one has even been released yet. I've read about in a gun magazine.'

'What exactly is it?' Spencer was getting a little bored with all the gun talk.

'This is the Mossberg 500 shotgun. It has I think, a five-cartridge magazine. Twelve gauge. This can really do some damage. Has to be close up,' he warned.

'Why close up?'

'It's a shotgun. You must have used them, surely?'

'Actually no. In fact, I'm not the greatest shot in the world.'

Gus threw him the Mossberg. 'Here, catch. This can be yours. If you're not a marksman, you just point this at central body mass and pull the trigger. The recoil is a doozy.'

'What about me? What can I use? 'Buzz's eyes flashed between the two men.

'Buzz. How old are you?' Spencer asked.

'Eighteen?'

'Oh yeah. When?' Spencer grinned.

'Ok, next birthday.'

'And when's that?'

'January,' Buzz said defensively.

'Good one, Buzz. It's August. So next year you will be eighteen. What do you reckon, Spencer?' Gus asked.

'Let's just leave it for the moment. How about we grab the Plymouth and go and pay the ungodly a visit in good old downtown Warbonnet.

CHAPTER THIRTY-SIX

SAVANNAH MAKES A VOW

'You're coming with me, bitch. And darling we're going to have so much fun.' Con-Rod leered as he grabbed Savannah by the scruff of her neck and her belt, frog marching her out of the hall into the cool night air. 'Hey there Hugo, Jerry, make yourselves useful and grab that piece of shit, FBI biker.'

Ty groaned. He was now sprawled on an old divan, semi-conscious, his hands and feet bound with rope. Hugo threw a jug of water over him, followed by a slap across the face.

'Wake up asshole. You're going for a ride.' Hugo slapped him again for good measure. 'C'mon Jerry, give me a hand.'

Jerry and Hugo grabbed Ty Brookman and dragged him across the floor, out to the waiting Dodge Van.

'One two, heave.' Jerry and Hugo threw him onto the hard steel tray. He groaned as his head smacked against the van's side.

Savannah yelled. 'Go easy, you gutless bastards.'

'Shut up, slut.' Con-Rod stuck his head through the side opening of the van and leaned up close to Savannah who was propped up against the van's wall, her hands tied behind her. He grinned and licked his lips. 'I guess I'm going to find out what it's like to really fuck the FBI.' He reached out and stroked her face. 'Normally I like, 'em a bit younger, but like I said, you and I are gonna have some fun.'

The van's sliding door slammed shut. Savannah could hear Con-Rod and, she thought, Hugo cackling as they both climbed into the front of the van. She shuddered at the thought of what Con-Rod had in store for her. Ultimately, she knew they were going to kill her, but she suspected death would only come after they'd had their fun. She wondered where Spencer and Gus were, and what about Dale Fletcher and the backup. She'd overheard Con-Rod telling Hugo about Warbonnet; by his descriptions it was a town. She vaguely remembered reading about an old mining town nestled in the Black Hills.

'So, tell me about Warbonnet, Con-Rod.'

'Ahh Warbonnet, Hugo, that's our little town. The Black Hill Demons' little playground. We got everything: our own saloon, courthouse, bike repair shop. Hell, we even got our own jail and courthouse.'

'Tell me about your cocaine setup.'

Savannah's ears pricked up.

'I tell you Hugo, Tolstoy is a fucking genius. We've got this underground factory where we turn the leaf into coke. It's amazing.'

'So, who does the work? It's fairly specialized?'

'We've got these wetbacks, some Columbians and some other beaners who know their stuff and they turn out pretty high-grade gear.'

'These guys wouldn't come cheap.' Hugo asked.

'Let's just say, they sort of do the job for the love of it.' Con-Rod chuckled.

'You're kidding? For the love of it? Get real.'

Con-Rod chuckled again. 'Yeah, what I mean is, for the love of life. If they don't produce…' He ran a finger across his throat.

Hugo roared. 'You son of a bitch.' He shook his head. 'Tolstoy thought of that?'

'You betcha.'

Hearing this conversation only reinforced Savannah's view that they were going to kill her. *But not without a fight.*

Ty was still unconscious as the van left the blacktop. Savannah sensed, or felt the different surfaces. The Jeep bounced over what seemed like a rutted cart track, like the one they'd been on down in Mexico with the burro. The ridged floor of the van made for a very unpleasant ride as they bounced, banging their heads. Tyrone began to stir, his breath wheezing.

'Hell, my damn head hurts. Where are we?'

'This isn't good news I'm afraid Ty. It seems as if the jig is up, as they say in the movies.'

'What the fuck happened? How the hell could they possibly know who or what we are?' Ty whispered.

'No idea. But they do.'

'What about Dale and all the backup?'

'Not a clue. But we're on our own.'

'What about Marlowe and Gus? Do you reckon they've been grabbed?'

'I don't reckon they have Spencer, or Gus for that matter, but even if the boys are free to help us there's no way they could know where we are going. So…Tyrone, it's just me an thee and so far, the deck seems to be stacked against us.'

The van bounced over a deep rut. Con-Rod and Hugo shared a laugh at the thump of Ty and Savannah's heads bouncing on the floor and the cries of pain that followed.

'Hell, that damn well hurt. I feel like I have the worst hangover ever. Those bastards really gave me a whack.' Ty grimaced.

'Hey, we're slowing down.' Savannah glanced at Ty. 'This could be the end of the line.'

'We're dead, but maybe not yet. They may have other plans.' Ty tried sit up as the van rolled to a halt.

Con-Rod jerked open the van's doors. Light from the adjacent building flooded in.

'Hey there, Sleaze, Rabbit, give us a hand will ya? Get these pieces of shit into a cell!' Con-rod yelled.

Two bikers placed their cans of Budweiser on the timber decking and obediently sprung up from their bentwood chairs.

'Hey Con-Rod, what we got here. A bit of entertainment?' the tall skinny one asked, hopefully.

'Play your cards right and she's your next date.' Con-rod chuckled around his ever-present toothpick.

Rough hands grabbed them and dragged them from the vehicle. Savannah and Ty now standing at the front of a redbrick structure with a broad timber veranda. They could see a hitching rail and a horse trough. The sign emblazoned on a slab of weathered timber bolted to the wall read "Sherriff" and below that "County Jail." A quick glance down the unpaved main street revealed a true Western town, with a livery stable, a haberdashery, barber shop, in fact everything you would expect to see in a John Wayne movie. The two-story rubble stone and Ponderosa Pine Long Branch Saloon was placed at the far end of Main Street, which was actually a cul-de-sac. Savannah grasped immediately the strategic location of the Long Branch. The hotel, with its handsome timbered balconies had a commanding view over the town. The hexagonal timber cupola on the wood shingle roof would double as a lookout and an excellent location for snipers.

The two jeans-clad bikers, presumably Rabbit and Sleaze, marched them into the jail.

Tall and thin, covered in the obligatory tattoos, Rabbit had all the charm of a rattlesnake. The acne scarred skin looked like bubbly paint, his worn jeans and denim shirt looked and smelled like they'd been glued on, and never washed. The incongruous comb over booked ridiculous, plastered to his head with oil that needed a change. Sleaze was similarly clad but was short, and dark, with a generous gut hanging over his studded belt, his fingers adorned with a collection of garish, chunky rings.

Everything about the interior of the jail resembled a Hollywood Western, except for the small black and white Tokyo Deluxe black and white television. A gun rack with 0.44 Winchester lever action rifles and two shotguns added to the decor. A solid scarred oak desk, cluttered with a stack of motorcycle magazines and a comfortable leather-bound swivel chair occupied the back of the room. Below a pine shelf laden with photos of vintage motorcycles was a worn leather chaise lounge. Pinned to the notice board, a collection of vintage wanted posters, the pungent smell of marijuana hung in the air like a shroud.

Con-rod nodded to his two henchmen. 'Put the slut into cell number one and this one,' he pointed to Tyrone, 'into cell five down the end. He'll still be able to hear the little lady's moans of pleasure. You and I are gonna have so much fun, darling.'

'You listen to me you big prick, you…' Tyrone yelled.

Con-rod drove the butt of a Winchester rifle he was holding, brutally into Ty's stomach. 'Who the fuck do you think you're talking to? Fucking FBI. You're not so fucking tough now, are you?' Con-rod screamed, unhinged enough that the toothpick tumbled to the floor. 'Throw the fucker into the cell. Move it, you guys.'

Sleaze and Rabbit grinning in unison grabbed Savannah and Ty. Con-rod opened the rear door that opened onto a corridor, revealing a number of steel barred cells.

'Hey, Con-rod!' Rabbit yelled, 'Do I get a turn?' He stroked her face and grinned, exposing a mouth full of twisted, nicotine-stained teeth.

'Of course, my man, I'm a good sharing boy. Hey, you're all gonna get a turn. Don't worry bout that.'

Con-Rod grabbed the keys from a big steel ring attached to his belt, and opened the cell door. 'Put her down gently, Sleaze, we don't want unsightly bruises now, do we?'

'I'm gonna be next after Con-Rod, darlin.' Sleaze grinned as he pushed Savannah into the cell.

Savannah plonked on to the hard bunk, watching intently as Ty was marched down to the last cell. She thought all the fight had been drained out of him. He didn't glance at her, his head seemed to bounce on his chest as Rabbit pushed him to the end of the corridor. She heard the metallic sound of the cell door opening, then slamming shut. She felt truly alone.

Tyrone neutralized. *Spencer and Gus? Who knows?* And Dale, where in hell was Dale?

She sat on the bunk, her hands still tied behind her. A part of her was scared, but overwhelmingly she realized the main emotion was anger. Anger and hatred. She vowed, then and there, that whatever happened, Con-Rod at least was going to regret ever touching her and her people.

CHAPTER THIRTY-SEVEN

WE NEED A PLAN.

Spencer drove. An excited Buzz sat next to him, pointing the way. Gus sat in the back; the slate grey, hinged wooden box of grenades next to him. Gus was making sure all the weapons were loaded. Spare mags rested on the far side of the bench seat. The metallic sound of the magazines being slotted into place made Spencer wonder just what sort of firefight they were likely to be swept into.

'Hey Spencer, you said you're not a great shot. Can you throw?'

Spencer immediately had a vision. *A scorching day. He's dressed in white. He's hurling a red leather clad ball. The ball has six rows of white stitching. He's already rubbed the ball on the leg of his white trousers, leaving a dull red stain. The ball flies through the air, it bounces. A grinning young man swings a bat. At the last second, the ball, as if controlled by an invisible puppet master, lurches to the right and smashes through three wooden wickets. The batsman is dumfounded. The crowd roars.*

'Oh, yeah. Can't shoot. But I can throw all right.'

The lights of the Plymouth danced across the forest of aspen, birch and ancient oak that had been around when other battles were fought. Some of these encounters were between the white man and the red man. But tonight, was different, this time there was no confusion about who were the good guys.

'How far is Warbonnet, Buzz?' Spencer asked.

'Not far. We should be there soon.'

At that moment the heavy timber fell away to reveal a tundra of rolling treeless meadows.

'Over that small rise, there's another small stretch of trees, then we come into an open plain, and in a bit of a valley you'll be able to see Warbonnet.'

'So they'll be able to see us coming. That's a worry.' Spencer turned and glanced at Gus.

'They don't have lookouts or anything like that. Most of the guys will be in the saloon, shooting pool or playing cards. Outsiders stay away.'

Gus pursed his lips. 'They might be on their guard. Let's cut the headlights and take her real slow on the way in, right?'

Spencer agreed, and flicked the lights off. A near-complete darkness swallowed them up.

Spencer chuckled as he pointed back at a sign. 'You blokes missed the sign. "You are about to enter Warbonnet. If you don't have no invite, fuck off."'

CHAPTER THIRTY-EIGHT

CON-ROD'S NIGHT OF PASSION

Savannah had already explored every nook and cranny of her cell. She'd concluded there was nothing Old West about her accommodation. It was clean, harsh and spartan. The floor of the cell was drab grey concrete, the wall rendered brick, and painted antiseptic green. The bunk was a hard slab of steel with a utilitarian olive green, canvas-covered mattress. Two robust chains secured it to the wall. There was no escape. Nothing loose. Nothing she could unscrew and turn into a weapon. All she could do was sit and wait. She didn't have to wait long.

'Stay here and mind the store, Sleaze.'

Savannah braced herself. She heard the door to the front office open, then close. Con-Rod's heavy boots clunked on the polished concrete floor of the passage. He stood at the cell door, holding a steel ring of keys in his hand. *Sure is a big son of a bitch.*

Wearing the uniform of black jeans and a Harley Davidson T-Shirt, his calculating, cold eyes surveyed the scene. He was running his tongue over his full fleshy lips, Savannah figured that was meant for effect. A matted black beard touching the top of his shirt. The physique was powerful, with weightlifter arms. He looked like he was designed to hurt people.

'Well, darling, it's your lucky night.'

Savannah rose to her feet as Con-Rod slotted the key into the lock and with a clang the door opened.

'Con-Rod, my mama said to me if you're going to be raped, lay back and enjoy it. Anyway, I have a proposition for you.'

Con-Rod leered at her. That God damn toothpick shifted from one side of his mouth to the other and back. 'You got nothin to bargain with.'

'Well, maybe not. Ok, you hold the winning hand, I've got the aces and eights, just like Wild Bill.'

'So, what you got?'

'I want to live. Yes, you can do what you want. You have the muscle. If that's what you want, then, that's that. But…'

'What's the fucking but, bitch?'

'Con-Rod, I can give you a real good time. The best you ever had,' Savannah purred. She now licked her lips. 'I guarantee, after we're done, you're going to want more. You're going to want to keep me around. I don't know what you've experienced before, but you've never had a gal like me. Undo these ropes and I'll take you to paradise. I just hope you've got what it takes.'

Con-Rod froze, raking his eyes over her yet again. The only thing moving was the toothpick. Back and forth it went, back and forth. A metronome for the big lunk's brain.

Savannah saw the gleam of lust in his eyes and pounced. 'The ropes Con-Rod, undo the ropes,' she whispered.

Without another word, he untied her.

Savannah sat back down on the bunk. 'I'm going to take off my boots. Then my jeans. My shirt. My bra…you going to watch…Con-Rod?'

'Yeah.' His voice hoarse.

'You can help.' Savannah held out her left leg. 'Pull the boot off.'

Con-Rod knelt on the floor and grabbed the boot.

Savannah knelt down and snatched the stiletto out of her right boot, she then kicked him in the head, sending him sprawling across the floor. He grunted in pain, the pointed toe of the boot ripped open skin on his cheek. Blood spattered onto the floor.

'You…' His words cut short as the razor-sharp blade sunk into his abdomen and Savannah put her left hand over his mouth. At the same time, she sliced the blade across his stomach, the dark red intestines slithered like snakes across the concrete floor.

'Was that good for you?' Savannah murmured.

The wound was fatal, but Con-Rod was strong and tried to raise himself from the floor. One iron hard hand shot out and grabbed her around the neck, squeezing. A puddle of blood swirled. He coughed. It seemed to take ages, but finally his eyes rolled in the sockets and the hand fell limp. Savannah held her hand over his mouth, watching as his life force ebbed away. Con-Rod swiftly bled out.

'Time to go.' Savannah removed the knife from the mess and in a final slick motion she slashed his neck, severing his carotid artery. Unnecessary but satisfying.

She grabbed the keys. Her boots thudded along the corridor leading to the office. Quietly opening the door, she could see Sleaze, his feet up on the desk as he watched the small black and white television.

"Marshall Dillon, you gonna go after them varmints all on your lonesome." Chester entreated, on the TV show, Gunsmoke.

'That you Con-Rod? That was quick. My turn, right?' Sleaze didn't take his eyes off the TV.

Just as Sleaze turned his head around, his eyes like saucers, Savannah grabbed him by his thick greasy black locks and slashed his fat neck. For a few fleeting moments his legs and arms thrashed, then he was still.

'Yep. It's your turn all right, sweetheart,' Savannah whispered..

She ran to the window and counted at a glance at least a dozen bikers strolling down Main Street. The saloon was noisy and clearly packed with a motley collection of leather jackets and blue jeans. *Why the hell aren't you guys at the God damned big event?* She knew the answer though: they were here for her, and for Spencer. However they'd found out they were law, they somehow had.

Locking the front door of the office, Savannah ran down the corridor to the cell where Tyrone was locked up. He was sitting on his bunk, head in hand.

'Tyrone dear, time to go.'

'What the…Jesus, what's going on? Savannah, I don't believe it. Is that blood?'

'Believe. Now we gotta move.' It took an infuriatingly long time to find the correct key, but eventually she opened the cell door. Tyrone jumped to his feet and followed Savannah along the passage.

'Where the hell is everyone? What's happening…Oh my God. You did that? How on…'

Ty had paused at Savannah's old cell and stared at the grisly mess that had once been Con-Rod Jackson.

Savannah opened the door to the office. Once again Tyrone was stunned, this time by the sight of Sleaze sprawled on his swivel chair with his feet on the desk. His head lay back, the slash on his neck looking like a bloody smile.

The front door of the office rattled. The puzzled face of a biker peered in through the barred glass window. 'What the fuck?' He hefted a shoulder against the door, at the same time screaming, 'The bitch is out of her cell! C'mon guys, get over here. Quick smart.' He continued trying to force the door. Fortunately, it was designed to repel intruders. Thick oaken slabs with bars of iron that had defied angry lynch mobs one hundred years ago.

'You betta open this fucking door, bitch. And just where the fuck are Sleaze and Con-Rod?'

'They don't sound happy.' Savannah just loved when bad people weren't happy. Furious faces crowded the small, barred window.

'C'mon, open up. I won't tell you again.' The owner of the voice had a big head and a very distinctive Mohawk hairstyle.

There was a moment's silence. Ty and Savannah could see huddled men whispering.

'Ok, here's the deal. You open up or we're gonna set fire to the joint!' Big head yelled.

'Shit. That's going to make things a little difficult,' Ty said.

'I don't think they'll do it. They don't know that Sleaze and Con-Rod have gone to that big Harley dealership in the sky.'

Savannah strode over to the gun rack, hidden from the sight of the window, selecting a Winchester repeating rifle.

'Full mag. Here, catch.' She threw it to Ty.

Next, she grabbed a shotgun. 'I will say Tolstoy has taste. This is the model 1911 SL, just about the most dangerous shotgun ever invented. An oldie but a goodie. Yoo hoo, sweetie, we want to talk.' Savannah's voice carried into the street.

'I thought you'd see…' The mohawk appeared at the window.

Kaboom! The shotgun exploded, sending the full load of 12-gauge buckshot through the window.

'They don't call it the widow maker for nothing.' Savannah chuckled.

'God dammit, Savannah, I'm not sure that was completely legal. I mean, he may not have been armed. I…can't just stand by and let…I mean what do I tell Dale Fletcher? Look, I…That, God damn, Savannah, that was, it was murder.'

Savannah turned on Tyrone with a snarl. 'You listen to me. They already threatened to burn this place down. They want to kill us. Don't you get it? Con-Rod was going to rape me and then hand me over to his boys for a bit of fun. And then they were going to finish us off. And as for telling Dale, we still have to get out of here. They still want to kill us and they have more weapons and people than we have. So how about you stop wasting your breath and figure out what our next move is. Ok?'

CHAPTER THIRTY-NINE

RAMIREZ FRETS

'What a fucking turnup, hey boss?' Jerry, grinned like a greasepainted circus clown. Hugo and Jerry had burst into Enrique Ramirez's comfortable room at the incongruously named Grand Hotel situated in the main street of Warbonnet. The room was tasteful in a chintzy way, sort of 1870's Americana meets Holiday Inn. The floor was polished mahogany. A tasteful geometric rug graced the centre of the room. A roll top writing desk a four-poster bed and some tan Chesterfield sofas added a warm homely touch, along with some Old West Remington prints hanging on the walls.

The plan had been for Tolstoy to show Ramirez the underground cocaine factory two miles into the adjoining forest. He'd been told that Savannah and Tyrone were in jail, and languishing in the lockup cells.

'Who woulda thought that tough broad Savannah was FBI? Well, we got her just where we want her, and the other jerk, whatever his name is?' Hugo was all smiles.

'Tyrone,' Jerry chipped in.

'Listen to me you fucking idiots. You don't mess with the FBI. It should be obvious even to you two morons that Marlowe and Steele are just the tip of the FBI iceberg. That clown Con-Rod will whack them for sure. It's a capital crime.'

'Capital?' Jerry echoed.

'Yeah, dummy. Capital! That means the death sentence.'

'Hang on, hang on, boss. This has nothing to do with us. If Con-Rod or Tolstoy want to waste them two, it's nothing to do with us, right?' Hugo spoke.

Ramirez sighed. 'Dumb and fucking dumber,' he whispered. 'Listen to me, you two boobs. The FBI obviously know about us and Tolstoy, or Marlowe and the broad wouldn't be here. If they get whacked, and I'm sure they will, everyone involved will be facing the death sentence. Do you understand?'

Hugo's face paled. 'Well, what do you suggest?'

'Ok, here's the thing. I don't know exactly how much the Feds have. It seems to me that Marlowe and that Savannah babe were setting us up with the band, the drugs the whole shebang. I reckon they were going to swoop, probably at the concert, cookout. For all we know they may have had hidden mikes. We just don't know. But.' Ramirez pointed his cigar at his two henchmen. 'At the moment I don't think they have much of a case against us.'

'Hell, boss, as far as we know there are only four of them. Come on?'

'That's four we know about. There may have been more, maybe more were on the way. It's obvious that the whole scene that Marlowe set up. And had me pay for. Son of a bitch. It was designed to incriminate Tolstoy, me and any of the bikers who participated, but now that's all fallen apart.'

'How do we know Marlowe and the woman are definitely FBI?' Jerry asked.

'I'm not sure. Something Tolstoy picked up from his nephew, but apparently, it's kosher.'

'So boss, what now?' Hugo was swigging on a can of Budweiser.

'What now? I tell you what now. Jerry, go grab the Lincoln. Try and be inconspicuous?'

'Inconspicuous?'

'For fuck's sake you ignoramus, try not to let anyone see you, ok?'

'Then what?'

'I'm going to meet you downstairs with my luggage. Give me ten minutes to pack, and then the three of us head back to Chicago. We'll leave these fucking hillbillies to sort out the mess.'

CHAPTER FORTY

PARTY NIGHT IN WARBONNET.

Gus was practically in the front seat with Spencer and Buzz as they slowed the big Plymouth to a crawl and inched toward Warbonnet. The twinkling lights of Warbonnet showed them a bunch of parked choppers at the far end, up the hill at the hotel. No sign of their owners, yet.

'How the hell do we handle this?' Gus peered ahead.

'We have to find where Savannah and Ty are. Hold up here. If we march right up Main Street they'll have us like sitting ducks. Buzz, are you familiar with the layout?'

'Yeah, pretty much, I've been here a couple of times. You see the bank and the haberdashers, there on the left?'

'Got it,' Spencer replied.

'Well next to that is the sheriff's office and jail. My uncle showed me over it. He was pretty proud of it. It has about six cells at the back. He had them built, God knows what for.'

'Hey, something's going down. Gus, have a look at the jail.'

They could see at least ten bikers at the front of the jail. A man lay on the sidewalk, blood pooling around him.

'Someone's been hurt,' Buzz said.

'What's the bet Savannah is behind it all?' Spencer chuckled.

'So far they haven't noticed us,' Gus said.

'They soon will. Let's have a wongi with those nice gentlemen.'

'What in hell is a wongi?' Gus asked.

'Sorry, Gus, it's aboriginal for having a chat. Pass me the shotgun.' Gus handed it over he'd already explained the mechanism.

'We could go around behind the main row of buildings," Buzz said.

'That'll take too long. Stuff these cartridges into your pocket. I'll grab an M14 and one of the Colts.'

'What about me?' Buzz questioned.

'Buzz, you're just a bit young. So please, stay here. Anyhow I reckon we'll sort these guys out. Ok?'

Gus and Spencer warily clambered out of their vehicle, the bikers were still huddled around the sheriffs, office. They noticed several of the men were brandishing pistols.

'FBI. Drop your weapons and move away from the door,' Gus barked.

Twenty eyes swivelled in unison. 'What the fuck?' A thug with a red bandanna turned and raised his pistol. Gus's M14 exploded and the man's chest blossomed into a plume of red.

Bikers scattered every which way. Fire was returned, but Gus and Spencer had already gotten to cover to either side of the street.

'You heard the man!' Spencer yelled. 'Nobody else needs to be hurt.'

Savannah's shotgun protruded from the smashed window. 'You heard. Now drop 'em!' She yelled.

One of the bikers dropped down below the horse trough, gun in hand. 'We've got the pricks outnumbered.' He raised his pistol. Spencer squeezed the trigger of his shotgun; the man's face dissolved into a mass of bone and brain matter. Splinters and wood went flying. The recoil just about pushed Spencer off balance. Three of the others threw down their weapons, while the rest bolted in panic to the security of the Long Branch Saloon at the far end of Main Street.

Spencer balked at the idea of shooting the men in the back.

'On the ground, now!' Gus screamed.

The remaining bikers glanced wildly around, dropping their pistols, and then one by one they threw down their weapons and spread eagled.

'Ok Buzz, make yourself useful. Come over and search these men for weapons,' Gus turned and yelled.

'You bet.' Buzz flew out of the Plymouth.

The door of the lockup swung open. Savannah, still wielding the shotgun, emerged, followed by a white-faced Tyrone brandishing a Winchester. 'Into the cells now, motherfuckers. And please just give me a reason to shoot.' Savannah winked at Spencer.

'How did I do Mr Marlowe?' Buzz turned to Spencer.

A solitary shot rang out from the Long Branch Saloon. Buzz screamed. 'I've been hit.' He fell to the ground clutching his leg, moaning in pain.

Spencer knew he couldn't help Buzz until he'd neutralized the three bikers, who fortunately hadn't moved a muscle. It seemed as if the fight had gone out of them. He realised there was no point trying to return fire. The Long Branch was way out of range for his shotgun, and up an incline as well.

'On your feet now. You heard the lady. Into the cells. Now move it.' Spencer yelled at the men.

One by one they clambered to their feet. A short stocky guy with a red bandanna snarled, 'You're still fucking outnumbered. What are you gonna do, shoot all of us?'

'Maybe not, darling, but I might just make an example out of you.' Savannah smiled.

'You wouldn't fucking dare you FBI bitch.'

Savannah grinned again as she levelled the shotgun at him.

Spencer watched as the man's eyes looked like saucers and his face turned a ghostly white. Savannah pointed the gun above his head, and squeezed the trigger.

'Into the jail. And I mean now, you sons of bitches.' Savannah yelled.

The men ran, stumbling into the hoosegow.

Gus and Spencer used the men as shields as they were hustled into the lock up.

As soon as the cell doors were bolted, Spencer rushed back to the street. Buzz groaned and clutched his leg, his face drained of colour.

Spencer grabbed him by the arm. 'Can you walk?'

'Yeah, but it hurts.'

Spencer pulled him to his feet. Buzz clung to him like a drowning man. Several more rounds thwacked into street and the wall of the lock up as they stumbled like two men in a three-legged race. Spencer helped him into the safety of the jail. He slammed the door shut and bolted it.

The three remaining bikers, now compliant, were silently escorted into the cells. Spencer heard some curses as they saw the body of Sleaze and then as they entered the corridor, Con-Rod's butchered remains.

With the immediate threats locked away, Savannah inspected Buzz's leg. It was like the sight of her made him forget all about his wounded leg. He fell right into a trance.

'I think you're wonderful. Maybe we could catch a movie some time?' he asked hopefully.

'I think you'll be Ok.' Savannah kissed him on the forehead. The well-equipped jail had a supply of bandages, painkillers and some Vaseline. 'It's a flesh wound. The slug went straight through.' Savannah turned to Gus and Spencer.

'Buzz, lie down on the couch, and elevate your leg. There's a good boy.'

'I'm not a boy,' he said angrily.

'He'll definitely be ok.' Savannah grinned.

'Guess what I found?' Gus brandished a bottle of Jim Beam.

'Life saver.' Savannah opened a drawer on the desk. 'Eureka!' She produced three grubby shot glasses.

'I could do with a drink, but I'm not sure I want to sit here with the late unlamented…' Spencer felt his stomach heave at the sight of Sleaze, his gashed neck and the vacant eyes staring at the ceiling.

'That was Sleaze,' Savannah said happily.

'Hey, Tyrone, give me a hand. We'll drag him into the cell with his old buddy.' Gus and Ty pulled him off the chair; he fell with a thump. They dragged him by the feet through to the cells, a trail of blood smeared across the floor. Savannah found some gun cleaning rags and did her best to mop up Sleaze's liquid remains.

CHAPTER FORTY-ONE
WAR

'You ok, Buzz?' Savannah gazed anxiously at the boy. His feet were up and he was reading a motorbike magazine.

He turned a hopeful face up to her. 'I'm all right. You're a life saver! It hurts a bit, but I reckon I'd soon be ready for a romantic dinner and dancing.' Buzz blew her a kiss.

Savannah glanced sideways at Spencer and grinned. 'He's going to be a lady killer. Now back to business, it's been pretty darn quiet. They're probably planning their next move. Buzz, do you have any idea how many gang members there could be here?'

'Nah, impossible to say. There are at least thirty guys living here. But hell, some could be at the show.' He hiked his shoulders and winced.

'Meaning we are outnumbered, outgunned, trapped in here, with no supplies or food," Savannah said. 'This building is only meant to allow people in or out through a single door, and that door is clearly visible all the way up Main Street where there are a bunch of heavily armed outlaw bikers. Does that sum up the situation pretty well?'

'Yeah, you're right but the Long Branch is a fair way away and we are at right angles to it. It makes it pretty difficult for them to have much of a shot at us. I have a suggestion.' Spencer nodded at his companions.

'Ok boy wonder, let's hear it.' Savannah's face was grim.

'It seems as if they have the whole street covered. That slug that hit Buzz, I saw a flash from the cupola on top of the Long Branch. If that guy is any good…'

'Or woman,' Savannah corrected.

Gus picked up a magazine and threw it at her, grinning. 'They're outlaw bikers. God dammit Savannah. A female sharpshooter. I don't think so.'

Savannah threw the magazine back at him. 'Yeah well guess what, I'm a woman, and I'm a sharpshooter.'

'Boys and girls, cool it. Like I said, I have an idea.'

'Sorry Spencer, we're all ears.' Gus gave him a thumbs up.

'Here it is. The first thing is they're not going away. All they have to do is wait until we move out of here and then they can pick us off.'

'Yeah sure. So?' Ty rolled his eyes.

'Savannah really is a sharpshooter. The whole street is lit up, the streetlights are definitely not old west. As long as the lights are on we can't move. So how about, if possible, Savannah can plug most or all of the globes…'

'Hang on, hang on,' Gus growled. 'I'm a pretty fair shot, and I don't think I could do that even with a telescopic sight. The only rifles we have are these 0.44 Winchesters and my M14. Nah, it can't be done.'

'Yes, it can,' Savannah said quietly.

'Leaving that for a minute, we have the Plymouth loaded with firepower. If Savannah can knock out most of those lights?'

Right on cue, an explosion of gunshots and the dull sound of rounds as they slammed into, what?

'The hell they shooting at? Idiots, we're in here.' Gus threw his hands into the air.

'The God damn Plymouth!' Tyrone exclaimed. He peered out of the window. 'They've hit the front tyres, the windscreen and the radiator. We're not going anywhere.'

'No matter. Like I said, if Savannah can knock out the streetlights. It's a moonless night. And we have some serious firepower in the trunk. They're not going to expect us to go to the car. So, what do you reckon?'

'Sounds ok to me.' Savannah grabbed a Winchester.

'We'll turn out the lights so the veranda will be pretty much in darkness. Savannah, if you crawl behind the horse trough, you should be able to get a bead on the streetlights. Are you ok with that?' Spencer was concerned for her safety.

'What do you Aussies say? "She'll be apples, mate."'

Lights extinguished, Spencer stealthily opened the door and peered down the street. 'All clear.'

Savannah dropped to the ground and carefully crawled behind the water trough. Spencer, Ty, and Gus stood by the open-door holding rifles and a shotgun.

Not a sound, then the Winchester barked and the closest streetlight smashed, sending a tinkle of glass fragments onto the street. Immediately a barrage of bullets slammed into the water trough. They heard the sound of the lever action chambering another round into the breech. Another light exploded. Once again gunfire came from the bikers, but less this time. One by one every light was extinguished, each time drawing less enthusiastic retorts from their enemies. The last light, Savannah had to fire twice. She crawled back into the jail.

'That was amazing, I've never seen anything like it.' Gus stood open mouthed.

'Who's a clever girl?' Spencer grinned at Savannah. 'How about we cool it for a few minutes. There's no reason for them to expect us to make a dash for the car.'

They sat in silence, 'Who's going to go?' Tyrone eventually asked.

Spencer spoke. 'We're going to need at least two. There's quite a stash.'

'I'm pretty quick. How about you and I Spencer? Tyrone's a shuffler, aren't you Ty?' Gus grinned.

'Yeah, I'm not built for speed, but I'm happy to try.'

'Let's do it.'

Spencer opened the door; he and Gus made a dash for the Plymouth. Spencer opened the trunk, grabbing the box of grenades, at the same time stuffing two Colts into his jacket pockets. Gus opened the rear door. The interior light burst into life. Just as he snatched the machine gun a volley of shots flew through the air. Flames could be seen snaking out from under the bonnet of the car. He managed to grab the M14 as well, and some extra ammo, including two belts for the M60. They both sprinted headlong back to the safety of the jail. The weight of the weapons in Spencer's arms slowed him down. He stumbled and almost fell. A dozen guns seemed to be firing at once. Bullets whizzed through the air.

'Christ, that was bloody dangerous.' Spencer couldn't help laughing as they fell into the jail and slammed the door shut.

The Plymouth had erupted in flame, throwing eerie shadows through the jail door window.

'Bastards, I loved that car.' Savannah held the bars of the window as she gazed at the stricken Plymouth.

'I'm sorry about the car Savannah but we have some more pressing problems.' Tyrone joined her, peering out of the window, just as a round whizzed past. 'Hell, that was too God damn close for comfort, that's for sure. There's someone in that cupola who knows how to shoot.'

'What now?' Gus asked.

'Let's just wait until they've stopped firing.' Spencer picked up the shotgun and chambered another round into it.

'I'd like to take out the guy in the cupola. From where he is, he controls the whole street.' Savannah weighed the M14 in her hands. 'Nice weapon. Just a little too heavy. I'm going to whack him with the Winchester. Just like the old-time cowboys. Meanwhile, just look at the God Damn Plymouth. Hell, I loved that darned car.' Savannah peered again out of the window at the flaming wreck of her beloved automobile.

'Attention fellow gunslingers.' Spencer's face was grim. 'Let's look at what we have. All the firepower is coming from the Long Branch. Agreed?' The space around Main Street was nothing but a barren plain, and it would only take a hint of light to expose anyone to deadly reprisals. Savannah and Ty had already judged it to be a death trap. Eventually they would be in sight of the Long Branch and picked off by their sniper.

'Yeah agreed,' Savannah repeated. Gus and Ty nodded.

'Parked out the front I saw a Chevy, and a Ford pickup, and a couple of Harleys. You enter the building through some batwing doors. It's just a big room with a bar, some pool tables and there's a big picture window. That pretty much sums it up I think?'

'Yeah, don't forget, the sharpshooter in the cupola.'

'Sure.'

'The lights are out in Main Street. If we mosey, along and keep to the sidewalk, the shopfront roofs will give us some cover.' Spencer grinned. 'If Gus, spots anyone coming out of the Long Branch and opens up with the M14. That's going to scare the hell out of them.'

'What about you, Kangaroo Man?' Ty questioned.

'I'll take the shotgun and grenades. Savannah is going to try and pick off the sniper on the roof. Sound like a plan?'

'What about me?' Buzz grimaced as he tried to move his leg.

'Stay here. There's another shotgun, and you have a Colt as well. If anyone tries to break in, shoot 'em, ok? You have FBI permission.' Gus winked at him.

'Let's do it.' Savannah hefted the Winchester and grabbed two boxes of cartridges.

The door of the jail creaked open. Spencer stuck his head out and peered carefully down the street. All was quiet at this end of town. The Long Branch was ablaze with light. A chandelier was clearly visible with multiple tiny globes illuminating bikers at the bar, drinking, with not a care in the world. He could see the flashing lights of poker machines and the sound of Elvis belting out Jailhouse Rock from a juke box. It seemed like it was party night.

'They don't seem to be taking things to seriously.' Savannah frowned. Immediately a volley of shots poured from the cupola.

'I'm surprised they haven't tried a frontal attack on the jail,' Ty said, brows knitted.

'Why do it at night? Let us stew until morning. They know we won't get any sleep. We sure as hell aren't going anywhere. And of course, they know one of us has been hit,' Spencer replied.

They shuffled silently along the timbered sidewalk. Ancient timbers creaked, as the three warriors trod, carefully, meticulously, eyes straining as they peered into the shadows, looking for gunmen who may be lying in wait. The body of the faceless biker lay where it had fallen, draped over the water trough.

Bang, bang, bang. Three shots broke the silence. Spencer could just see the shadowy outline of the shooter silhouetted in the cupola. The rounds had no chance of hitting them as they were protected by the veranda.

'I'm going to get that son of a bitch,' Savannah muttered. 'Gus how about you cover me with the M60? I'm going to the centre of the street. Fire for about ten seconds. When you stop, he'll stick his head up.'

'Jesus, Savannah. That's pretty high risk.'

'Just do it. Please?' She smiled sweetly.

Gus glanced sideways at Spencer. 'What do you think, Spencer?'

Spencer shrugged. 'Yeah, go for it.'

'Here goes.' Savannah rushed into the street. Shots rang out from the cupola striking the ground near Savannah's feet. The M60 erupted as the massive 7.62 mm rounds thudded into the Long Branch, shattering the window and slamming into the roof. Gus ceased fire. There was a moment of eerie silence. The stink of cordite hung in air.

Savannah stood motionless; the Winchester locked onto her shoulder. *Bam!* One shot.

'I got the bastard.'

Elvis had stopped singing. The lights went out. Party night at the Long Branch was over.

'Hey Marlowe!' an unidentified voice rang out. 'Throw down them weapons. Put your hands on your head and walk towards us. You guys are outnumbered. We was gonna wait till mornin, but, fuck you.' An array of rifles now protruded from the shattered main window. Without warning a ragged volley of shots rang out, peppering the buildings around them.

'Stalemate.' Savannah was now back in the safety of the veranda in front of Honest Abe's General Store. 'They can just wait us out. Where the hell did Dale and the crew get to?'

'I have an idea,' Spencer murmured.

'Gus, cover me with the M60. It's about time our friends find out about my Aussie throwing skills.'

'Hey, yeah. The grenades. God damn, just like Mexico, Spencer. That was really something. You saved our bacon then.' Savannah grinned.

'Mexico. Really?' Spencer had no idea what she was talking about. Except maybe he did. He had a flash of memory involving him in a rickety old farm cart, holding one of these same grenades. It disappeared just like all the others, but he snorted laughter regardless.

Spencer grabbed two grenades from his pocket and pulled the pin out of each, making sure he held the levers down.

'Ok. Say when.' Gus fed the last belt of ammunition into the machine gun.

'Now!'

Gus stepped into the street and let it rip. The deep throated chatter of the M60 was deafening as it sprayed bullets into the Long Branch.

Spencer dashed into the street, a grenade in each hand. He estimated the distance at about 120 feet. Not an easy throw. The first pineapple sailed majestically through the air and clattered onto the sidewalk in front of the Long Branch, exploding in a burst of smoke and shrapnel. Spencer immediately followed through with the second. All gunfire had stopped. This one sailed through the shattered front window. *Kaboom!* Then silence.

The screaming started. Panic stricken men flew out of the building.

Whomp, whomp, whomp. There are few things scarier than the sound of the Huey attack helicopter. Search lights blasted their white light over Main Street and then like a lion going for the jugular of an antelope the helicopter swung onto the Long Branch.

'Throw down your weapons. Lie on the ground, hands on your head, cross your legs. Do it now.' The chopper hovered like a prehistoric bird of prey. The loudspeaker blasted out its impersonal message like a pre-recorded telephone bulletin.

With machine guns poised for action and the grenade launchers clearly visible it was like omnipotent aliens taking over the planet. Scary as hell.

'Fuck you!' A bare-chested biker in blue jeans, holding a BAR Browning, sent a flurry of bullets at the helicopter. Immediately the two-front mounted M60 machine guns of the first chopper opened up. The biker looked like a rag doll that had come alive. His body thrown around as if invisible wires were creating a macabre dance. The bullet ridden body finally collapsed in an untidy bloody heap.

The few remaining bikers straggled out of the Long Branch and joined their brothers lying on the ground. The two Hueys gently descended to the ground, and with a hiss, and as the whine of the rotors finally ceased, ten black-painted Rangers sprung out of each chopper, their M14's at the ready.

'Better late than never.' Tyrone chuckled.

Alighting from the second Huey was the familiar figure of Dale Fletcher wearing fawn chinos and a crisp white y-front shirt with a paisley tie. Next to him strode a big man with greying hair, wearing a military style cargo shirt and cotton fatigue baker pants.

He held out a hand to Savannah, a broad grin cracked his face, 'Well, if it isn't Mrs Moretti, and, as I live and breathe. Mr Moretti, how about that?'

Spencer's head swivelled looking behind, 'I'm sorry, did you say Moretti? You have the wrong person.'

'Buck Randall. Is it really you? This really is something. How in hell…?' Savannah turned her gaze to Dale. 'Kiss my go to hell, Dale, how in hell did you manage this?' Before he could answer she turned her gaze to Buck. 'I can't believe it, all those years ago in Tokyo. When was that?'

'That Savannah was 1955, a full decade ago. Mr Moretti here seems to have forgotten.'

'Spencer has amnesia and remembers nothing.'

'Jesus, that's a bitch. You don't remember, Spencer? You were Mr Moretti, the mob's lawyer, and you helped the Rangers with that Jap nationalist idiot, what was his name? Watanabe, something like that.'

Spencer shrugged. 'Nothing, a complete blank. How come my name was Moretti?'

'Hang on, Spencer,' Dale chipped in, 'Savannah can fill you in on the details a little later.'

'Dale, how in hell did you manage to get the Rangers at such short notice?' Savannah's eyebrows raised.

'Buck and I have always kept in touch. He's now stationed at Fort Benning in Georgia, and would you believe the Rangers were just involved in night exercises just outside of Rapid City. Our vehicles were totalled in Spearfish Canyon. When I was able to get to Deadwood, I made some calls.'

'How in hell did you know we were in Warbonnet?' Spencer piped up. At the same time, he ran a curious eye over Buck.

'Well…you might say, I…that is we, sort of leaned rather heavily on a couple of the Black Hill Demons and let them know they could be spending the rest of their natural on Rikers Island. So much for the brotherhood.' Dale chuckled. 'One of them claimed you broke his arm tonight, Marlowe.'

Spencer grinned in response. 'Poor fellas, those two.'

'Now let's go and inspect the debris. How many dead?'

CHAPTER FORTY-TWO
DONE AND DUSTED?

The following week passed in a whirl of officialdom. An army of law enforcement descended on Sturgis, arriving on the last day of the motorcycle rally.

'Lester Barrington, you are under arrest for suspicion of murder. Hands behind your back.' Dale beamed from ear to ear when he recounted the arrest of Tolstoy. I tell you it was just about the best moment of my life.'

'What will happen to him?' Spencer asked.

'This trial will be bigger than the Capone one in in '31. Lester Barrington was lawyered up when we arrived. Say, that ranch of his is something else, isn't it?'

'What about the cocaine factory?' Savannah was anxious for the details.

'Jesus wept. I've never seen anything like it. Sort of what you could imagine a WW2 slave factory might be like. Those poor bastards. Mexicans, Columbians. He worked them to death. They knew they'd never get out alive. I tell you it was horrible.'

'Do you think he might get the death sentence?" Savannah's eyes gleamed.

'Look, it's hard to say. Already he's denying just about everything. Puts the blame on the late Leopold Jackson AKA, Con-Rod. There is one little thing, Savannah?'

'That is?' She scowled.

'You, ah, you're the one who killed Jackson. Right?'

'Yes, and don't start Dale. We want to stay friends. *Don't we?*'

'I'm sure you had to do what you had to do…well, it's just…'

'Just what? Great God damn horn spoon. The bastard was going to rape me then hand me over to his buddies. Tell me, Dale, what's your lovely wife's name again?'

'Clementine. You've met her. Why do you ask?'

'You just run the gory details past Clemmie, get another girl's reaction. Do you know what she'll say?'

Dale shrugged. Spencer thought he looked as if he wanted to dig a hole and pull it in after him.

'Umm, no, I guess not,' he said weakly.

'She'll say "It was too good for the bastard."' Savannah yelled.

'Yes, umm perhaps. Of course, Clemmie doesn't swear. Now moving right along. We have more than fifty locked up at the moment. More arrests will follow. Unfortunately, we can't pin a whole lot on the big four, but we dragged in a few Desperadoes, Comancheros, Outlaws and Hells Angels, and we'll work on them. See if we can't get some of the lower-level ones to flip on their superiors.'

'What about Ramirez?' Spencer asked.

'That's a little tricky, actually.'

'Tricky? C'mon Dale.' Savannah looked puzzled.

'Well, we have the recordings made at the hall. They're a bit incriminating but…'

'How the hell can they be a bit incriminating?' Spencer demanded.

'Look, it's obvious they were talking about drugs, but dammit, Ramirez doesn't at any time use the words, heroin, drugs, smack or anything else. We can already hear the defence, "Oh no your honour, Mr Ramirez thought they were talking about the sale of alcohol," or God damn ladies' underwear, or anything else they care to dream up.'

'You gotta be kidding me. Anyone with half a brain would realize what they were talking about.'

'Savannah, all I'm saying we'll have a fight on our hands.'

'Where is the lovable Enrique?' Spencer inquired.

'He's skipped town. I imagine he'll be on the interstate back to Chicago, as we speak. Along with Hugo and Jerry.'

CHAPTER FORTY-THREE
THE HOMECOMING

A weary Savannah and Spencer waited impatiently in the Hertz office in Pierre, South Dakota. Spencer grinned at the cheesy advertising sign, "Hertz got me to the church on time." It featured a gleaming red pillarless Chevrolet and a bride and groom with a smiling little bridesmaid waving a bunch of flowers.

Dale Fletcher had driven them the 500 miles from Sturgis to the capital in a borrowed police black and white, a battered Ford Fairlane Interceptor.

'I'm sending the Harleys back to Chicago. So, take your time, you are both on leave for the next two weeks.' Dale clapped them both on the back. 'Drive safe, you hear?'

He waved as Savannah steered the Hertz Buick onto Airport Road, Pierre.

The canary yellow Buick Electra laden with their luggage tore down the interstate towards Sioux Falls and then on to Chicago.

'Slow down, Savannah, I want to get there in one piece.'

'Whine whine. I've phoned Inez and I'm not about to waste any time. You could have flown. Dale did offer us flights.'

'I really felt the need to unwind. It's just, just all a bit rushed.'

'Yes, me too, Spencer. It was one hell of a time, wasn't it. Not a bit like Mexico. God, remember when I shot that bastard Bustillo? That felt good. Sorry, I keep forgetting your amnesia.'

'I'm riding with a serial killer. Just how many people have you killed?'

'I'm not exactly sure.' Savannah chuckled. 'Not enough.' She roared with laughter. 'Anyway, you've knocked off a few bad guys yourself.'

Spencer sighed. 'I guess now is as a good a time as any to fill me in with all the details. The details I missed the first time round.'

For the rest of the journey Savannah answered Spencer's questions about their exploits in Manhattan, Tokyo, LA and Mexico. She got further into details about what they had really been up to in their adventures.

'My God, I'm…I'm stunned. And I really did kill a cop. That's terrible.'

'For God's sake, Spencer, the cop was working for the cartel. You only killed bad guys.'

'The worst of it is, I just don't remember a thing.'

'I feel sorry for your poor wife and daughter, wherever they are,' Savannah added.

'You and me both. I keep wishing I could see their faces. If there was a photo, maybe it would kick the old brain back to life.

'Well, you have, or did have, a wife.'

'I know. Michiyo. She's Japanese. I believe you, I've just got nothing.' No flash of memory came this time, and he pouted.

'How can you not know about her? I don't understand.'

'You don't understand! Hell, I don't understand. You used to mention her. You wouldn't say much. I thought she was a figment of your imagination.'

'You said, "I have, or did have" a wife. She could be dead?'

'Spencer, I have no idea. The fact is we don't know much about you. Every time you were questioned, you'd just say "It's a long story."'

'This is very disturbing. I don't remember a thing. She must be worried silly. What about that daughter you mentioned, Trilby?'

'You're asking me, Mr "It's a long story"?'

They drove in silence, deciding to spend the night in the Country Side Motel in the pretty little town of Alden, Minnesota.

Spencer had a headache as he tried to remember. *Michiyo, Michiyo. I have a wife. How do I find her?*

After the ever-present breakfast of bacon, eggs, a short stack with maple syrup and freshly brewed coffee, they set off on the 320-mile trip to Chicago. Even with the windows wound down, it was hot, damned hot. Spencer didn't mind the sweat; he felt the stress rise up and out of his skin with each molecule of evaporating water. Tolstoy, Con-Rod and hopefully Ramirez, all neutralized. They passed rustic farms and fields of corn and soybeans, but Spencer was oblivious to the rural beauty. He couldn't stop thinking. *Michiyo. Trilby.* He couldn't summon them to the forefront of his mind. They drove in silence, lost in private thoughts.

The Buick turned into Old McHenry Road. 'Just about there, Spencer. Inez said she'd be cooking Bistec a Caballo.'

'Sounds good, that's steak and…?'

'You got it. Steak with a tomato and onion sauce, topped with a fried egg.'

The road shimmered in the heat; tiny specks of dust seemed to dance in the shaft of afternoon sunlight slanting through the car window.

'Summer in Illinois. Too damn hot,' Savannah grumbled as she steered the Buick up the drive. 'California here I come. I just hope Dale's happy. I'm not a fan of Chicago.' Savannah turned the engine off and shifted into park. 'The winters are brutal and the summers too darn hot. Hey, Spencer, do you know the only thing that grows on the South side of Chicago?'

Spencer shook his head.

'The crime rate.' Savannah cackled at her little joke. 'What about you Spencer? What are you going to do?'

Spencer felt like he'd been hit by a sledgehammer. What was he going to do? He couldn't envision a life without Inez and Savannah.

'I don't know. Dale said we had two weeks leave. That would imply that he had some plans for me.'

Savannah favoured him with a smile full of emotions. Bittersweet was the word he wanted. 'Go find your girls?'

He tried not to show the bleakness welling inside him. He didn't *know* his girls. He only knew this woman and her significant other. And justice, brought about by violence.

He managed a weak, 'Maybe.'

Savannah gave him a quick smile. 'Well, we're here.'

The next-door neighbour waved as he snipped his hedge with his shears.

Sweet-smelling petunias unhappy in the heat, lined the drive adding a splash of colour. The Kentucky bluegrass lawn looked a little brown, and in need of a cut.

'If we're going to be here for a while, we'll have to mow the God damn lawn, I guess. Hell, it's good to be home, Spencer.'

'I'll grab the bags.' Spencer opened the trunk and grabbed their two suitcases. He left Savannah's bag of mayhem. Honestly, he wasn't entirely sure how she'd slipped all the hardware out from under the noses of the FBI, but he had a hunch it was on account of Dale.

Savannah couldn't wait as she ran to the front door. Spencer heard her call out, 'Hi darling, we're home.'

Spencer followed close behind; he was looking forward to seeing Inez. He was already savouring the steak and cold beer.

Spencer closed the front door. No music? No fragrant cooking odours.

'Inez, where are you?' Savannah called out.

'I'm…in the kitchen.'

They padded along the short passage. Everything looked the same. The homely Norman Rockwell print, titled "Young love walking to school" featuring two schoolkids and their dog, hung still slightly lopsided. Their shoes made little noise on the buff cobbled cushion vinyl. Savannah glanced at Spencer. Holding a finger to her lips, she slid the Magnum out of its holster. She stepped back from the kitchen door and motioned Spencer, mouthing, 'Now!'

With an almighty crash the soft pine door tore off its hinges and smacked to the floor. Spencer's kick left the door in two pieces. Savannah bounded into the kitchen; gun drawn.

'Drop the fucking gun, dyke.'

A grinning, gun-toting Hugo stood behind Inez; a nickel-plated 0.38 revolver pointed at her head. She was lashed to a dining chair.

Jerry leaned against the kitchen sink, cigar in one hand, a gold lighter in the other. 'Spencer, Savannah, nice to see you both. Great entrance, Spencer. Very dramatic, I will say. First things first. Do you happen to have an ash tray? No?' He laughed. 'I don't suppose it matters, really, does it?'

'I'm impressed, Jerry, how the hell did you find out where we lived?'

'Oh dear, Spencer, that is your name? Or is that fake just like the rest of you?'

'It's for real.'

'Knowledge is power. We have a contact at Hertz Chicago. When he told me the FBI hired a car in Pierre, South Dakota, and it was travelling to an address in Long Grove, it wasn't too difficult to join the dots.'

'So, what is it? Revenge? Ramirez isn't happy? Why didn't he come himself?'

'Hell, he's the boss. He doesn't need to get involved in the messy stuff, and, yes, the fact is we're all a little pissed off. I guess that sounds a bit childish. But dammit, you've caused us all lot of grief. Also, you have to understand on a practical level, there's no doubt the word will get around that you, and you.' He pointed his cigar at Savannah. 'Yes, you little lady. You made us look like fools. The thing is, Ramirez's business is all about image, you understand? If he allows you two to live, well what would people say, eh? The other thing is of course you're going to testify against us.'

Jerry lit his cigar and blew a plume of blue smoke. 'This's one of the bosses special Havanas. I guess it's a thanks for whacking the three of you.'

'Hang on, Jerry… you, Hugo and Ramirez haven't been charged with anything,' Savannah threw in.

'Ha ha, true, true. But I'm sure we will be. And you know what they say about dead men? The last I heard; they still don't tell tales. And let's face it, Spencer would enjoy telling the grand jury all about our conversations.'

'Inez hasn't done anything. She's completely innocent,' Savannah pleaded.

'Don't be so damn stupid. She'd be a God damn witness.'

'Ok Jerry, there is one little thing.' Spencer's mind raced. It seemed that Jerry was the man in charge.

'Really?' Jerry yawned.

'Do you want the opals?'

'You must think we're idiots.' Hugo entered the conversation, but Spencer caught the flitting eye contact the two shared.

They're not sure. Spencer smiled at Hugo and Jerry, trying to appear nonchalant.

'You really need to understand, I'm not and never have been FBI. Without going into too many details, you might say I am a sort of conscript. A lot of what I told you at our first meeting was actually the truth. Popeye and I were in partnership. I did shoot the silly fucker and, well it's a long story, but the nuts and bolts of it are that I was offered the job of going after you in exchange for my freedom. Just ask Savannah.'

Savannah's eyes were like dinner plates as she listened to Spencer's story.

'Whoa, hang on. The bitch is FBI. I know because we had her checked out. She and the other dyke are from LA. So, what the fuck's going on?' And, how come the two of you are together? What is it, Savannah, are you a team player? You bat for both sides? You and Spencer, is that what it is? You like a bit of cock, right?'

'I was there to make sure Marlowe did as he was told and didn't do a runner or get ideas. As you know, he's a smart guy,' Savannah said, face hardened.

'What about the fucking opals?'

Savannah stared at Spencer, her face blank. She shrugged. 'Look guys, I'm afraid I have to say, I haven't got a clue. This is news to me. We both know Spencer is one tricky son of a bitch. So, you'll have to ask him.'

'Well either way we sure as hell don't need Dickless Tracy and her girlfriend.' Hugo grinned.

'Sorry fellows, but that's not the deal. You want the opals, the ladies live. That's it.'

'You think you can call the shots. Fuck you. Shoot them, Hugo.'

'Hang on, hang on. Remember what Enrique said when we were in Warbonnet, about the FBI? I'm not sure I want to kill them. Anyway, I reckon Marlowe's telling the truth. There's no way he's FBI. He was seen with Popeye. Let's see if we can get the opals first and then make a decision.'

Jerry splashed some ash on the floor. He turned and gazed out of the kitchen window; it was now dusk. The Flintstones theme song could just be heard from the neighbour's television. Fred Flintstone was yelling "WILMAAA!"

Jerry grabbed one of the laminated kitchen chairs. Sitting down heavily he clicked his lighter and applied the blue flame to his stogie.

'Hey, you, what's your name again?' he pointed the glowing cigar at Inez.'

'My name is Inez.'

'Make me a coffee, sweetheart.'

'Savannah, please. I don't think I can.' Inez's voice was shaking.

'I'll make the coffee, if that's all right with you guys.'

'Yeah sure. Don't forget, do anything silly and Hugo will shoot. Won't you, Hugo? And just in case.' Jerry opened his jacket pocket, revealing a pearl handled six shooter in a leather shoulder holster.

Savannah stepped over to the Frigidaire, opening the door she grabbed a bottle of milk from the rack. Spencer was motionless. Hugo's pistol was still pointed at Inez's head. Jerry's coat was open, one hand dangling too close to his open jacket. Spencer knew even with his extraordinary reflexes he had no chance. He was surprised Savannah actually whistled as she filled the electric kettle with water and plugged it in. She spooned four heaping tablespoons of coffee into the French press. She slid open the glass door of the overhead cabinet and withdrew five coffee mugs. Spencer watched fascinated as she withdrew the last mug. One hand rested on the laminated marble effect bench top.

'How do you have your coffee, guys? Happy days, eh.'

Savannah spun around; the matte black 0.32 Beretta semi-automatic pistol in her hand. Crack, crack. Hugo appeared to have a third eye, and a hole in his chest. He dropped to the floor, his 0.38 still clasped in his hand.

'What the…?' Jerry had already grabbed his pearl handled revolver when Spencer's clenched fist slammed into his throat. Jerry's eyes bulged. He dropped the pistol and held a hand to his neck. A wheezing sound filtered out of his mouth. Clambering unsteadily to his feet, he reached out to Spencer. They could just hear a rasping voice like fingernails being scratched along a pane of glass, 'You…'

Savannah ran to Inez and put an arm around her. Spencer stood, stunned at what he could see. He'd forgotten about Savannah's hidden pistol. Hugo lay face down on the floor in a pool of blood. Spencer knelt beside Jerry, who had collapsed. He felt for a pulse. Nothing.

CHAPTER FORTY-FOUR
AFTERMATH

Law enforcement swarmed over the Long Grove house.
Spencer wondered what the neighbours were thinking. A few lights in the quiet street flashed on. Residents in dressing gowns and pyjamas gazed nervously as three matching pale blue Pontiac Parisienne sedans pulled in front of the house. Grey men in grey clothes sombrely strode to the front door.

Subtle, definitely subtle. Spencer counted eight serious FBI types, including Dale Fletcher, quietly combing the house. Looking for what, he wasn't sure.

Just as the cuckoo clock announced midnight, a Ford Econoline Clubwagon rolled silently up the drive. Behind the Ford, a gleaming black Oldsmobile hearse glided to a halt.

***

The dawn chorus of melodious birdsong drifted into the kitchen. Golden fingers of sunlight lit up the peaceful Long Grove streets. Dale Fletcher, Savannah Steele and Spencer Marlowe wearily sipped their umpteenth coffee. Inez had long since retired to the upstairs bedroom.

'My wife will kill me but, dammit.' Dale squashed another Lucky Strike butt into the cast aluminium Smith and Wesson ashtray. The outline of their famous Model 13 boldly outlined on the base. 'Clementine has a lovely set of Noritake ashtrays with pictures of pussycats on them.'

'I'm sure they're lovely.' Spencer noticed this was followed by an eyeroll from Savannah.

'Moving right along. What's next, Dale?' Savannah's fingers drummed on the Laminex tabletop.

'We still don't have enough on Ramirez, and now that his two trusty lieutenants are…well…'

'The word you're looking for is *dead*, Dale. Defunct, deceased. They are departed, slain, slaughtered. They are no more.' Another eyeroll from Savannah.

'Yes, sad, of course. And I understand you may go through a period of depression, remorse…'

'Dale!'

'Oh, yes. Perhaps not.'

'Ramirez?'

'Here's the thing. The FBI have already been to see Ramirez in his Chicago office.'

'And?'

'Gone. Skedaddled. Like, I mean nothing.' Dale frowned, making his cigarette bounce comically in his lips.

'He can't have just disappeared?' Spencer threw in.

'Well, he has. And we haven't got enough on him. So, until we find out where he is, our hands are tied. We can subpoena him, of course. But without knowing his whereabouts…' Dale shrugged.

'I'm not giving up. His goons were going to kill us. Jesus Dale, they had a gun at Inez's head. They crossed the line.' Savannah scowled.

'Special Agent Steele. As far as you're concerned, it's over. At least for the time being. We'll find the bastard and we'll…'

'We'll what? Interview him? Question him, with his high-priced lawyer telling him to take the fifth? C'mon Dale…'

'That is it. Finished. I'm leaving two agents on guard at the front of the house…'

'Dale, Dale, you really don't need to do that. If Ramirez sends some more thugs, they're not going to be a problem.'

Spencer could swear he saw the slight bags under Dale's eyes fill out and swell before his eyes. 'I get it, Steele. More corpses. Right?'

Savannah looked sideways at Spencer. 'I give up.'

'I'm out of here. Both of you come to the office tomorrow for a debrief. Inez will need to come in, too.' He held his hands up to ward off a tirade from Savannah. 'It's a formality. After that, take the rest of the month off. Spencer, great job. I'm sure we'll have something for you. When you and Savannah come in, we'll discuss other things.'

'Anything in mind, Dale?'

'This isn't the time or place, but you two are a remarkable team. There is a possibility of something coming up in San Francisco. That may need both of your talents.'

Spencer was intrigued. He knew he needed a reason to be. He had nothing else.

The debrief was predictable, boring and repetitive. Savannah knew what was coming and had warned Inez and Spencer.

'All right, dears, this's what's going down. Because there are dead people, we will be interviewed separately.'

'Estoy molesto. We are the victims. Is this necessary? Why can't they just take our words for it?' Inez was in tears.

'Inez darling, it's procedure. Now listen up. We all must tell the same story. Comprende?'

Inez looked to Spencer and made a face, as if to underscore how out of her element she was with all this.

'We don't have to lie at all,' Savannah went on. 'We haven't done anything wrong. All that needs to happen is you say how it went, and when they ask again, you repeat the same thing. Hugo and Jerry were in the kitchen with the intent to murder all three of us, Spencer distracted them with some cockamamie fast talk about the opals, and I used it as a distraction to go for the gun in the cabinet. The end.'

Inez nodded, but still looked like she was seeing ghosts.

The interviews took place in the impressive art deco FBI field office at Dearborn Street in Chicago's loop. Escorted to the ninth floor by a taciturn officer in a grey flannel suit with a conspicuous bulge in his upper coat pocket, they were indeed led to adjoining rooms. Inez smiled bravely at Savannah as she disappeared into a stark room where an unsmiling agent with a recorder waited.

Five hours of nonstop interrogation followed.

***

The evening sun cast long shadows, the rays bouncing off the pillars of steel and glass.

'That wasn't so bad.' Savannah grinned.

Spencer pitied the agent or agents that had grilled Savannah.

'They weren't too tough?' Spencer inquired, genuinely curious.

'God damn pussies. Never shot anybody, I'll just bet.' Savannah's hand went for the shoulder holster that wasn't there, and instead rubbed her side like she'd been laughing herself sick. 'Inez, are you ok, darling?'

Inez nodded. 'It was all right. They were quite nice. Mine spoke Spanish.'

Spencer had no trouble fielding the questions and answers.

'It's time to celebrate. I'm buying.' Savannah grinned, then got the door for her darling Inez.

The rest of the night passed in a whirl. Rare steaks and red wine at Gene and Georgetti's restaurant at North Franklin Street, followed by a night of blues at Kingston Mines at North Halstead Street.

'You my babe, I got my eyes on you.' John Lee hooker's words were ringing in their ears as they bounced out of the club at one AM

They strolled through downtown Chicago on a high. The bad guys were mostly dead and they weren't.

'See that hotel? That's The Lexington.' Savannah pointed at a gracious neo-classical old building as they strolled along Michigan Avenue.

'Yep, nice.' Spencer and Inez paused to stare at the ten story Victorian era pile.

'You'd never guess who used to live there?' Savannah said.

'I give up,' Spencer replied.

'Al Capone.'

'Like our tabby,' Inez replied.

'Yeah, but he was no pussy cat,' Savannah growled. Then she froze.

'I think I know where Ramirez is.' Spencer and Savannah both said at the same time.

CHAPTER FORTY-FIVE

WE HAVE A MISSION

'Inez. Bacon, scrambled eggs, hash browns, orange juice and coffee. Come and get it.'

Four weeks had passed since the death of Hugo and Jerry. Now in late September, the weather had cooled. The days had plateaued to the low sixties. Spencer the chef surveyed his culinary efforts with pride. He had flashbacks of prepping meals in a restaurant, another time another place.

'Mil gracias, Spencer, you are such a good chef.' Inez poured herself coffee from the French press as she took her place at the kitchen table.

'Savannah left early this morning?'

'Yes, she had a meet in Chicago with Dale.' Inez crunched on some bacon and buttered a slice of toast.

'She said she'd be back early. Spencer, lovely breakfast.'

'There she is.' Spencer heard the sound of a car door slamming.

'Hi, I'm home. I can smell food. Great, I'm starving.'

Savannah bounded into the kitchen. 'Can you believe what they've given me to drive? A God damn Plymouth Valiant. Heap of crap. 6 cylinders. That's unAmerican. Hell and damnation, I miss that old rocket of mine.'

'Sit down, darling, let me get you some breakfast.' Inez jumped up.

'Spencer, we have a job. Woo hoo!'

'Awesome. Tell me more.'

'Awesome might be a bit over the top. Is that an Australianism?'

'Don't know. I guess it must be.'

'Here it is. It looks like we were right, Boy Wonder. Capone's old mansion on Palm Island Miami was sold recently to a shell company.'

'So, what? That could be anybody.'

'Yeah well, I spoke to the realtor. I pretended I was an interested buyer; in case the deal to buy Capone's mansion fell through.'

'Go on, obviously there's more.'

'Get this. The guy, the realtor, described Ramirez to a T.'

'So, I guess the FBI in Miami will go round and arrest him, subpoena him, or whatever?'

'No, here's the good bit. Dale wants us to go down there and bring him in.'

'Why in hell would Dale do that? I don't mind going, I've never been to Florida. At least not that I remember.'

'Hey, I wasn't about to argue. Dale wants us to go to Miami and pick the slimy son of a bitch up and bring him back. So that's what we do. Ours isn't to wonder why, and I forget the rest.'

'Language at the breakfast table.' Inez frowned at Savannah.

'Ours is but to do and die,' Spencer quoted.

'Yeah, whatever. Some bacon would be nice. You do great scrambled eggs, Spencer. What's the secret?'

'Cream. Charge of the Light Brigade. Alfred Lord Tennyson.'

'What are you blathering about?' Savannah forked bacon and eggs into her mouth.

'Cream, is what you put into the scrambled eggs. "And the Ours is but to do and Die", from the Charge of the Light Brigade. Tennyson.'

'What the hell is it with your memory? How do you remember some rubbish poetry and God damn Latin and not the stuff that counts?'

'Maybe I was a professor of English literature. How would I know?'

CHAPTER FORTY-SIX

MIAMI BOUND

'Here's your ticket.' Savannah handed Spencer his airline ticket. United Airlines 727, direct flight to Miami.

'I need this coffee. My bag weighed a ton.'

'I wonder why?' Spencer's eyes gazed heavenward.

Bags checked in, Spencer and Savannah had found a seat at the Metropolis Coffee shop.

'I can't get over all these people carrying suitcases. Weird.' Spencer took a sip of his coffee and grimaced.

'Coffee not up to scratch, again?' Savannah grinned. 'And what's with the people carrying suitcases. It's a God damn airport. What do you expect?'

Spencer's head swivelled; he took in the broad concourse. The hustle and bustle. The overpriced gift shops. Flags from all nations were hanging from the ceiling like somebody's washing.

'No, I mean, why don't people have their suitcases on wheels with extendable handles so they could just pull them along? Obvious really.'

Somewhere in Spencer's subconscious there was a vision. Another airport. Another time. Another place.

Savannah looked at him strangely. 'That's one hell of an idea. Did you just think of that?'

'I guess. What can I say?' Spencer gave her an exaggerated shrug.

'Do you know what I think?'

'No idea. Does it feature firearms?'

'I'll ignore that. I reckon you must be some sort of inventor. I mean you have no idea what in hell your real job was, or is. That thought of having a suitcase on wheels, is just brilliant. Perhaps we should patent it, eh?'

'Take time off from killing people, perhaps?'

'Time to change the subject,' Savannah growled.

'That was nice of Inez to drop us here at O'Hare. I saw her whispering in your ear when she dropped us off. She looked sort of concerned.' Spencer knew a mention of Inez would get Savannah back on track.

'You know Inez, she worries.'

'I'll bet I know what she asked you.'

'All right, smart ass.'

'She asked "did you pack your usual assortment of field artillery?"'

'You're right. Of course. Again.'

'And the answer?'

'Just, you know, the usual.'

Spencer put his head in his hands. 'Why do I get the horrible feeling this is going to be a small war? Anyhow, surely you can't take guns on a plane?'

'Kiss my go to hell. This is America. The land of the free. What the hell's wrong with you? Actually, it's funny you should mention it, but they are trying to bring in rules.'

'Heaven forbid. What's the world coming to?'

'Don't start. How many times have my guns saved your ass, eh?'

'I don't remember. But speaking of Inez, will she be, ok?'

'She'll be fine, Dale has kept a guard at the house. Anyway, I'm sure now Hugo and Jerry are finito and Ramirez is in Miami, there isn't going to be a problem. Anyhow, speaking of guns and things, here's an interesting story. Do you have any idea how O'Hare Airport got its name?'

'Not a clue. But it involves guns, right? I can hardly wait to hear this one.' Spencer feigned a yawn.

'There's a connection, sort of. Regarding our mission.'

'Really?'

'Shut up. You might just learn something.'

'I'm all ears.'

'O'Hare airport is named after Edward "Butch" O'Hare, the US navy's first medal of honour recipient.'

'Riveting.'

'You bet your sweet ass it's riveting. He, all on his lonesome, attacked nine, nine for Christ's sake, Japanese heavy bombers about to attack his aircraft carrier. His Grumman F64 Hellcat was shot down. Never recovered.'

'Good old Butch, eh? I can see the connection with our current mission. I think.'

'There's more.'

'There would be.'

'Here's the kicker. His father, Edward, was a lawyer. Edward the elder. Butch was Edward Junior.'

'Fascinating.'

'Elder Edward worked for Capone. They called him Easy Eddie.'

'Well, well.'

'His father turned on Capone and played a big part in getting dear old Alphonse put away for tax evasion.'

'You're right. That's one hell of a story. I'll bet Scarface wasn't very happy.'

'Poor Edward was driving home and another vehicle pulled alongside and somebody filled him with buckshot. Anyhow, that's the story, and it's time to board.'

CHAPTER FORTY-SEVEN
LIFE IS A BEACH

'Welcome to the Fontainebleau Miami, Mr and Mrs Winchester. The bell boy will take your bags.'

The beaming desk clerk handed Savannah's Diners Club card back as if it was the original Declaration of Independence.

'What in hell was that all about? Mr and Mrs Winchester. You're kidding,' Spencer whispered.

'Shut up. I'll explain in a minute. How about you handle the tip?'

The bell boy, a smiling black man in a striking scarlet jacket with brass buttons that gleamed like freshly minted gold coins, showed them around the two-bedroom suite. Like a conjurer pulling a rabbit from a hat, he pressed a button on the wall. The creamy brown curtains slid noiselessly open save for the faint whir of an electric motor. Like a cinemascope production, below them lay the lagoon of Biscayne Bay, the beach alive with holiday makers. Coloured umbrellas dotted across the sands. A congregation of clouds lit up the blue. Spencer blinked at the sudden rush of sunlight; he grinned as he gave Savannah a thumbs up.

The strong browns and forest greens lent the room a sense of calm and serenity.

'And Sir, Madam, we have, ta da!' The bellboy switched on the television. 'Colour TV.'

A stirring guitar solo echoed around the room. A map appeared on the screen, immediately bursting into flames. Savannah's eyes went wide and she actually clapped in delight. 'Hey, that's Bonanza. Inez just loves this show.'

The suite was the perfect array of homey hues. *Definitely sense of home away from home. But what's going on?*

Spencer handed the man two crisp one-dollar notes. His one act play over, the smiling bellboy silently exited the room.

Savannah grabbed the hotel compendium. 'Hey, guess what? They have a swimming pool and a beauty salon.'

'Whacko, you'll be in the beauty parlour at the first opportunity.'

'Is sarcasm a big thing in Australia?'

'No comment. What else?'

'We have access to their exclusive lounge, serving free drinks and food, all day.'

'I'm confused. This isn't at all like the usual FBI accommodation.'

As if she hadn't heard Savannah continued exploring. 'And the bathroom, marble and dinky chrome fittings. It's really something. Not as good as Tokyo, but not bad.'

'We were in Tokyo.' According to her; he still couldn't recall anything other than dizzying and disjointed glimpses.

'The hotel we stayed at. Of course, you don't remember. That was absolutely ace.'

'How about we just sit down and you clear up a few things?'

Spencer perched on the chaise lounge with its fancy splayed legs and scatter cushions. He patted the space next to him 'Sit,' he commanded.

'What?'

'Mr and Mrs. Winchester? Give me a break. You use a nom de plume named after a gun?'

'Nom de plume?'

'It's French. It means name of the pen. And what's with the Diners Card. A fake ID?'

'Get with it, Spencer. I don't know what sort of reach Ramirez has, but for all we know he could have people letting him know if anyone by the name of Steele or Marlowe makes an appearance.'

'Ok, I still don't get it, but what's the plan? There is one.'

'Remind me never to go to Australia. Yes, there's a plan. Sort of. But first we're going on a picnic.'

***

'We have a picnic basket. Just have a look at the goodies the hotel has packed for us. Wow, Cuban sandwiches, cold conch fritters, strawberries, key lime pie.' Savannah rummaged through the wicker basket.

'A day off? A picnic? Excellent. Where are we going?'

'We…are going down to the marina. There's a tourist ferry. We're going to see the sights. The sun's shining, we're going to cruise around Biscayne Bay, see the homes of the rich and famous.'

'This doesn't sound like you. The Savannah we know and love doesn't generally do fun things like that. The next thing I know you'll be saying you want to visit a dress shop.'

The Chevrolet yellow cab deposited them at the marina the car radio blaring Barry McGuire's rasping voice howling about the eve of destruction, Spencer wondered if it was an omen.

The driver, a skinny Puerto Rican kid, spent the ten-minute journey complaining about the damage that Hurricane Betsy had wreaked across Florida. 'Ay bendito, you shoulda seen it. The waves just about swamped Palm Island. I tell ya, it was awesome.'

Savannah nudged Spencer and whispered, '"Awesome" he must be an Aussie.'

'Two dollars ninety, chacho.' The driver said with a grin as the Chev jerked to a halt in front of the Miami Marina where the millionaires parked their luxury yachts.

Spencer handed the driver a five dollar note. 'Keep the change.'

Spencer carried the basket as they strolled along the broad jetty, to where the Poseidon Miami Beach ferry waited. The old clinker-hulled vessel, a veteran of the brine, resplendent in gloss white and varnished timber, marked time with its twin diesels burbling a low comforting *thump thump thump*. One of the crew, in his sparkling white trousers and side cap emblazoned with the name "Poseidon" snapped photos as they boarded, with a cheery, 'Ready when the cruise is over folks. Only five dollars.'

Packed with chatty holiday makers, the atmosphere on the old ferry exuded gaiety. Spencer was still getting over his surprise at Savannah pausing to smell the roses, so to speak. Or in this case the brisk tang of salty air. A pretty yacht with sails billowing ripped through the brilliant blue water in front of them.

'What's with the field glasses?' Savannah wore flared jeans with a casual striped ribbed T shirt. Around her neck dangled a pair of powerful Zeiss binoculars.

'Well, you, know, we might see some whales…maybe.'

Curiouser and curiouser, whales? Really? Spencer's eyebrows raised. *Something's not as it seems.*

Savannah and Spencer squeezed onto the polished timber bench seat, next to a bubbly chatterbox of a lady, who enthusiastically introduced herself as Margaret, from King's Lynn in England. 'And this is my hubby, Andrew.'

Spencer smiled and nodded, about to offer his hand, when Andrew stood and bolted to the stern, where he vomited enthusiastically into Biscayne Bay.

'He does get seasick, my Andrew, he does,' Margaret said breezily.

'Coming up on the starboard side shortly you'll be able to see Palm Island.' A tinny voice crackled from the loudspeaker.

Spencer found his suspicions suddenly confirmed. 'Whales, huh? This isn't a pleasure trip. I wonder who lives on Palm Island? Boy, am I stupid?'

'Palm island is man-made. It's only eighty acres. This is very expensive real estate.' The captain's cheerful description boomed from the speaker.

'Hey, just take a peep. That's it.' Savannah peered through her binoculars.

Simultaneously the captain announced, 'The white mansion that's coming into view used to belong to the infamous Chicago gangster Al Capone.'

'Today wasn't rest and recreation at all, was it?'

'What are you talking about? Here we are on a boat, having a tour. It's a lovely day. How's Andrew doing, Margaret?' Savannah asked, as she slipped Spencer a sly grin.

'Changing the bloody subject,' Spencer whispered.

'Thanks for asking, dearie. He's having a little lie down. One of them crew has taken him below to a bunk. I offered him a bacon sarnie and he was off again.'

'Hey, this is interesting. Have a look.'

Spencer glanced skywards, at the drone of a single engine float plane. The aircraft flew over the ferry and made a smooth descent to the jetty outside of the Capone Mansion.

CHAPTER FORTY-EIGHT
ARTURO DIAZ

Arturo Diaz leant against the railing on the upstairs balcony, also gazing through binoculars. The *Poseidon* caught his eye as it rocked in the slight swell. Brightly attired tourists waved, a few raising glasses in acknowledgment. Arturo grinned and waved back. Focusing on the single engine Cessna being moored to his jetty, Arturo shook his head. He watched his new employee Gabriel Lopez bent double as he hauled the plane to the jetty. Rivulets of sweat trickled down Gabriel's back, making his skin glow. Arturo imagined Gabriel swearing in frustration as he grappled clumsily with the mooring rope, tying it to a cast iron stanchion. Arturo saw him put a foot on the stanchion, jerk the rope and secure it. He turned and waved at Arturo, who waved back. *What a klutz.*

'Another successful run, Yesenia.' Arturo turned to his companion.

Yesenia was a stunning Latin beauty, many years Arturo's junior. Posed suggestively on a teak deckchair, and wearing a gleaming string bikini, she looked like she would be at home on the cover of a magazine. Margarita in hand, she blew him a kiss. Arturo was the latest in a string of older lovers for the beguiling Yesenia.

'Arturo, darling?' her wheedling voice was beginning to grate on suave, fifty plus Arturo.

'What is it?' His gaze was again focused on the Cessna. The pilot and Gabriel were manhandling burlap sacks onto trolleys.

'You said I could have one of those cute Cadillac convertibles for my birthday. And that's tomorrow.' Depending on timing, Yesenia often had several birthdays every year.

'Sure thing. Tomorrow we'll go to the dealership.'

'Gracias, mi amor.' Yesenia placed her margarita on the side table and threw her arms around his neck. 'I think it's time for siesta, you lovely man,' she whispered in his ear.

Arturo disengaged himself. He could feel a stirring in his loins. The full-busted Yesenia in her tiny black bikini still had the capacity to ignite passions in Arturo that made him forget his age.

He wished she has suggested a little afternoon fling even ten minutes earlier. 'Sorry babe, I gotta go talk to the boys.'

Arturo made his way downstairs to the cellar. The spacious, light, and airy mansion made every day feel like a holiday. It seemed as if every room had a view of palm trees and stunning Biscayne Bay. *Who needs Chicago?* He thought about the stifling summers and the brutal winters. *I shoulda done this years ago.*

He wrenched open the stout oak door leading to the basement. Skipping down the stairs his voice boomed as it echoed against the limestone walls. 'How was the flight, Justin?'

Enrique Martinez, aka Arturo Diaz, always felt a slight shudder when he saw Justin. The man just looked evil. Martinez knew in the grubby world of drug dealing, sometimes things went wrong. The biggest problem wasn't law enforcement but unscrupulous drug dealers. One look at

Justin's villainous face, enhanced by a vivid scar running diagonally from forehead to sneering mouth generally nipped arguments in the bud.

Justin Ginder, a lanky ex-marine chopper pilot, had decided to leave the armed forces when he figured he was likely to see active service. Uncle Sam was happy to see the back of Justin Ginder. He'd been arrested and charged with a vicious rape. The victim, a nurse from Minnesota, had decided not to proceed when the lovable Justin had managed to speak to her. He'd simply convinced her with the old 'drop the charges or I'm gonna slice you up real good' routine. Threatening to turn a woman's face into a freakshow attraction always had the intended effect.

'Yo boss. This's like taking candy from a baby. I…ah…had a slight disagreement with, that guy Benito. You remember him boss? Short guy. Had a big mouth?'

Arturo shook his head. There were a lot of suppliers south of the border.

'Yeah,' Justin persisted. 'You should remember him. He had five fingers on each hand.'

'Had?'

'Yeah Boss, had.' Justin threw his head back and cackled.

'Well, I guess you gotta do what you gotta do, Justin.'

'Fucking spics. I gotta tell you Boss, the little fucker, screamed like a stuck…'

'I get the picture. Apart from that, all good, eh?'

'You betcha. All good.'

Arturo surveyed the mounting burlap sacks with satisfaction.

'I shoulda got into this years ago. Smack was just one big fucking headache. Always a problem with quality. I had to pay off the cops. It was a fucking nightmare I tell you.'

'What's next, boss?' Chubby Gabriel sweated with the exertion. He never complained about a little hard work.

'Tomorrow Gabe, grab the Econoline. Take ten sacks to Biloxi, Mississippi and see Ronnie Fabian. You know where to meet him?'

'Yeah, sure boss. What If the cops catch me? You know I done time already. I could get a ten stretch for this,' he whined.

'The cops will be fine. Don't worry. I want you to drive nonstop. It's about…I don't know, maybe eleven hours, twelve tops. And after you have the cash, check into the Buena Vista. It's a real swell joint. Just one night, mind.'

'Hey, thanks boss.' Gabriel grinned ear to ear, exposing teeth that looked like an unpainted picket fence with some of the boards missing.

Arturo clapped him on the shoulder. *Sharp as a bowling ball, but at least I can trust him.*

Arturo wasn't concerned Gabriel would do a runner with the hundred G's. He'd found him the day after he'd been paroled. Arturo had tested him with a hit on a small-time dealer. Without hesitation Gabriel had put a bullet in the man's head as he was climbing out of his car at the front of a grubby apartment complex in Little Haiti.

'It's none of my business, boss, but why get Gabe to take the blow all the way to Mississippi? I mean, it's becoming real popular hear in Miami. I mean…'

Arturo glared at Justin. 'Yeah, you're right. It's none of your business.'

'Ok, ok, sorry I asked.' Justin shrugged.

'I'll tell you. It's not a state secret. We've been selling too much locally and it's forced the price down. Also, the local law was getting a bit nosy. By sending it to Biloxi, it passes the heat elsewhere. You follow?'

'Hey, that's pretty smart. Up there for thinking, eh?' Justin tapped the side of his head and grinned admiringly at Arturo.

Arturo kept thinking, *this is too good to be true*. No dealing with junkies, just a plain old wholesaler. Aircraft are the answer; no chance of being pulled over. At the moment the Cessna could fly from Cartagena to Miami in five hours, fully laden. *But with a bigger airplane. Hey, why stop there? More aircraft. More pilots.*

CHAPTER FORTY-NINE
SAVANNAH PLOTS

'You should at least try the water. It's great.' Spencer towelled himself off before plopping on to the candy-striped deck chair next to Savannah.

Every deck chair was taken. In sharp contrast to the tanned locals, pale-skinned tourists from the northern states seemed to want to expose as much flesh as possible. Spencer had the odd certainty that the beach shouldn't have had so many fit people of all ages. He vaguely understood that there ought to be a lot of not-so-tiny men and women in some tiny bikinis.

The day wasn't so hot due to a slight breeze gently touching people's faces. The water in the Fontainebleau pool was as blue as the sky and as clear as crystal. The pool was busy, crowded with guests. Youngsters jumped into the water, fingers pinching their noses, screaming, 'I'm gonna do a cannonball! Watch me, Mom.'

Pale yellow, red and vivid gold gerberas crammed the flower beds along the fence, adding colour to an expanse of tailored lawn. The hot dog stall was doing a roaring trade, the tantalizing odour of fried onions and sauerkraut made Spencer's mouth water.

'How about a hot dog and a soda?'

'What? Oh, yeah ok. Heavy on the mustard. How about some fries as well?' Savannah reluctantly placed the Miami News on the wicker table next to her.

'I've just been reading. Apparently Miami is being swamped with high grade cocaine.'

'Really,' said Spencer. 'Fascinating.'

'For God's sake Spencer, this is my job. You know? Bad guys. Drugs? Ring any bells?'

Spencer leaned forward; his head swivelled. He lowered his voice, 'I've never told you this. But…I have to tell you. I used to sniff coke.'

'I gotta hear this. Go on.'

'Yep, used to sniff coke, but the bubbles got up my nose.' Spencer laughed uproariously.

For a moment Spencer thought Savannah looked like a Pekinese trying to learn French.

'Oh, right. I get it. Bubbles, Coca Cola. Yes, very funny. I must go to Australia one day. Not. But meanwhile I have to figure out what our next move is. I've made some enquiries with local law enforcement and Enrique Ramirez isn't on their radar. It's almost as if he doesn't exist.'

'That's right. Enrique Ramirez doesn't exist.'

'What the hell are you talking about?'

'Guess what. While you were checking with the local law, I've been doing my own sleuthing.'

'And?'

'Lovable Enrique has changed his name.' City records had entirely too much information freely available to the public and he loved it.

Savannah's face coloured. She closed her eyes. 'Jesus, how damned elementary is that? Alright, smart ass, the name, por favor?'

'Arturo Diaz. And he's as clean as a whistle. He has a live-in girlfriend named Yesnia, or Yesenia, something like that. The local parole board love him because he's given a recently released thug a job as a handyman. His name is Gabriel, and from what I have been told he bears no resemblance to the angel of that name.'

'Really, that is interesting. Tell me more about this Gabriel?'

'His parole officer said he had the mental agility of a soap dish, but he seemed to think Diaz would keep him on the straight and narrow.'

'Good to know.'

'While we're on the subject, I still don't understand the subterfuge.'

'What subterfuge? What's to understand?'

'Why aren't you simply knocking on dear Arturo's door? "Hello Mr Diaz, FBI here. You're coming with us."'

'As I have said, we aren't at all sure we can get a conviction on what we have. There's no doubt he's up to something nasty, agreed?'

'Sure, obviously.'

'So, let's just play it cool. There's no way local law is going to do anything. No judge will give them a warrant. There is no probable cause.'

'But there will be,' he said.

'Precisely. You and I know it has to be drugs. We're very close to South America. My guess is it's probably coke.'

'I thought heroin was the name of the game?'

'It still is, but I have been saying for some time that blow is the next big thing.'

'Blow, really?'

'Yeah, blow, nose candy, flake, snow. They just love their drug slang.'

'What then do you want to do?'

'I'd like to sniff around his mansion, I reckon that's where the action might be.'

Spencer nodded. 'Yes, I've come to the same conclusion. It's on the water. Easier to smuggle stuff in. And…and he has an aeroplane, it would seem.'

'For starters, let's just grab a cab and have a drive around Palm Island. It's pretty small. We can check out Ramirez, sorry Arturo's pad, perhaps using your field glasses. Just maybe we might see some coming and goings, suspicious characters?'

'Oh yeah. Suspicious. I got it. Trench coats, fedora hats and carrying violin cases. Give me a break,' Savannah chortled.

CHAPTER FIFTY

GOT AN INVITE?

'So, the plan is?' Spencer and Savannah settled into the Chevrolet Yellow cab, as it turned into Biscayne Boulevard Way.

'I've already explained,' Savannah testily replied. 'We're going to recce the joint. Understand?' She gave Spencer a wink.

'Palm Island please, driver. I guess you know where the old Capone Mansion is?'

'Sure lady, everyone knows the Capone joint. You got an invite?' The driver was a stolid guy, late fifties, grey hair and a world-weary manner.

'We're not going inside, we're just looking. Checking out the real estate, we…are maybe looking at buying on Palm Island.'

'That's pretty ritzy real estate. Like I said, you gotta invite?'

Spencer glanced at Savannah and mouthed, 'What's he talking about?'

Savannah shrugged and made a finger twirling motion around her ears.

The cab turned into the MacArthur Causeway leading directly on to Palm Island. Up ahead surrounded by lush palms they could see an impressive, stunning white three level fountain, sparkling water tumbling into a white marble pool.

Beyond the fountain lay a Spanish styled arched gatehouse with a uniformed guard.

'Isn't that just gorgeous?' Savannah whispered to Spencer.

The cab glided to a halt in front of the steel gates. The guard, a very fit Latino gentleman strode up to the cab. A Colt revolver strapped to his waist. He nodded at the driver and knocked on the rear passenger door. Spencer wound down the window.

'Who are you here to see, sir?' The driver asked. His Zapata moustache made him look like an extra in a Spaghetti Western.

'Ah…no one in particular. Just having a look around. You know? We're perhaps thinking of buying some real estate here.'

'Sorry sir, madam. This is a private estate. No one's allowed here unless they're invited.'

'Who the hell do you think you are, I'm…'

'Shut up, *dear*.' Spencer could see the steely glint in the guard's eye, and the hand that now rested on the butt of his revolver. They had made the mistake of giving out their names too often. 'I'm very sorry, sir, we had no idea. We'll make arrangements through our realtor. Have a nice day.' He sat back heavily. 'Driver, could you please take us back to our hotel?'

Savannah's jaw was clenched, her mouth a hard line. 'Why the hell didn't you tell us we weren't allowed in? Didn't want to miss out on a fare, eh? You can whistle dixie for the tip. Kiss my go to hell. What sort of Mickey Mouse town is this?'

'Hey, lady, I thought everyone knew the rules. I arxed you twice whether you had an invite.'

'Sorry driver. Our fault. Yes, you did ask whether we had an invitation. It's cool.' Spencer glared at Savannah, mouthing, 'Enough.'

Savannah stormed into the lobby of the Fontainebleau, oblivious to the magnificent polished black and white marble flooring and the soaring gracious gleaming gold columns. The verdant foliage that rose in organic swirls that had entranced her the day before now went unnoticed.

'God dammit, I need a drink.' She strode up to the bar and climbed on to one of the chrome and leather high backed bar stools.

Spencer slid into the chair next her, chug-a-lugging an ice-cold Budweiser, while Savannah moodily sipped on her Jacks on the rocks. 'This is God damned annoying. I can't believe we can't get on to that stupid island.' Savannah took a hefty swig of her whiskey.

'Nil desperandum, I say.' Spencer motioned the bartender to bring him another beer.

'What the…nil?'

'Nil desperandum. It's Latin. It means "Don't despair."'

'Jesus, I'd just love to know what you were in a past life. Latin. Give me a break. Speak American.' Savannah sipped at her drink again to kill her scowl.

'Ok, ship face.' Spencer grinned.

'Who the hell are you calling shit-faced? One lousy Jacks on the rocks. Listen, buddy, I can drink you under the table any day of the week, and twice on Sundays.'

'Whoa. Hold on,' I said, 'Ship face. Not shit face. Ship face is a small boat hire firm. When we were on the pier the other day, I noticed them. They have rowboats, canoes, dinghies with outboard motors. An apology, perhaps?'

'Oh Spencer, you are so clever and I'm just the little woman dazzled by your manly…manly what? Yeah, got it. Manly bullshit.'

Spencer barked out a laugh. 'I'm going to take that as a compliment.'

'Yeah. Jokes aside, that was well spotted. Let's go and sort out the son of a bitch.

CHAPTER FIFTY-ONE

BILOXI

'When the people beat their feet on the Mississippi mud,' Gabriel Lopez sang the old Bing Crosby song, enthusiastically if a little tunelessly. The lumbering Ford Econoline sped along the Florida turnpike. The sweet of citrus flowers melded with the leaden odour of trucker's diesel.

Gabriel tapped his fingers on the steering wheel, the just risen sun shone softly. Early morning traffic sprinkled unevenly across the black top. He was happy enough. Prison had been tough for the barely literate Latino, but that was behind him. He was now a trusted employee of Arturo Diaz. He rolled the name around his mouth sounding the syllables AR-too-roh Dee-azz. In awe of his employer, Gabriel was like a big, happy, slobbering Labrador. Whatever Arturo wanted was ok with Gabriel. If it meant cold blooded murder, no problem. Gabriel couldn't believe he'd been entrusted with the task of delivering the cocaine to small time Biloxi hoodlum Ronnie Fabian. Five hours later Gabriel passed through Jacksonville on the Atlantic coast, he really could have used a coffee and a sandwich, but Arturo's words rung in his ears. 'Stop for gas, and that's it. Don't leave that van. You follow?'

Four pm and Gabriel could see the beautiful Miami Sound. His mouth watered as he thought about the oysters, lobster and crab dishes that would certainly be on the menu at the Buena Vista. *But first I gotta drop the toot, and pick up the loot.*

Gabriel had met Ronnie Fabian when he and a couple of his goons had visited Arturo at the Capone mansion. He didn't like Fabian. Or that pilot with the slashed face. He only liked Mr Diaz. And his supermodel girlfriend, Yesenia. He liked her a lot.

The dusty Econoline crawled along Bridgeview Drive as Gabriel peered at the house numbers, *Son of a bitch, just look at that motherfucker.* The bold white mansion stood there as if the surrounding nature had embraced it. Oak, hickory and pecan trees dotted across the spacious grounds.

The Econoline slowly advanced up the winding drive. Gabriel had a moment of panic as he stopped in front of the impressive oak double front doors. *What if? What if he doesn't give me the money?* Gabriel climbed slowly out of the van.

Before he could knock, both doors swung open, Ronnie Fabian swung the doors open. 'Come in. Buenos dias. That's what you wetbacks say?' Fabian grinned but Gabriel shuddered, Fabian's sunken eyes reminded him of a rattler seeking his prey. Everything about him was scary, the deep shadows under protruding cheekbones, and the fake smile when he turned on the charm.

'Well, ah, Mr Fabian, it's afternoon, so it's buenos tardas.'

'Gotcha, who gives a fuck eh? Anyway, you've had a long drive. Come in. Have a drink. Something to eat?'

'Well sir, I got orders. Mr Diaz, he say, don't leave the van.'

'I understand. We gotta shift it.' Fabian called out. 'Hey Clint, you lazy fucker, come and shift this van.'

'Yeah, hold your horses, Ron.'

Gabriel remembered seeing Clint when Fabian and two other men had visited at Diaz's house. *Jesus, how tall is this hombre?* Gabriel eyes rotated upwards as he took in Clint's height. He figured Clint was some way short of thirty, a wide neck and a physique that reminded him of the gym junkies in prison.

He wore a vivid paisley shirt and fashionable flared jeans, incongruous with his greasy 1950's Elvis's style hair.

'Mr Fabian, I really gotta, you know, stay with the…'

'Keys.'

'Yes sir, Mr Fabian.'

With a sinking feeling, Gabriel watched as Clint opened the timber garage doors, whistling as he crammed his height behind the wheel, calling out. 'Hey Ron, this is made for fucking midgets.'

'Like I said, c'mon have a drink. I reckon you'd be hungry. My housekeeper has made us some po'boys, crabmeat and cheese. Not your typical beaner food. You'll love it.' Ron gave him a friendly wink.

'Mr Fabian I gotta go, you know, I gotta get the money. I'm checking in to the Buena Vista,' He said proudly.

'Sure thing, Pancho. The Buena Vista eh? It must be, be nice to wetback week, eh.'

'Gabriel, sir.'

'What was that?'

'My name, Mr Fabian. It's Gabriel.'

'Yeah sure.'

Gabriel's mouth was dry, and he had a tremor in his hand as he followed Fabian downstairs to a cellar. He heard the front door slam, and Clint calling out, 'We're in the playroom, right?'

'Yep, come through Clint, Margie's prepared some food, and we got cold beer.'

Gabriel sighed with relief as he gazed around at the spacious white-walled entertainment area. Obviously, the playroom. In the centre stood an oak pool table. Crafted into one corner stood a beautiful carved maple bar. On the wall behind was a gigantic mirror with the Confederate flag etched into the glass. Gabriel's mouth watered at the sight of the po'boys stacked on a wooden serving rack.

'Help yourself, son. I'll get you a beer.'

Gabriel grabbed a sandwich, sinking his teeth in as Fabian, with his back turned, poured him a beer.

'Have a seat.' Ron gestured at one of the comfortable lounge chairs.

Gabriel sank into the delicately modernistic padded chair. He poured half of the frosty Budweiser down his throat.

'You must be pretty important for Arturo to send you here to good ole Mississippi, and put you up in the Buena Vista?' Ron whistled in appreciation. 'Yes sir, pretty God damn important.'

Gabriel's chest swelled. The po' boy and the beer had allayed his suspicions.

'Yes, sir, Mr Fabian. Mr Arturo, he trust me. Sure thing.'

'I mean, he's a pretty wealthy man, right?'

'Yes sir, Mr Fabian.'

'I'll just bet he has a heap of cash in the house. I mean he couldn't just stick it in the bank. Now, could he?' Fabian chuckled as he took a swig of beer.

Gabriel leaned forward and lowered his voice. 'Mr Fabian, he got millions, I tell you. He can buy whatever damn thing he wants.'

Gabriel had no clue what money Diaz kept in the house, but he was bathing in the reflected glory.

Clint watched on from a matching chair, as he took huge bites from his po'boy.

'Mr Fabian, thank you for the beer and the food, but I really gotta go. I gotta , I gotta…

The last thing he remembered was Clint laughing.

CHAPTER FIFTY-TWO

SHIP FACE

'That one. What do you reckon, Spencer?'

Spencer knew as much about boats as he knew about cars.

'Yeah. I guess.' Spencer gazed uncertainly at the aluminium dinghy equipped with a small outboard motor and a pair of oars.

'You folks doin' a bit of night fishin'?'

Bix Flanagan was the old salt who owned Ship Face. Short and wiry with sun bleached hair, tattered jeans, disreputable deck shoes and a pipe jammed into a toothless mouth, he looked like Popeye the Sailor Man. Spencer imagined him opening a can spinach.

Bix shuffled around, showing them how to start the outboard, 'I guess you be city slickers, am I right?' He pulled the pipe out of his mouth and tapped the ash out on a pylon.

'Is it that obvious?' Spencer smiled sheepishly.

'When ya'll done, if it be the early hours just tie her up with this here padlock, k? Good luck to ya. There's plenty a snook and wahoo just awaitin' to be caught.'

'Thanks, Bix. We might just take her out now for a bit of a run just to get the feel.'

'Ya'll paid up till tomorrow night. So, she's all yours.'

Spencer stepped gingerly onto the small craft and held out a hand to Savannah.

'Did I mention I get seasick? Ugh, it smells of dead fish. Yuk.' Savannah grimaced.

Spencer jerked the starter cord and the little two-stroke *putt putted* to life. He untied the dock line and pointed the dinghy towards open water.

'Hey, this is a blast. Awesome.'

'There you go again. It's many things but awesome doesn't quite cut it. And I feel sick.'

After twenty minutes Spencer felt like a true ship's master.

'Let's have a go at the oars.'

'Let's.' Savannah groaned and heaved her breakfast into Biscayne Bay.

Spencer realized he must have done some rowing in a past life as he confidently placed the oars into the rowlocks and propelled the little dinghy forward, his muscles rippling under his white T-shirt.

'Enough already. You can row, you can drive the damn thing. That's it. Take her back. Geez, I don't like boats.'

CHAPTER FIFTY-THREE
CONFUSED

Gabriel's head hurt. His mouth was dry. He opened his eyes. Early morning light streamed into the room through a small barred rectangular window at ground level. He could just make out a row of golden marigolds swaying like hula skirts in a light breeze. The big forward-looking window was shuttered. He lay on the settee. *I'm sure I was sitting on a chair last night.*

Gabriel went to get up, his leg jerked. He realized it was cuffed to the leg of the settee.

'Mr Fabian, please, what's happening? Help me.'

'How you doing, Pancho? I reckon you can sit up. I've brought you some bacon, eggs and coffee. We believe in looking after our guests.' A beaming Ron Fabian strode down the stairs, holding a tray with a plate, cutlery and a steaming coffee mug.

'Mr Fabian, what I do? You angry with me? Why am I cuffed?'

'Angry, hell no. You had a little too much to drink last night. Oh man, you were out like a light. I tell ya.'

'Well, I thought I had one drink?'

'One, hell you had at least a half bottle of my best bourbon. Why, me and Clint had to carry you onto the settee.'

Gabriel shook his head. Mr Fabian seemed like a nice man.

'But why did you…?'

'Why did I chain you to the settee? Well, I figured if you woke up in the middle of the night, you wouldn't have known where you were and you might have panicked. Understand?'

'Can I go now?'

'Clint discovered your van has a radiator issue. Water has leaked out all over my garage floor. Son of a bitch, eh?' Fabian nodded sympathetically.

'It was ok when I got here.'

'Sure, but these things happen. Just like that. It's a good thing it didn't happen on the way back to Miami. You mighta cooked the motor.'

'I better ring Mr Diaz. He'll know what to do.'

'Already done, Pancho. I spoke to Arturo first thing.'

'Gabriel.'

'Huh?'

'My name, Gabriel.'

'Of course. I'm terrible with names.'

'So, what Mr Diaz say?'

'We're going to take you back to Miami. This morning.'

'Who is, Mr Fabian?'

'Well, let's see. There will be me, and Clint of course and a lovely guy called Pedro. He's never been to Miami so he asked if he could come too.'

'We go in the van?'

'No, no, like I said the van has to be fixed. We'll be taking my Caddy. Lots of room. It's air conditioned. You'll ride in style Pa…I mean Gabriel.'

Gabriel shook his head as he tried to get his head around his changed circumstances.

'Um, what about the cash?'

'I've got it. Nothing to worry about,'

'Can you undo me please, Mr Fabian?'

Ron felt through the pockets of his jeans. 'Wouldn't you just know it? Clint has them. He's gone to town. He'll be back in a minute, then we'll all be off to Miami. How's that? Just one little thing?'

'Yes Mr Fabian?'

'To get past the security on Palm Island. Is that a problem?'

'No, sir, no problem,' Gabriel said boldly. 'Those fellas they know me. And anyway, I gotta pass, if it's someone new. See.'

Gabriel reached into his pocket, pulling out a rectangular card with his photo on it.

'This is the official entrance card. It has my photo and everything.'

'Like I said before, you're an important guy alright. Can I have a look?'

Gabriel handed it to Ron, who studied it before putting it into his pocket.

'Can I have it back please, Mr Fabian?'

'The thing is, Clint will be driving, so if the guard asks for the card…you see what I mean?'

Gabriel wasn't entirely sure he did understand, but he nodded vigorously. Mr Fabian was such a nice man.

CHAPTER FIFTY-FOUR
FISHING

'What time do you want to go out then?' Spencer wasn't happy about the new plan, but he knew Savannah wasn't likely to budge.

'If we get going at about nine…nine thirty. Pull the dinghy up on the beach near the jetty. If the Cessna's there, we might be able to poke through it. If I find anything in it, that would be probable cause to enter the house.'

'I get it. Sure thing. If you find a kilo of coke that they had just simply forgotten about?'

'Spencer, leave the real police work to me. How the hell do I know what we might find? Mr God damn negative.'

***

'Miami looks like one big party town. Doesn't anyone ever sleep around here?'

Spencer and Savannah strolled casually out of the Fontainebleau at five past nine. The streets were alive with vibrant clothes and noisy people.

If the concierge or bellboys thought anything odd about two of their guests, dressed like funeral directors heading off on to busy Collins Avenue, they didn't bat an eye.

'Black trousers, black shirt, we look like we're off to a far-right Nazi rally.' Spencer chuckled.

'I'm so sorry you can't wear that hideous Hawaiian number you bought in their gift shop. But I don't think it's a great idea to prowl around Enrique's Garden in your snappy shirt. God damn you just about need sunglasses to look at it.'

'I assume that lurking under that chic black jacket of yours, the blunderbuss awaits in its custom spring-loaded holster?'

'If you mean the Magnum? You bet your cotton picken socks I do. And the jacket, chic? Do you really think so?'

Spencer glanced at her shapeless black polyester jacket, that had neither style nor grace.

'It's um, how can I put it? Let's see. Hang on there's a cab.' Spencer held a hand up and whistled.

The prowling Checker Cab swerved towards them.

'Good evening driver, the Bay Walk Jetty please.'

'What about my God damn jacket? What's wrong with it?' Savannah whispered.

The driver turned up the radio, in his Chevrolet. 'Hope you don't mind folks, I love this song.' Jan and Dean belted out one of their hits, *the little old lady from Pasa deeeenah.*

'Well, this…song sort of describes it. If you know what I mean?'

'Old lady, you son of a bitch. I bought this jacket when I graduated. I'm very fond of it.'

'Here we are folks. Two bucks fifty. And I think your jacket is swell. My gran has one just like it.' The driver said with a smirk. Spencer could see the man's laughing eyes in the rear-view mirror.

Savannah handed over two one-dollar notes and two quarters. 'Oh, and I mustn't forget the tip.' She scrabbled in the pocket of her jacket and placed a nickel in the driver's hand. 'That's just for you.' Her smile was as cold as frost on a window pane as she slammed the door.

***

Silence slid in like a bolt, their rubber soled shoes noiseless on the worn timbers of the jetty.

Spencer mentally kicked himself for his tactless comments, but he knew Savannah never held a grudge. Well, not where he was concerned. But he feared Savannah held Ramirez responsible for Hugo and Jerry holding a gun on Inez and terrifying her.

Sure enough, it seemed all was forgotten.

'I have a good feeling about tonight. I reckon we'll get the goods on Enrique. Just you wait and see. Look, there's our little runabout. You have the key Bix gave you?'

They clambered unsteadily aboard; the little craft rocked in the slight swell. Spencer cast off. They took their seat; Spencer pulled the cord on the old matte grey Evinrude two-stroke motor and the little engine burbled happily to life. The palpitating pulse of the sea was steady and peaceful as Spencer pointed the bow to the windward side of Palm Island. Spencer didn't share Savannah's optimism, he figured Ramirez would have some sort of contingency plan, particularly where intruders were concerned.

***

'Um, guys. I need a bathroom break.' Gabriel leaned forward to speak to Clint, who was driving the Cadillac.

'Tie a fucking knot in it.' Pedro glared at him.

The Cadillac swished silently along the interstate. The Ray Conniff singers softly warbled *Stranger in Paradise*. Clint drove. Ron Fabian dozed in the seat next to him. The new addition to the entourage was Pedro, a thin, thuggish Mexican with a 38th Street Gang tattoo inked across a bulging bicep. Gabriel avoided eye contact with the Mexican. Flat and hard, the eyes looked like *la Muerte*.

Gabriel knew the gang well from the time he spent in a Tijuana jail. Gabriel was afraid.

'Wake up Ron.' Clint shook Fabian awake as the Cadillac approached the security stop.

The guard peered in, giving Gabriel a wave. 'How's tricks, Gabriel?'

The black limousine entered the lush, manicured grounds of Palm Island, the safe enclave of the super-rich. Nestled in the woodlands, mansion after mansion came into view. Spanish American haciendas with tennis courts and swimming pools. Houses here weren't crammed together like the Chicago and New York townhouses that so many of the residents had left behind in a past life. This is where the obscenely rich went to retire, and tonight, to die.

***

'Hell, the Cessna's gone.'

280

'Never mind I'm sure you can figure out some reason to invade poor old Enrique's pied-a-terre.'

'Stop with the Greek already.'

The night sky was clear. The full moon, a glowing yellow-white, was the backdrop to the inky sky and the millions of stars were little white pinpricks, illuminating the way for Savannah and Spencer just enough to see where they were going but also to provide a convenient camouflage to prying eyes. The ocean waves lapped lazily as Spencer hauled the dinghy on to the beach.

'French.'

'What?'

'Pied-a-terre. It's French.'

'Jesus, who gives a…'

'Language.'

'Are we on a mission, or a God damn language lesson? Did you bring the 0.45 I gave you?'

'Well, no. Not exactly. I figured…'

'Fair enough. You probably would have missed the bad guys and shot me.'

The mansion was in darkness as they stealthily made their way across the manicured ground, pausing behind clumps of Buccaneer palms and scanning the area for possible armed guards.

'Enrique, or Arturo as he now is, obviously doesn't think he's in any danger,' Spencer whispered. 'Hang on. Something's coming.' Spencer grabbed Savannah's jacket, pulling her to the ground.

A black limousine snaked silently up the long driveway, only its park lights illuminating its way. It glided quietly to a stop. The doors opened and four men climbed out.

'Cast your peepers on the driver. He's one big dude.'

Spencer and Savannah watched as the men warily scanned the surroundings and quietly padded to the front door of the house.

Now safely out of earshot, Spencer whispered to Savannah. 'What do you make of that, Special Agent Mrs. Winchester?' Spencer chuckled.

'The guy next to the driver, I reckon he's the boss. Mean looking prick.'

'What about the others?'

'Well, I reckon the chubby little Latino guy is some sort of hostage.'

'Really? How did you work that out?' Spencer was puzzled.

'You notice how the driver and that thin Mexican looking guy are standing so close to the fat one.'

'Yeah, I see that.'

'I reckon he's definitely some sort of hostage. I tell you; he didn't look happy.'

'We're about to find out. They're at the door. That big guy's knocking. Hey, look, they've pushed fatty to the front of the door, and the others have fanned out. The Mexican and the big guy have both drawn pistols. Jesus, something's going down.'

The hall lights flashed on, and the door opened.

'Mr Diaz, they got guns!' the tubby Latino man yelled.

Spencer and Savannah watched spellbound as the person inside tried to slam the door shut. The big guy kicked it open.

A flash and the boom of a gunshot followed. At the same time the Mexican put his pistol to the chubby man's head and pulled the trigger. *Kaboom*, the man fell into a heap.

'That's it. If murder isn't probable cause I don't know what is. We're going in. Dammit.' Savannah grabbed her Magnum and checked the load.

'Not yet. They're hyped up. We're outnumbered. Just wait a minute,' Spencer cautioned.

CHAPTER FIFTY-FIVE
BREAK AND ENTER

'How about we circumnavigate the house? There may be more bad guys. I think the neighbours must be too far away to hear the gunshot. Maybe Ramirez has some bodyguards inside. I We don't know what's happening.' Spencer was cautious.

'You're right.' Savannah reluctantly holstered her pistol.

The front door opened; they watched as the big man scanned the grounds. He leaned down and grabbed the corpse by the legs and dragged it roughly inside. The hall light went on for a second. He stepped back out on to the porch, wiping his hands on a handkerchief, rolling it into a ball and throwing it into the garden. A light flashed, they heard the click of a lighter, he cupped his fingers around the flame. Drawing hungrily on a cigarette, puffing out a plume of smoke.

Spencer placed his index and forefinger under his eyes and then pointed towards the far side of the house, the special forces signage. Savannah grinned and nodded. They crept away to warily scout around the unlit mansion.

'Over there. The flower bed.' Spencer pointed.

Clearly visible was the light from a small rectangular window behind the blooms.

'That has to be the cellar. I reckon that's where they are,' Spencer whispered.

Lying full length on the lawn, they peered into the cellar. A composed Enrique Ramirez sat on a chaise lounge, nursing a whiskey glass. The television was on. Sprawled on another settee, they could see the Mexican with a Colt pointing at Ramirez. The one Savannah designated the leader was talking.

Savannah nodded to Spencer, they carefully backed away and hid behind a clump of firebush.

'This is what we've got. It's obvious the dead guy worked for Arturo, or Enrique, whatever you want to call him. The Mexican is a street thug. I don't know if you saw his gang tatt. But anyway, he's a bad guy. We know that. That other mean looking son of a bitch is the boss. They're here to rob Ramirez, kill him, or whatever. It's obvious there is no one else in the house.' Once again Savannah grabbed her revolver. 'So, I reckon we go in.'

'Aren't you forgetting something?'

'What, am I forgetting?'

'The gorilla at the front door.'

'Hmm, yeah.'

'You can shoot him. But that's going to be tricky. He'll see you coming, and there's a good chance the shot will be heard inside.'

'What do you suggest?'

'Well. I think we walk up to the front door. Bold as brass. And I have a little chat, and possibly get him to see the error of his ways.'

'Get real.'

'Seriously, it'll work. Trust me. I'm a people person. We'll get on like a house on fire.'

Spencer jumped to his feet and strode off.

'I don't believe this,' he heard Savannah mutter.

Savannah caught up to Spencer as he was about to turn the corner and make his way to the imposing double doors of the Arturo Diaz mansion.

'I just hope you know what you're doing,' Savannah whispered.

'G'day mate.' Spencer boomed in his best Australian accent.

'Hold it right there.' The big man held up a warning hand. 'What the fuck do you want?'

'My name's Marlowe. I'm here to do a little business with Arturo. Know what I mean?' He gave the thug a friendly wink. 'I'm his Australian business connection. I guess you must work for him, right?'

'Yeah, but, Mr Diaz, he's ahh…busy right now. In a conference. I'll tell him you called.'

Spencer drew closer, a silly grin on his face. 'Well, you see cobber, I've got some cash here for him.'

'You can give that to me. I'll be sure he gets it.'

'The thing is, he specifically said to give it to him personally.'

Spencer had long since realized he didn't look scary. He sort of missed his temporary tattoos. But, although he was tall with an undeniably muscular build, well the fact was he looked like a nice guy.

'What's your name, sport?'

'Name's Clint. I won't ask you again. Give me the dough.' He held out a hand.

'Spencer!' Savannah growled.

Spencer turned and grinned at Savannah, he wheeled around, slamming the heel of his palm under Clint's jaw. The jawbone snapped. Blood gushed out of his mouth. Clint dropped like he'd stepped into a vacant elevator shaft.

'Jesus H, I thought you two were going to chat forever.'

'A bit of gratitude would be nice.'

Savannah reached into her jacket pocket and retrieved a pair of handcuffs, 'How about you cuff his ankle to his wrist, and I'll gag him. I don't want him calling out when he wakes up.'

From another pocket Savannah pulled out large squares of material.

'Hey, I'm impressed. That jacket isn't just haute couture. Function as well as style, eh.'

'Sarcasm. It's an Australian thing, right?'

Savannah retrieved the blood-stained handkerchief from the garden and stuffed it into Clint's mouth. The large square of cotton fabric she rolled into a strip and bound it tightly around his face.

'Hey, hang on. That's a little tight, isn't it? The guy might have trouble breathing. There's a lot of blood. He could bloody well suffocate.'

'That would be a shame.' Savannah rolled her eyes.

'I didn't want to kill the guy, dammit.'

'You listen to me. He wakes up he's gonna scream blue God damn murder.'

'Well, I'm not happy about it.' Spencer knew when he was defeated.

'Look at it this way. He can't get to heaven if he doesn't die, now, can he?'

CHAPTER FIFTY-SIX

RAMIREZ SMILES

The solid oak panelled door swung open, the only sound a squeak from a rusty hinge.

Savannah and Spencer paused for a moment, eyes adjusting to the gloom. In front of them a broad staircase. To their left a large sitting room. Alongside the staircase, a long-tiled hallway disappeared into the shadows. At the end of the hall a faint light slid under a closed door. The corpse of a dumpy man lay face down on the tiled floor, 'Poor sod. Looks like that guy, Gabriel.' Nearby lay another corpse, that of another man, but older. Savannah checked, but the man wasn't Ramirez, or Arturo Diaz for that matter. *Probably a house servant.*

'Not our problem, Spencer,' Savannah hissed. 'It's what these guys do.'

Spencer tapped Savannah on the shoulder. She was holding the revolver in two hands, the classic shooter's stance.

'What?' she hissed.

'You can't just go in guns-a- blazing. The guy with the gun might have moved. He might get the drop on you.'

'Well, what then?'

'Seeing as I've already demonstrated my people skills, I reckon we try the same approach. I'll walk in like I own the place. I've come to see Arturo. They will see I'm unarmed.

They're going to figure Clint must have been ok with me coming in. It'll work, fair dinkum.'

'Then what?'

'You can listen at the door. I'm going to tell you where the Mexican with the gun is. You come in and shoot the bastard.'

'You're ok with me shooting him. Really?'

'Look this is different. Stop arguing.'

'Oh, and you're going to yell out "Savannah, he's sitting down at the left of the room" That'll work.'

'Leave it to me, woman.'

'God damn suicide,' Savannah snarled.

They padded silently down the hallway, stopping at the closed door. Muffled voices could be heard.

Spencer turned to Savannah. 'Wish me luck.' He reached into his trouser pocket and briefly touched the cornicello. *Bring me a little more luck, old friend.*

Spencer opened the door and stood on the landing. The scene hadn't changed. The Mexican sat on a chair to his left. Arturo still nursed a whiskey glass and the tall thin man reclined in another chair facing Enrique Ramirez.

'Arturo, my old mate,' Spencer boisterously announced. 'Stone the bloody crows, eh. We seem to be a little short of brotherly love here. Who's this fucker on my left with the pistol? Looks like the bloody Cisco Kid.' Spencer's voice resonated like the bells of Big Ben.

'Who the fuck are you?' the thin man enquired.

'And who the fuck are you exactly, Sport?' Spencer replied.

'My name…is Ron Fabian.'

'Really? Never heard of you. What's happening Art, old mate, are you thinking of cutting the Aussies out and dealing with these pricks instead?'

The Mexican pointed his pistol at Spencer 'You want me to waste this hombre, Ron?'

'No, no, hang on. I need to know who he is, and what the hell he's doing here. I gather Clint gave you the ok to come in?'

'Obviously.' Spencer gave him that disarming, nice guy smile.

'Arturo, who is this guy exactly?' Ron Fabian stared at Ramirez.

Ramirez chuckled. 'As always Spencer, it's a pleasure. Your timing is perfect. Yes Ron, Spencer is an Australian buyer. Always full of surprises, aren't you?'

Spencer was just beginning to think he'd run out of dialogue when the door burst open. Savannah screamed, 'Drop the pistola estupido!'

Pedro wasted a millisecond as he glanced at Ron Fabian. The Magnum boomed, twice. The sound bouncing around the room like a thousand cannon blasts. The Mexican slumped backwards on his chair, his chest a bloody mess and most of his throat ripped away.

'Fuck you.' Ron Fabian reached under his jacket. The Walther PPK had just come into view when Savannah unleashed another round. The hollow point slug obliterated most of his face. Blood and grey brain matter spattered over Ramirez's white shirtfront.

Ramirez grimaced as he glanced at his glass of whiskey and noticed specks of blood and brain matter floating on the surface.

'Spectacular entrance, Spencer. And Savannah, so nice to see you again.'

He went to rise from his seat.

'Stay right where you are,' Savannah barked.

Ramirez shrugged. 'I was about to fix myself another whiskey and soda. This one is…a little contaminated. Where are my manners? Would you both like a drink? I'm sure shooting people is thirsty work.' He said with a grin.

Spencer leaned against the bar and tried to avoid looking at the blood and the gore.

'Spencer, could you give me a hand please? And don't you so much as bat a God damn eyelid.' She glanced menacingly at Ramirez, who shrugged. They grabbed the remains of Ron Fabian and dragged him off his recliner. Savannah took a hand towel from the sink behind the bar, folded it neatly, and carefully laid it over the chair, before taking a seat.

'That's better.' She beamed. 'It's been a tiring day. So much happening, eh Enrique?'

'Indeed, lots of fun. First things first, what's this about someone named Clint? I gather he is or was, standing guard at the front of my house?' Ramirez wagged a finger. 'Of course, Spencer, you took him out with some of your fancy martial arts bullshit. That's why we didn't hear anything. Right? And my man Gabriel, they've whacked him for sure. Nice little guy. Yeah, he only had two brain cells and both of them fought for third place.'

Spencer nodded. 'The Mexican shot him at the front door. I'm surprised you didn't hear it.' *Compassion isn't in this guy's vocabulary.* 'Your house servant too, I'd guess.'

'Shame about that one. Rodrigo was his name.' Ramirez reclined back in his seat, his hands linked behind his head, he burst into laughter.

'What's so funny?'

'What's so funny? There I was watching Hogan's Heroes with the sound turned up loud. I reckon I've gone a little deaf in my old age. And I didn't hear this idiot Ron Fabian and his Mexican hitman who'd come here to rob me, and I've no doubt they were going to kill me. And then I get saved by a God damn FBI dyke and an Aussie who I still can't figure out exactly what his game is. Just out of curiosity, who the hell are you, Spencer? There's no way you could be FBI. Are you with some Australian law enforcement? I don't get it. And while we're on the subject, what about that scumbag Popeye Gordon? Did you kill him? Is that what it is? The FBI have recruited you in exchange for being a snitch?'

Spencer threw his head back and chortled. 'Ahh, it's a long story.'

'Jesus, here we go again,' Savannah mumbled.

'Well, I don't really give a fuck. I'd like another drink.'

'Let's have a little chat first.' Savannah leaned forward in her chair. 'Where's the Cessna, as we speak?'

'You've been watching me obviously. None of your fucking business. Am I under arrest?'

'No, you're not under arrest.'

Spencer stared hard at Savannah. His stomach knotted. He had a bad feeling.

'In that case, I'm going to get that drink, and guess what?'

'I couldn't possibly.' Savannah smiled. Spencer remembered that smile. He didn't know where, but he had a memory flash. A restaurant. A short swarthy man, a smirk on the man's face that morphed into gut wrenching fear. The sonic boom of a gunshot. Once again, he felt for the comforting outline of the cornicello.

'Well, thanks and all that, but seeing as I'm not under arrest, I suggest you phone the Miami Police. Tell them there's some stiffs here. Of course, I'd like you to explain that I had no hand in anything. I'm the innocent victim.' Enrique rubbed his hands together with glee. 'This is just perfect.' Again, he went to rise from his seat.

'Sit down.'

Ramirez's mouth snapped shut. He turned his gaze on Spencer, and mouthed, 'What the fuck's going on?'

'Aren't you forgetting something?' Her eyes narrowed to slits.

'No, nothing springs to mind. But like I said, I have to…'

'Warbonnet? I was meant to be entertainment for the Black Hills Demons.'

'Hang on. Not my fault. I can understand you're pissed. Sure, who wouldn't be? But that wasn't my doing. Anyway, I heard you sorted 'em out.' He said with a wink.

'Well, I'm prepared to move on, but…? There's the little matter of Hugo and Jerry.'

'Hugo and Jerry are dead, for Christ's sake. You and Spencer, hell I don't know who did what, but they're both finito.'

'But what I can't forgive, is your goons went to my house. They put a gun to Inez's head. They intended to kill all of us. Spencer and I…well, it sorta goes with the territory. But Inez, you crossed the line.'

'Fucking dykes,' Ramirez muttered.

'What was that?'

'You fucking heard. Anyway, they're dead. You can't pin that one on me. So, like I said. Phone the cops, the FBI. The phone's on the bar there.' Enrique pointed to a red handset on the bar.

Spencer's mouth was dry.

'No, Enrique, this is between you and I.'

'What, what, what do you mean?' he stammered.

'Enrique Ramirez, you have lived too long.'

CHAPTER FIFTY-SEVEN
DEATH

Spencer stumbled along the hallway in a daze, the sound of the two Magnum rounds ringing in his ears. The look of surprise and then terror when Ramirez realized what was about to happen was indelibly imprinted in his mind. 'We have to talk. You're not going to call *anyone*, are you?'

'Let's just get out of here. We'll talk back at the hotel. I don't know about you, but a Jacks on the rocks would go down pretty well. What do you reckon?' Savannah smiled.

'We still have Clint to deal with. I don't believe this. What's it going to be? A bullet in the head? And Ramirez, that was simply murder. What the hell are you going to tell Dale? We don't even know this guy, Clint. Obviously, he's a thug, but it doesn't mean he should be executed. I'm not happy, Savannah.'

'All right, all right already. I'll undo his cuffs, give him a kiss goodbye and send the guy who killed poor little Gabriel on his way. Make you feel better?'

Spencer yanked open the heavy front door, and peered out.

'There's Clint. Right where we left him. Hey Clint, wakey wakey.' Spencer shook him by the shoulder. Spencer felt for a pulse. 'Bloody hell. He's dead. Look his face is blue.'

'Oh, well. Accidents will happen.'

'Accident! Bullshit. You stuffed that hankie into his mouth. The poor bastard never had a chance.'

'We'll talk about this later. Can you hear what I hear?'

The roar of the air-cooled Lycoming engine of a Cessna could be heard.

'That'll be the late Enrique's plane with a shipment of coke.' Savannah grinned. 'How's that for timing? Now, shall we do something about that, or do you think we've been too unkind to the bad guys tonight?'

They set off at a gallop towards the jetty.

The gentle murmur of the waves hitting the beach sounded like a lullaby, but the brutal images of the recent carnage he'd witnessed were at the forefront of his mind.

As the plane dipped, the line between shadow and light moved. The hum of the single propellor grew louder. Savannah and Spencer crouched behind a clump of Pindo palms. The Cessna swooped low and circled. They could just make out the thin pinched face of the pilot.

'He's a cautious son of a bitch, I'll give you that.' Savannah chuckled as she spun the chamber of her revolver.

'No more killing. Ok?' Spencer pushed her gun hand down.

'Mr Goody Two Shoes. What do we do if he has a gun, eh? Any bright ideas?'

'I'll take care of him. Just…leave it to me.'

Obviously satisfied, the pilot gently touched down on the calm water with perfect precision. The Cessna glided up to the jetty. Spencer and Savannah watched as the tall pilot threw a rope around a bollard, hauled the plane close and climbed onto the decking.

Cupping his hands, he lit a cigarette and scanned the surrounds. Afterwards, he clambered back into the aircraft and began throwing out small cotton sacks onto the landing.

In a crouch Spencer and Savannah ran silently down the jetty towards the plane.

They positioned themselves by the open door of the Cessna as sack after sack landed on the jetty.

'Take your time sport. Don't leave any behind. We have all night.'

'What the fuck?'

A head appeared, with lank greying hair and a face as hard as an executioner's axe. 'Did Arturo send you?' he said hopefully.

'You could say that.' Spencer smiled.

The pilots' eyes flashed wildly, he leaned down, and turned on the ignition switch. The engine belched blue smoke; the propeller whirled.

'Why don't I just shoot the bastard?' Savannah yelled over the roar of the motor.

Spencer leaned down and grabbed the pilot's collar, hauling him onto the jetty.

'It's over, pal.'

'Fuck you?'

The pilot yanked a Bowie knife out of a sheath on his belt. Advancing on Spencer, and with a rebel yell, went for a simple but powerful thrust at Spencer's chest. Spencer sidestepped and grasped the knife hand in a grip as strong as a steel vice. The knife clattered onto the jetty. Spencer let go of the pilot's hand, kicking the knife into the water.

'I'm still happy to shoot him,' Savannah yelled.

'That won't be necessary, will it, buddy?'

Holding his hand and cursing, with a bellow he launched himself at Spencer.

Spencer grabbed him by the lapels, hurling him towards the water, and the waiting aircraft.

There wasn't so much as a murmur. The propellor blade sliced through the pilot's body like a machete through a ripe water melon. Savannah and Spencer dripped with dark blood.

'Jesus Christ Spencer. What a mess. That was real clever. Yuck! My God damn jacket is ruined. Son of a bitch.'

Spencer gazed white-faced at the remains of the pilot. He leant over the edge of the jetty and puked.

'Something you ate?' Savannah's eyes twinkled.

'I never intended that to happen. This's just awful, awful.'

'Well, I did offer to shoot him. Would've been a lot less messy.'

TRUTH

The wind gusted with the tempo of a fiddlers bow as the little dinghy sped across the bay, the two-stroke motor chugging noisily.

Savannah and Spencer were lost in thought. Spencer steered the little craft into its slot. He clambered onto the deck and held out a hand to Savannah. She rose unsteadily to her feet, and carefully climbed on to the jetty.

***

'Ok, out with it.'

Spencer and Savannah had flopped exhausted onto the steamer chairs of their hotel balcony. A third of the bottle of Jack Daniels had mysteriously disappeared. Ice cubes in the silver bucket had begun to melt.

Spencer gave her a long look. 'I don't think you've been completely honest with me.'

'Well, I guess. I...um might have left a few things out. Perhaps...'Savannah hesitated.

'Here's what I think,' he said.

'What do you think Spencer?'

'I don't think Dale knows anything about this, this, what would you call it? This bloody criminal vigilante attack.'

'What makes you say that?'

'Mr and Mrs. Winchester? Come on? You used someone's Diner's Card. You have fake ID. Does Dale know about that, eh? Dale said nothing to me. He hasn't been in touch. He hasn't phoned. What the hell is going on? As far as he's concerned, we're still on leave. That's right, isn't it?'

'All right, Jesus have another drink. You're right. As far as Dale was concerned, we didn't have enough to get Ramirez into court. And by the way, the ID and Diner's aren't fake, they're legit.' Savannah giggled. 'They belong to a dead mobster. Getting back to Ramirez, aka Arturo Diaz, you and I, knew absolutely he was guilty. Didn't we, hey? That's correct, isn't it?'

'Yeah, sure but…'

'But nothing. The son of a bitch was guilty.'

'You can't just go on being judge, jury and executioner.'

'Really? Why not?'

'It's, it's not civilized. This is a civilized society. We have courts for this sort of thing.'

'You and I have had this conversation before.'

'Have we? When?'

'It was a long time ago.'

'My God, how many dead? Ramirez, Fabian, Clint, that chubby guy Gabriel, the Mexican, the pilot. This has been like a bloody war.'

'Hang on, you killed the pilot.'

'That was an accident.'

'And what about that big bruiser, Clint? You hit the son of a bitch.'

'And you suffocated him.'

'This is really splitting hairs.' Savannah slammed her whiskey tumbler down on the side table. 'You listen to me. As I said to Ramirez…'

'Before you shot him.'

'Moving right along. Ramirez crossed the line. His thugs broke into our house. Our house, dammit. They held a gun to

Inez's head. You and I had no idea whether or not Ramirez wasn't going to try again. If you think I was going to wait, just because we didn't have enough evidence, and allow him to have another go, you don't know me very well.' Tears came to her eyes. 'Spencer, I've had nightmares about that night. Inez means everything to me. Attack those I love and there's no mercy. So, you do what you like. If you want to tell Dale, that's up to you. He's already mentioned he wants us to tackle something in San Francisco and New Orleans. If you want out, I'll understand. If you want to do your disappearing act again, well that's up to you. Make up your mind. We've been here for days, I want to get back to home and Inez.'

'I'll do a deal with you.'

'This'll be good. Let's hear it.'

'I have no intention of disappearing. You and Inez are all I have. I have no job prospects; I don't even know who I really am. What we achieved in South Dakota was fantastic, if a little messy.'

'Hey, you were the one who picked on Trunk and beat him to a pulp. Oooh that was nasty.' Savannah shook her head. 'That poor man. Innocently eating his noodles.'

'Fried rice, in fact.'

'Important detail.' Savannah rolled her eyes.

'What I'm saying is, if my memory returns, all bets may be off. I'm sure I have a real life somewhere. But until that day I want to keep working with you. But…'

'Let's hear it. Let me guess, you don't want me to carry, right?'

'Don't be silly. I know you need a weapon.'

'Multiple weapons, actually.' Savannah grinned.

'What I don't want is you killing people in cold blood, just because you've decided they're guilty.'

'Just one cotton picking minute…'

'That's the deal. Take it or leave it. I'm going to bed.'

Spencer glared at the ceiling. His partnership with Savannah was going to continue…. That's a good thing, I guess. He yawned. But sleep proved elusive. Plagued by insomnia that seemed like a form of PTSD, when fears were igniting ghosts, he'd tried to forget. increasingly his mind flashed back to Singapore, Hawaii, New York. Mexico. Machine gun fire, paralysing fear. A Japanese psychopath. A New York restaurant. Violent deaths. A man called Zachariah and his henchman Charlie.

As sleep gradually came, Spencer drifted in and out of a restless repose. His mind wrestled with the images that swirled haphazardly through his subconscious.

CHAPTER FIFTY-EIGHT
FUNNY MONEY

Visions of himself in New Orleans came so profoundly and with such realism, Spencer cried out in his dream. What's happening? Is this real? Spencer saw himself caught up in the Mardi Gras; the streets a riot of colour and music, hot and sweet blaring from every bar and juke joint. Spencer glanced at his watch; Jorge Simenson was late. Actually, Spencer didn't mind at all, packed like a sardine in Frenchman Street and captivated by the melancholic, melodic tones of blues musician Elliott Small as he sang The House of the Rising Sun. Hordes of bead wearing people danced as if possessed and drunk ladies laughed as they flashed bare breasts. The piquant scents of freshly fried beignets overlayed by the aromas of gumbo, jambalaya and crawfish etouffee wafting through the air and the tang of cayenne, paprika and bay leaves.

A black fedora caught his eye. Jorge Simenson with his distinctive hat and his grubby white suit jostled through the throng. Spencer screwed his nose up at the sight of the noxious little man. ' G'day Jorge. Enjoying Mardi Gras?'

Simenson glanced nervously around 'Fuck Mardi Gras. I've got the samples to show you, fifties and hundreds just like you asked for.'

'Great. Let's see them.'

'Nah, not here. No way of knowing who's watching. My car's parked a couple of blocks away.

Spencer followed the guy across streets until the crowd had thinned, he could just hear the soulful sound of Elliot Small as he sang about the infamous house of ill repute.

'This is it. Hop in.'

'Nice car, Jorge. Funny money must pay well.' Spencer admired the gleaming white MK 11 Jaguar sedan.

The smell of English leather greeted Spencer as the door closed with a subtle click.

'Ok, Jorge. Let's see what you got, eh?'

'Oh no. Not on your life pal. I don't know if you've been followed. Counterfeit money is a federal rap.'

Simenson turned the key and accelerated. The tires squealed.

'Hey, this wasn't the deal, mate.'

'Calm down buddy, I just want to make sure we ain't being followed.' The Jaguar roared as Jorge seemed to revel in the car's performance and handling. Spencer didn't know New Orleans well. He recognized the famous St Louis Cemetery No. 1, and wondered if that might end up being his final destination.

'Relax pal. Nothing to worry about. You want my play money and I want your real stuff. As long as you don't try and stiff me, we'll be cool.'

The Jag rocketed into Fulton Street, 'No one's following, my friend. How about you pull over and show me the samples.'

'You think I was born yesterday, Marlowe. They aren't on me.' The Jaguar turned hard right, and roared into a cavernous red brick warehouse, its double door wide open.

Spencer's stomach clenched. This was not the plan. Jorge bounced out of the car and slammed the garage door shut.

'Better safe than sorry eh mate?'

Spencer warily climbed out of the Jaguar, 'Ok, I'm impressed. You're very careful. Now show me the product.'

'Spencer Marlowe. Fucking FBI. Who woulda guessed.' Jorge Simenson grinned a 9mm German Luger held rock steady. 'On your knees, mate. Hands behind your head.'

His body moved numbly to obey. He reacted on autopilot; he was one finger squeeze from death. Spencer's eyes swivelled. Is this really it?

Kaboom. The 0.44 Magnum round had opened up Jorge Simenson's chest. Dark red blood flooded onto the concrete floor.

'Savannah.'

CHAPTER FIFTY-NINE
HOME AGAIN

'Savannah, how in hell?' Bathed in sweat, his heart pounding Spencer sat bolt upright.' Where…'

A gentle sunlight streamed through the window. Did he imagine the soft and nutty aroma of espresso coffee? The faint, precise ticking of his wristwatch was strangely comforting. 'New Orleans. So real. Just a dream? *Watch? I don't wear a watch.* He opened his eyes, lifting his head. *What's this?* The gold face of the timepiece said "Rolex". It was 7.04. A moment of panic. He jerked to a sitting position. *Something's not right.* Watching him, lying by his side, a bemused expression on her face, he saw a beautiful Asian lady, her long sleek black hair, obscuring part of her face.

'About time, Spencer darling. Trilby wants to bring you your coffee.'

'Oh my God. What on Earth…Where's Savannah? Who…'

The lady sat up in bed and stroked his face. 'You've been away, haven't you?'

Spencer nodded. 'Yes…Michiyo?'

'Dad, dad, I have coffee here for you and Mum. It's just the way you like it.'

In a rush, all the memories returned. It was like being bowled over by a wave at the beach. Tears ran down his face in a torrent at the sight of this delightful bubbly girl, a younger version of her mother, her face a study in concentration as she carefully carried two steaming mugs. 'Put the coffee down on the bedside table, I want to give you both a hug.'

She carefully placed the two containers on the side table and jumped onto the bed and kissed her mother and father on the cheek.

'Guess what, Dad! I've just been watching an awesome old movie on Netflix "Back to the Future". It's about a boy who travels back in time. Can that really happen?'

'Yes darling, it really can.'

If you enjoyed The Chicago Story a review or a kind word
on Amazon or Goodreads would not only be appreciated but
would guarantee more Spencer and Savannah adventures.

KELVIN WHITE AUTHOR

I'm a West Australian author, having been born in Perth and living in WA for most of my life.

As with so many authors my background is awash with many careers, taxi driver, musician, Roof tiler, shoe salesman and a plethora of others.

Given that I have always been an avid reader it was probably inevitable I would eventually put pen to paper. My first publication was the time travel adventure "The Singapore Saga" featuring central character Spencer Marlowe. I was delighted when positive reviews appeared on Amazon and Goodreads. I was hooked. The first "Spencer" novel was followed by the next instalment " The Hawaiian Intervention" and then " The Manhattan Sting" , introducing Special Agent Savannah Steele. Then The L A Confrontation, once again with Savannah Steele and now The Chicago Story with Savannah and Spencer once again wreaking havoc.

Amidst churning out the "Spencer" series I have also published along with co-author Allan Butler, our rock and roll memoir "Oh How We Rocked". This memoir complete with photos of the bands and musicians we worked with is a fun look at the music scene mostly in Perth in the 60's 70's and eighties.

Having enjoyed writing the musical memoir, my next project was the crime novel" Birthright", this time In collaboration with acclaimed Perth author Bruce L Russell.

Bruce added a whole new dimension to the writing experience. Having won the prestigious T A G Hungerford Award for literature and also holding a doctorate in creative writing, Bruce's writing skills are very evident in Birthright.

Bruce and I have also released our next crime novel. Published by Vivid Press, The King of San Francisco, set largely in the United States in the 1970's.

I have found the collaborative writing experience to be very rewarding and an extraordinary learning platform, as a consequence I have participated in another collaboration, "Undercover Heat" with American co-author Tali A Sandbridge.

Tali is the author of the 'Love Throughout The Centuries' series. The debut story, 'The Ghost and Mrs Smyth' featuring the lovers Jake and Angie, I found to be quite enchanting. This story was followed by book two 'The Great War' and then 'Peachtree Plantation.' The most recent addition is 'MacKenzie's Hope.'

The thought then occurred to me, why not write a crime novel with this lady who 'does romance' so well. The collaboration was a lot of fun as it incorporated Australian detective Gage Madden and NYPD cop Kimberly Biche. Undercover Heat is a crime story alternating between New York, Perth, Sydney and then finally Bali. It's very different, raunchy, sexy and gritty, and is available on Amazon in kindle and paperback.

Tali and I are also currently co-writing the sequel to 'Undercover Heat.' 'The Dogcatcher,' once again with Gage and Kimberly is a taut thriller with a surprise ending.

And now, a glimpse of the next Spencer Marlowe story.

THE SAN FRANCISCO AFFAIR
CHAPTER 1

'Wakey wakey. Jimbo, throw some water into the sonofabitch's face.'

Jimbo appeared to be a little too tall for his build. Were he a few inches shorter, he would have been considered well proportioned. As it was, he looked like he'd been stretched on a medieval rack. His thin face was largely obscured by a scruffy red beard that failed to conceal teenage acne scars. He smiled with a face devoid of warmth.

Filling a chipped ceramic jug from the faucet at a sink stacked with dirty dishes and take out containers, Jimbo grimaced at the sight of the remains of fried rice and clumps of rancid vegetables. Pizza boxes from Magoo's littered the worn linoleum floor. Huge black and white photos of The Beatles covered one wall.

'Sure thing, BBQ.'

The man giving the orders was Big Ronny Delgado, aka BBQ. Big? Yes. And tall. Once a taut-bodied football player for the Dallas Cowboys. But too much fast food had taken its toll. The hairy inner tube around his waist and the red veiny splotches across his flaccid face destroyed the image of what was once a strikingly handsome man.

Ryan Murray, the object of their displeasure, groaned and shook his head when Jimbo poured the water over him.

'C'mon Brucey baby,' Ronny exhorted, 'time for us to continue our little chat. Only it's not Bruce, is it?'

'My name's Bruce Murray,' the man in the chair groaned.

BBQ's methods of coercion lacked originality, but they had always proved to be effective. Bruce aka Ryan Tod no longer possessed ten fingernails. His hands were a bloody mess. Strapped on to an Adirondack chair, his laboured breathing came in short wheezing gasps. Beside him, a wooden trolley with a pair of everyday pliers and a bundle of bloody rags.

CHAPTER 2

Spencer Marlowe slept on a camp stretcher, long legs dangling over one end.

'Wake up sleepyhead,' a brusque female voice disturbed his dream.

'Michiyo please, it's Sunday, can't a man sleep? C'mon please, sweetheart.'

'It's not wifey and it's not Sunday, Spencer. It's Savannah, now wake up. Things are happening.'

Spencer groaned and glanced at his watch, 'What?' The Bulova watch told him it was 7:04. Bulova… oh shit. The Rolex. Gone. He knew. He was back.

'Good morning, Savannah, nice to see you.'

The owner of the voice grinned and handed him a styrene cup of coffee.

'Sorry princess, not your preferred drop of heart starter.'

Spencer sat up, relieved to see he was fully dressed in worn Levi's, a tie-dyed T-shirt and hip, tooled cowboy boots. He took a sip and spluttered. 'Stone the bloody crows. Instant.'

'Yeah yeah, it's instant. Like I said, things are happening. How the hell can you sleep, boots and all? Must be an Australian thing.'

Spencer's lips curled as he took another sip. 'Sorry, Savannah, but where exactly are we?'

'Kiss my go to hell. Don't do this to me.'

Spencer sat up and gazed around a spartan room. Savannah Steele peered out of the window, a pair of binoculars glued to her face.

'I'm not happy, Ryan hasn't called in as he was supposed to and I think he's in trouble. We're going to have to go in.'

Spencer knew immediately he'd returned, leaving his wife Michiyo and daughter in the next century. He was confused but alert.

'Savannah I'm sorry, but you know I have memory lapses and…'

'I don't have time for this. We have to move.'

Savannah stepped back from the window, pulling a small automatic pistol out of her shoulder holster. 'I think the 0.22 with a suppressor is what the doctor ordered.'

'Nice outfit,' Spencer said.

Savannah wore a pair of tatty low-slung flared jeans and a bold t-shirt with a picture of the British rock group The Who stamped on the front. She shrugged on a grimy army style canvas jacket, hiding the shoulder holster.

'Love the headband. It's very cool.' Spencer grinned.

'This is San Francisco, dear, peace love and all that bullshit. Now please get a wriggle on. Grab this damn coat, and this God damn hat, and get ready.'

Savannah handed him an unfashionable gaberdine raincoat and a plaid golf hat.

Spencer climbed off the stretcher and pulled on the coat, jamming the hat on his head.

'Ok, what's going down?'

Savannah closed her eyes and grimaced. 'You should know. For Christ's sake we've been through this. Ok,' she muttered, 'all you need to know right at the moment we're in an apartment overlooking 4 Haight Street.'

'You mean like San Francisco Haight Street?'

'Yes, dammit San Francisco. Did you think it was God damn Sydney or something?'

'Actually, I'm from Perth. Australia.'

'Really? Like I didn't know that?'

'I'm truly sorry Savannah, but I'm a blank.'

'Hell in a handbasket, now of all times. Here it is. The bad guys and our undercover guy are in an apartment above the record shop at 4 Haight Street. Ronnie Delgado is in the apartment with at least one other thug, probably that idiot Jimbo Kline. The problem is they have another one of their merry men standing watch downstairs, a big mother, who's definitely carrying. I want you to do as we discussed; immobilise him, quietly, efficiently, in your inimitable style. If you can remember how to do that.'

'Then what?'

'Oh well…I thought we might toddle upstairs and have a love in with Ronnie and Jimbo. What do you reckon?'

'Ok, I get it. I think. We then go upstairs and you shoot someone?'

'Don't start with the bolshie stuff, Spencer. Yes, very probably. But only as a last resort,' she added. Like she'd rehearsed it.

Spencer roared with laughter, 'Last resort. Yeah right.'

'Are you coming?' Savannah headed for the door.

Spencer followed meekly, glancing quickly at a big mirror on the living room wall. Yep, he looked the same, maybe needing a shave.

Early morning and San Francisco was buzzing with bearded men, flower power gals, but sadly no flowers in their hair, Spencer noticed. Big finned old Chevys and Volkswagen Kombis with ban the bomb signs on their spare wheel covers, rattled up the packed streets. The guys all had long hair the girls in miniskirts and long cotton dresses, the musky odour of patchouli oil mingling pleasantly with the heady aroma of marijuana.

Savannah pointed across the street at The Beat Box record store. 'Do you see what I see?'

'You bet, the sign in the window says Jefferson Airplane are playing the Winterland Ballroom in March. I'd love to hear Grace Slick live. Bloody hell, it's Baltic out here.'

'Poor Diddums. Anyway, I'd sooner Tony Bennett.' Savannah sneered. 'Stop fooling. Look at the entrance to the upstairs rooms next to the record store.'

They stared at a big guy lolling by the doorway.

About six foot two, Spencer thought. A long chin, prominent teeth, flared jeans, Cuban heels, aviator shades and a fleecy jacket almost hiding the bulky shape of a shoulder holster. Most of all Spencer saw confidence and instinctively recognised a street fighter. Nothing showy, but this guy knows his stuff.

'Jesus he's a big sucker. Can you take him, Spencer?' Savannah whispered. 'We can't have prolonged fisticuffs. It has to be quick, and quiet,'

Spencer noticed an overflowing trash can and an empty bottle of Jim Beam Bourbon in a brown paper bag. He grabbed the bottle and carefully wiped the rim.

The lights changed, Spencer tottered across the street, swigging from the empty bottle. The gaberdine coat and the stupid hat were great props, Spencer thought. He staggered up to the man, a silly grin on his face. Savannah followed surreptitiously behind and gazed with feigned interest into the Beat Box window. An SFPD helicopter clattered overhead.

'Shay buddy, can you spare a quarter?'

'Fuck off you old drunk.'

Spencer grinned and glanced skywards, 'Check out the chopper, buddy. I reckon it's gonna…'

Irresistible. Spencer knew no one could refrain from a quick look.

In the second the eyes went skywards Spencer drove fingers made of steel into the outstretched throat. The lightning thrust was silent and deadly. The thug collapsed in a heap, his hands clasped around his neck, eyes bulging.

Savannah sprang into action, opening the stairwell door. Spencer grabbed the man by the shoulders and began dragging him inside. A concerned old lady put a hand on Spencer's arm. 'Oh dear. Is he ok?' Savannah smiled winningly at the old girl. 'We're paramedics, dear. Sadly, Reverend Irving here has regular seizures.'

'Oh my gosh.' The lady exclaimed, 'a man of God. This is terrible. Should I call an ambulance?'

'Don't bother. Truly he'll be ok. The Lord will look after him,' Savannah added piously.

Spencer dragged the semi-conscious guard into a narrow foyer, while Savannah gave the old lady another reassuring smile, slamming the solid timber door shut.

'Hey, what the fuck's going on down there?' A strident male voice rang out from the top floor of the three-story building.

'We've been sprung.' Spencer glanced upstairs in time to see a tall red bearded man disappear. They heard the thunk of a door slamming.

The man on the floor groaned and tried to climb to his feet.

'I don't think so, petal.' Savannah grabbed his arm, dragging it roughly upwards and handcuffing it to the steel support of the post box holders. She relieved him of his sidearm next.

Savannah and Spencer bounded up the stairs two at a time. 'Did you see which door?' Savannah panted.

'First on the right.'

At the top of the stairs, Savannah leant against the balustrade, breathing hard. 'I'm not as young as I once was.'

Savannah grabbed her automatic, yelling, 'FBI, open the door!'

She nodded at Spencer who winked and slammed his booted foot into the worn timber.

The cold March wind swept through the open window leading to the fire escape. Threadbare curtains fluttered in the breeze.

'Don't even think about it, Jimbo.' The red bearded man looked wildly around, grabbing at a black snub nosed 0.38 on the sink.

Spencer rolled his eyes. 'Not again,' he murmured.

Phut phut, two rounds from the Hi-Power 0.22 smashed into Jimbo's face and chest. He dropped like a stone. A short exhalation of air and a moan, and it was the end of life.

Savannah climbed through the open window onto a rusty steel landing, in time to see the hurriedly retreating form of Ronny Delgado jumping off the fire escape and legging it down the alleyway.

'God dammit.'

Spencer untied the bonds of the unconscious Ryan Tod.

CHAPTER 3

'I don't even know if we have enough to arrest BBQ,' Savannah said moodily, pushing a taco salad around her plate.

Savannah and Spencer had been waved to a white tableclothed table in the corner of the homely Balboa Café by a friendly waiter who recognised Savannah, with a 'how y'all doin?' the Landmark Café on Fillmore was quiet, the lunch trade yet to arrive. Spencer gazed approvingly at the cosy old establishment, with its long walnut bar and white-coated waitstaff. The welcoming odours of fresh coffee and hamburgers on the griddle wafted across the room.

'Hey, this looks great.' Spencer munched on a burger and took a gulp of his beer. 'You've been here before. I guess?'

'What on earth is happening?' Savannah mumbled.

'What are you talking about?' Spencer stuffed a French fry into his gob.

'I'll tell you what I'm talking about. You and I have been here at least…I don't know. Five times, ten times. A lot. You always have the same burger. C'mon Spencer. What's the story? You don't remember? I don't get it.'

'Oh shit. I do have a confession to make.'

'I have a bad feeling. C'mon. Out with it.'

'It's my memory.'

'For Christ's sake Spencer, this is becoming just a tad annoying. What do you remember, and what don't you?'

'Ok. We're not in hurry, are we?'

'Of course not. It'll be happy hour in about six hours and the drinks will be half price. By the sounds of things, I'll be ready for some Jack's by then. In fact, I'm probably about ready now. The floors all yours.'

'Remember when you rescued me from the clutches of that cop Doolan, from the hospital in Chicago?'

'How could I forget? What a klutz that man was.'

'As you may recall, I had no memory of anything.'

'How could I forget?'

'Well, here's the thing. You'll be pleased to know my memory has completely returned. Well, almost.'

'Hallelujah, there is a God. So, you're telling me you remember when we first met in New York in '55?'

'Absolutely. I remember you coming out.'

'Here we go, you mean Inez and I and…?'

'No, no.' Spencer added hastily. 'I mean you coming out as a one-woman killing machine.'

'Oh that.'

'Yes that. It started when you killed Isaac the Jew and his pal Dutch …'

'Ambroos.'

'All of that. And the lawyer. It's a long list.'

'Goody goody. I'm delighted. What about LA? Mexico? You killing that Federale?'

'He was a crooked cop. Anyway, let's move along, shall we? You never said, but I figured you also killed Charlie and the movie guy Zachariah Colchester.'

'Stand up for a minute.'

'What are you talking about?'

'Indulge me.'

Spencer climbed to his feet. Savannah carefully ran her hands along his chest.

'Let's just have a peek under that shirt.'

'Savannah, people are staring.'

Spencer waved at the barman, mouthing, 'It's ok.'

'You're clean.'

'Seriously, you didn't think I was wearing a wire, surely?'

'It had all the hallmarks of a sting. A set up. What's with all this trips down memory lane? Anyway, I'm not admitting to Charlie and the lovable Colchester.' Savannah grinned impishly. 'Would I do such a thing?'

Spencer shrugged. 'Who cares? They're dead and that's a good outcome. But here's the thing. I remember everything after the hospital in Chicago. I remember Sturgis, that fabulous chopper, you as the tattooed biker chick. The shootout in Warbonnet. Oh, and Miami. That was bloody scary.'

'But?'

'I remember everything. Ramirez and the outcome in Miami late last year.'

'Great. So, what's the problem?'

'I might add, I also know everything that happened in Miami wasn't sanctioned by Dale Fletcher. And the fact is what we did was completely illegal.'

'I thought we'd sorted all that,' Savannah said sulkily.

'We have. But the only small problem is, my memory stalls right there.'

'What do you mean? That's everything, isn't it?'

'Not quite. I remember everything up until we went back to our hotel in Miami.'

Savannah gave up on her taco salad and took a swig from her Budweiser. 'So, what gives?'

'My memory stops, there. Late 1965 in Miami. It's now March 1966 and I have a gap of about three months.'

'It could be worse, I guess. I'm going to have another beer. You?'

'Ok.'

She motioned to the waiter, holding up her bottle of Bud and two fingers.

'This seems slightly ridiculous, but here goes. You and I went back to LA. Inez was safely back in our home in Marina Del Rey. Dale Fletcher was as happy as a clam. You and I went to New Orleans in February for the Mardi Gras weekend. Undercover of course.'

'What was going down in the Big Easy?'

'You seriously don't remember? I mean it's just a couple of months ago?'

'Savannah!'

'All right already. It was a counterfeit racket. Nasty brute. Jorge Simonson. A little guy, but wicked as. Everyone was scared of the bastard.'

'What happened? Oh, let me guess. You shot him?'

'It was a righteous kill. I was cleared. Jesus Spencer, he had a gun pointed at you.'

'Bloody hell. A white Jaguar.'

'Come again?'

'Jorge Simenson. He drove a Jag. Nice. White duco, red leather trim. Maple dash.'

'That's right. You do remember?'

'Thank God. Yeah. Bourbon Street. The music, the food, it was great. It's all come back. Christ, I thought I was dead, until…'

'Yeah, until I shot the creep.'

'So you did. And thank you Savannah. But here's the thing. I remember all of that. Standing in Frenchman Street, listening to a black guy play the harp and singing The House of The Rising Sun. Simenson driving like a lunatic. And then the warehouse and you appeared like magic. How did you do that?'

'I'm not going to run through it all now. There're obviously still some gaps.'

'Actually, that's all I remember. The next thing I remember was waking up just before this little skirmish.'

'Not much more to it really. We flew back to LA. We had a meet with Dale and he sent us off to the Golden Gate City, and he we are.' Savannah smiled.

'I don't want to be difficult but I have absolutely no idea what's happening right at the moment. I have no idea what the job is. I remember waking up yesterday on that stretcher and wham, we're into it. Who exactly are the bad guys? I mean BBQ. Seriously, he cooks folk and eats them?'

'Ronnie Delgado aka BBQ. Dear Ronnie is an ex-football star. The Broncos, no sorry, the Cowboys, I think it was from memory. He was a real pinup boy. The BBQ stands for Big Beautiful Quarterback.'

'Wouldn't that be BQB?' he asked.

'We did that joke two months ago,' she told him, unamused.

Spencer gave her finger guns. 'The upside of having memory issues. Anyway, he's a bad guy?'

'You betcha.'

'Bad how? I mean drugs? Holdups? What exactly?'

'I don't know?'

'Oh, isn't that simply topping? You don't know. Really?' Spencer gave an imitation of an English toff.

'Well for a start he was torturing our guy, Ryan Tod.'

'I don't want to be difficult, but all you saw was a big guy jumping off a fire escape and hot-footing it down the alley. And I might add in your inimitable fashion you shot his partner in crime.'

Savannah grabbed a sugar cube from the stainless-steel container and threw it hard at Spencer.

'Hey. That bloody well hurt.' Spencer yelped.

'Good. He was going to shoot us.'

'You used to love the Cisco Kid, as I recall.'

'Give me strength. Where exactly is this going?'

'Well. As I recall, dear old Cisco used to shoot the six gun out of the bad guys hand, didn't he?'

'Oh, I see. Silly me. Just like the movies I shoot the gun out of his hand. Australia must be such a wonderful place.' Savannah said sotto voce.

'Well, why not? Your shooting skills are Olympic standard.'

Savannah daggered a finger, 'This is it. For the last time. When I shoot, I shoot to kill. Our training teaches us "Centre mass. Centre mass." Got it?'

Spencer turned smiling at the other diners who appeared to be hanging on every word, 'It's ok folks, we're rehearsing for a TV show.'

'Now that we've covered the lefty peace, love and all of that crap did you also forget that Dale Fletcher was meeting us here? And speak of.'

Spencer peered out of the window to see a tan Pontiac Catalina sedan swerve into a parking space.